GILDA JOYCE
Psychic Investigator

GILDA JOYCE
Psychic Investigator

JENNIFER ALLISON

SCHOLASTIC INC.
New York Toronto London Auckland Sydney
Mexico City New Delhi Hong Kong Buenos Aires

ISBN-13: 978-0-439-02389-4
ISBN-10: 0-439-02389-0

12 11 10 9 8 7 6 5 4 3 2 1   7 8 9 10 11 12/0

Printed in the U.S.A.   40

First Scholastic printing, January 2007
Book design by Richard Amari

For Michael, who always makes me laugh,
and in memory of Paul and Louise Allison

ACKNOWLEDGMENTS

I am grateful to stellar editor Meredith Mundy Wasinger for her editorial insight and outstanding work on numerous aspects of book production; to assistant editor Margaret Woollatt for her astute suggestions; to Richard Amari for his stunning design work; to Dutton Children's Books president and publisher Stephanie Owens Lurie; and to Diane Giddis and others at Dutton for their copyediting efforts. I owe a special debt of gratitude to literary agent Doug Stewart. His expertise, hard work, and ongoing support are immensely appreciated.

I would also like to thank my talented friend Carolyn Parkhurst, whose encouragement made all the difference. The outstanding writers and teachers I met at American University's M.F.A. program deepened my understanding of the writing process, while my husband, Michael, who loves books more than anyone I know, inspired me to keep writing even during times when he was my only reader. The girls at Connelly School of the Holy Child deserve thanks for their vibrant personalities and for their enthusiasm about this book and good stories in general. Finally, I would like to acknowledge baby Max for thoughtfully waiting to be born after my manuscript was complete, and just for being the cutest thing I've seen in diapers.

CONTENTS

GILDA JOYCE
Psychic Investigator

PROLOGUE

by Gilda Joyce, Psychic Investigator

If you've ever been in a real haunted house (not one of the fake ones with recorded screams and ghosts projected from cameras), you know that they're actually very quiet.

Mr. Splinter and his daughter, Juliet, lived in just such a haunted house: a house where a Gothic tower rose up from the back garden like a witch's hat; a house of ponderous draperies, dark wood, and long, silent hallways lined with locked doors; a house where fog stalked the neighborhood like a serial killer pursuing a busload of cheerleaders. It was a house that concealed a terrible secret.

Like many people who live in haunted houses, Mr. Splinter and his daughter didn't want to believe in ghosts.

They needed my help. It was the first case in my illustrious career as Gilda Joyce, Psychic Investigator.

1

It's Not a Lie If It Comes True

In the back row of Mrs. Weinstock's eighth-grade English classroom, Gilda Joyce chewed on a lock of her dark hair and pretended to listen as her classmates described their plans for the summer on the last day of the school year. Gilda paid little attention to the discussion, because she was secretly absorbed in reading a small, dog-eared book called *The Master Psychic's Handbook: A Guide to Psychic Principles and Methods.* Ever since she'd found the book at a garage sale, Gilda had been a big fan of the author, Master Psychic Balthazar Frobenius, who had grown up in one of the most dangerous neighborhoods in Detroit and who claimed to have used his psychic gifts to help detectives solve numerous crimes.

As the other students chattered about visiting places like Lake Michigan or Florida or the caves of Kentucky, Gilda perused a chapter entitled "Following Impulses, No Matter How Illogical," in which Balthazar Frobenius explained how psychics sometimes get distinct physical sensations:

. . . impulses that seem arbitrary at the time, but which actually lead to some fortuitous event or crucial piece of information. For example, a psychic might suddenly experience a craving for an unusual food that leads her to a neighborhood that she would never visit under normal circumstances. What does she discover in this neighborhood besides food? *Most likely a person seeking the help of her psychic abilities or a clue leading to the resolution of an unsolved crime.*

For the psychic, it is often the *unexpected impulse* that leads her to people in need of help, clues that solve crimes, and even spirits seeking her attention.

Over time, you will recognize your own physical cues: you may have headaches, itches, aches, twitches, or other physical sensations that become your own personal signals—a kind of *psychic radar* that helps you perceive important information.

As she read the passage, Gilda felt an unusual itch in her left ear. She wondered whether this might be one of her own physical signals that she was about to have a paranormal experience.

Gilda glanced up from her book and realized that Mrs. Weinstock was looking at her.

"Gilda, how about you? What are *your* plans for the summer?"

At the moment, her only specific plan was to spend much of the summer spying on a strikingly unattractive young man she had nicknamed "Plaid Pants" who worked at a nearby convenience store, but she didn't want to admit this to Mrs. Weinstock. Remembering that her mother had recently spoken of her eccentric cousin who lived in California, Gilda blurted the first idea that came to mind. "I'm going to San Francisco," she said.

Everyone in the room turned to gaze at her with a combination of surprise and curiosity, causing Gilda to immediately regret the impulsive lie.

"And what will you be doing there? A vacation with your family?"

"I'll be writing a novel." Why did she tell Mrs. Weinstock that?

Gilda's pale, freckled complexion turned pink with embarrassment, and Mrs. Weinstock peered at her suspiciously. Gilda had been known to make up stories in the past, and she knew Mrs. Weinstock regarded most of her comments with a degree of skepticism. "Writing a novel is a pretty ambitious plan for a girl your age."

Mrs. Weinstock obviously didn't want to believe that an eighth grader could write a novel, even if it was Gilda, who had a unique talent for writing in a voice well beyond her years. In fact, because Gilda had used vocabulary words like *specious* and *trenchant* in some of her assignments, Mrs.

Weinstock had unfairly hinted that she thought Gilda had plagiarized on several occasions.

"I've already written a few novels," Gilda replied, "so it's no big deal." This statement was partly true; her bedroom closet was stuffed with bizarre stories that she hoped would someday make her famous.

"How interesting," said Mrs. Weinstock, crossing her arms over her chest. "Do tell us more."

Gilda chewed on her pencil, trying to think of something to say that would make Mrs. Weinstock and the entire class stop looking at her as if she were a toad that had suddenly explained it enjoyed singing opera.

After a few agonizing seconds, Gilda was saved by the last school bell of the year, immediately followed by the clatter of students rushing toward the door and fleeing the building.

As Gilda trudged down the hallway, she felt irritated with herself. Was her impulsive idea of traveling to San Francisco the product of a genuine psychic impulse, or was it merely a compulsive lie? Lately, Gilda had been making a genuine effort to tell the truth. At least, she had promised herself that if she *did* tell a spontaneous lie, she would do everything possible to make the lie actually come true. In order to maintain this resolution, she would now have to find a way to get herself from Michigan to San Francisco for the summer—a plan that suddenly seemed entirely impossible, given the fact that she had no money and that her mother would almost certainly veto the idea.

"Hey, *since when* are you going to San Francisco?!" Gilda turned to face her best friend, Wendy Choy, who was struggling under the weight of an enormous blue backpack.

"Look, Wendy, you're going to music camp, right? Do I ask you a million questions about that?"

"Yes, you do. And I'm only asking because—well, you know how you *are.*"

"If you don't believe I'm going to San Francisco," said Gilda, "just call my mom and ask." Gilda knew that Wendy would never call her mother. Wendy hated getting stuck in conversations with Mrs. Joyce.

"But just *yesterday* you told me that you were planning to spend a few months spying on Plaid Pants at the convenience store," Wendy persisted. "You said you thought he might be a serial killer."

"I wouldn't waste my time doing something that dumb," Gilda lied. In truth, Gilda had been looking forward to spying on Plaid Pants, particularly since she had just made two interesting discoveries: (1) Plaid Pants had a real name—Hector Flack (a name Gilda found far more scandalous than the nickname she had given him), and (2) Hector/Plaid Pants had recently gotten in trouble for eating candy on the job. Gilda thought he might be in danger of getting fired.

Lately, however, Gilda sensed that Wendy had lost interest in the "neighborhood surveillance" project they had started after reading *Harriet the Spy* back in elementary school. Wendy also seemed uninterested in the business she and Gilda had been planning to start—Psychic Investigations Inc. While Gilda had been diligently working to develop her psychic abilities, Wendy seemed increasingly skeptical about the whole enterprise. Besides, Wendy would be spending three months at a music camp in northern Michigan, leaving Gilda on her own all summer for the first time.

"Do you want to come over and spy on Plaid Pants just one *last* time before the summer?" Gilda ventured. "Or how about conducting a séance? We haven't done any psychic investigations for ages—"

"I can't. I've got to start packing for camp, and I haven't practiced piano nearly enough this week. We can't play these games forever, you know. We're almost in ninth grade!"

"Wendy, they aren't games; they're *careers.*"

"Maybe for *you,* but some of us have to live in the real world."

Gilda felt deflated. Wendy was abandoning her, and the real world was such a bore.

As Gilda exited the front doors of the school, she vowed that she would find a way to get herself to San Francisco. *Maybe there was a* reason *I blurted out that idea of going to San Francisco,* Gilda thought. *Maybe it really was a psychic impulse.*

2

The Magic Typewriter and the Bold Letter

Mrs. Joyce rushed down the hallway of the hospital and grabbed the telephone from her supervisor's hand.

"Sounds like your daughter again," said the head nurse irritably.

"Hi, Gilda!" Mrs. Joyce's voice rose to a high, nervous pitch over the phone. She always braced herself for either terrible news or requests for favors when one of her children called during her nursing shift. "How was the last day of school?"

"Boring."

"Have you put that meat loaf I made in the oven?"

"Not yet."

"Gilda, that meat loaf needs to go in the oven now."

"Okay," said Gilda, poking the loaf of uncooked ground meat with her finger.

"Boy, my feet are killing me tonight," said Mrs. Joyce,

lowering her voice so that the head nurse wouldn't over-hear her complaint. "They want me to work a double shift again this evening. The hospital's just been swamped, so I'm afraid it's going to be another late night for me."

"We'll be fine," said Gilda. She and her brother were used to their mother's erratic work schedule and had learned to prepare dinner for themselves some time ago. "Mom, I was actually calling because I need to get in touch with a cousin of yours—that strange one who lives in San Francisco?"

"You mean Lester Splinter?"

"Isn't he the one whose sister jumped off the roof of the house?"

"Yes—such a tragedy. It must have been ten years ago at least."

"Could you give him a call?"

"May I ask *why* you want me to call him?"

"I need to go somewhere exciting this summer, and I'd really like to visit him." Gilda decided not to bother trying to explain the psychic impulse that was pulling her toward San Francisco and the fact that she needed to make a lie she had just told her English class come true.

Mrs. Joyce sighed. "Gilda, Lester and I are not close. He's my second cousin, and I used to see him at family re-unions when we were kids, but we haven't spoken in ages. I'm sorry, but it isn't realistic to ask if you can visit him in San Francisco."

"But he's *family,* isn't he?"

"Why don't you just go spend some time with Grandma Joyce if you want to visit one of your relatives?"

Grandma Joyce lived only a few miles away, in a tiny house downriver in Detroit. She was the only person Gilda knew who actually owned a black-and-white television and who liked baking prune pies.

"Visiting Grandma Joyce is not my idea of fun," said Gilda. "She *smells.*"

This prompted a small lecture from Gilda's mother about bad language, the evils of ageism, and how, in the future, she herself might smell terrible, and how, in the event that turned out to be the case, she would hope that her own daughter would "show some consideration for the elderly."

"Okay, Mom, I'd better get going on my work," said Gilda, interrupting her mother.

"I thought today was the last day of school."

"I mean my *real* work. My career."

At the moment, Gilda's "career" encompassed several different activities: writing novels, spying on neighbors, and developing her psychic abilities.

"Oh, *that,*" her mother replied. "Well, you're certainly one unique kid, Gilda Joyce. I suppose you get that from your dad. He was a strange one, too, in his own way."

• • •

Gilda contemplated the chaos of her bedroom. A tornado surrounded her: hundreds of books threatened to spill from shelves, peeked from under the bed, and teetered in random piles throughout the room—everything from mysteries, ghost stories, and comic books to collections of poetry and plays. Empty soda cans, Mars bar wrappers, and several unopened bags of giant orange marshmallow peanuts that were several years old also littered the room. "You might as well eat Styrofoam!" Mrs. Joyce had yelled when she discovered the lurid orange candy. But Gilda refused to throw it away: she and her father had purchased it ages ago on a Saturday afternoon trip to the hardware store. Instead of buying a new toilet plunger, the two of them had left the store with several bags of orange peanuts. Now the fossilized candy peanuts preserved the memory of her father's small, whimsical indulgences.

In the middle of the room was Gilda's favorite possession—the old Underwood manual typewriter that her father had given her before he died of cancer two years ago. It reminded her so much of her dad: it was old-fashioned and reliable, like the horn-rimmed glasses and flannel shirts she remembered her father wearing. Gilda loved the way the clacking of the keys made them sound enthusiastic about the stories she wrote, as if the typewriter were cheering her on and saying "Great idea!" Sometimes Gilda even liked to imagine that her father's spirit was actually inside the old typewriter, telling her stories and encouraging her to write. Besides, she felt that her typewriter had certain advantages over a computer: it never fell prey to viruses or needed a "software upgrade."

On the day her father had given her his typewriter, Gilda had sat at his bedside in the hospital, listening as he struggled to breathe. She remembered that one of his eyes seemed to be looking right at her while the other gazed off in a slightly different direction—toward the window that overlooked a parking lot. Gilda had never seen her father's eyes look so strange before. *Dad isn't going to get better after all,* she thought. *From now on, he's only going to get worse.*

After a very long silence, her father whispered, "Gilda, I want you to have my typewriter."

Gilda's father had purchased it when he was just a kid, with the first money he ever earned. Gilda never grew tired of hearing how he had dreamed of becoming a writer; how he loved seeing words stamped out on real paper as he wrote and hearing the sharp *snap! snap! snap!* of the typewriter keys as he formed ideas. But instead of becoming a writer, he had spent his time building engine clutches by day and watching TV at night. "Sometimes life doesn't turn out the way you think it will," Gilda's father often warned. "You've gotta give life a real hard kick in the nuts to get what you want. And *even then*—prepare for disappointment."

But one day, a few months before he entered the hospital for the last time, Gilda's father had gone to his room after dinner instead of turning on the television. He locked the door, and then a few minutes later, everyone heard: *tap, tap, tap, tap, clack, clack, clack, clack, clack—zing!* He typed long into the night.

Mr. Joyce continued this routine for weeks. Each night, Gilda listened to the clattery sounds of her father's writing as she drifted into sleep; she imagined that she was traveling on a train toward somewhere warm and pleasant, and that the *click, clack, clack* of the typewriter was the sound of wheels moving quickly over the tracks.

"What are you typing, Dad?" Gilda asked one day.

"I'm writing a story," her father whispered.

"What kind of story?"

"Not telling."

Gilda never discovered what her father had actually been typing, but she remembered that he had seemed happy at that moment.

"You should have my typewriter," her father said on that last day in the hospital. "You'll do something really great with it."

Gilda remembered her mother's warning: "Your dad's on a ton of pain medication now, so he might not be himself." Perhaps her father was confused.

"It's a magic typewriter," he whispered. Then he drifted into sleep, and the nurse said visiting hours were over.

What had her father meant by the phrase *It's a magic typewriter*? The idea had given Gilda a childish feeling of hope at the time. Perhaps—in some way—the typewriter really was magic. Maybe she would find a way to stay in contact with her father even after he was gone.

Stored beneath her typewriter was a list Gilda had typed shortly after her father's death:

IMPORTANT: Some Things
To Remember About Dad
by Gilda Joyce, Author

1. When he took off his glasses and
   smiled, there were deep crinkles
   around his eyes.
2. He told ghost stories when we went
   camping, and insisted on calling hot
   dogs "weenies" even when everyone
   made fun of him.
3. At Christmastime, he left out
   cookies and a beer for Santa, and
   then he ate them himself but said
   that Santa had eaten them.
4. He liked costumes and "people
   watching"--just like me.

5. He was brave. He always reminded me,
   "Never turn down a chance to have
   an adventure."

The sight of her father's Underwood typewriter always reminded Gilda that there was no time to waste. Ignoring her mother's skepticism about the idea of visiting Lester Splinter, Gilda decided to seize the day by sending a letter to Mr. Splinter herself.

Gilda sat cross-legged on the purple carpeting of her bedroom and began typing at lightning speed on her type-writer, which was balanced precariously on top of a pile of books.

Dear Mr. Lester Splinter:
   Allow me to introduce myself. My
name is Gilda Joyce, and I'm a distant
relative of yours--the daughter of your
long-lost second cousin, Patricia Joyce
(you may have known her as Patty McDoogle
before her marriage to my father--a
marriage that ended tragically with
my father's untimely death).
   Let me come right to the point: My
mother would like to know if it would be

okay for me to visit you in San
Francisco this summer.

I realize this may seem presumptuous
of my mother--even a tad impolite--but
the situation in our little family is
such that the formalities of politeness
must be disregarded.

Let me explain. As a widowed woman, my
mother is struggling to support herself
and her two children. I'm sure you can
imagine the strains of raising a preter-
naturally gifted daughter (that's me) and
a uniquely unattractive idiot son (my
brother) on her own. Each day, my mother
labors in the harshly lighted rooms of a
hospital, her hands soaked in blood and
vomit. Even as she lifts truck-sized
patients over her shoulder to carry them
down to surgery, she manages to tell the
funniest jokes you've ever heard in your
life.

At the end of the day, my mother
returns home to relieve her talented
thirteen-year-old daughter of the duties
of feeding and harshly disciplining her

```
"special" son. On most days, my brother
entertains himself by flushing the toilet
repeatedly, but at other times he
requires constant supervision if we are
to prevent him from drinking all the
household cleansers under the sink.
```

Gilda paused to read the letter. She found it splendid so far, but wondered if she should tone down the part about her mother lifting patients over her shoulder, which might be just a *bit* exaggerated. She had also lied about her older brother, Stephen, who was by no means an idiot. Stephen was in fact annoyingly bright, particularly when it came to computers. However, Stephen had recently spilled the beans to Mrs. Joyce that Gilda had been responsible for three terrible things: (1) the gum stuck in the living-room carpet, (2) the disappearance of two whole boxes of Twinkies, and (3) worst of all—the disappearance of Mrs. Joyce's secret stash of cigarettes, which Gilda had flushed down the toilet. Consequently, Gilda felt that it was payback time. Her older brother deserved to be slandered in her letter.

Gilda concluded:

```
To make a long story short, Mr.
Splinter: My mother feels that I would
benefit greatly from a change of
```

scenery. Just today she said to me:
"A young lady with your talents isn't
meant to spend the summer wiping drool
from the mouth of a big, dull lug of a
boy. She should be out spreading the
sunshine of her presence to more glamorous
families in more attractive settings."

And as you can imagine, Mr. Splinter,
I can't help but agree with her.

As you can probably tell from this
letter, I am highly intelligent, self-
sufficient, polite, neat, ambitious,
energetic, lice-free, and, of course,
quiet. I can also prepare my own meals,
or exist solely on Froot Loops for
several weeks if necessary.

I look forward to hearing from you so
I can make travel arrangements and start
packing as soon as possible.

Yours sincerely,
Gilda Joyce

Gilda thought for a moment, then typed:

P.S. My mother would have written
this letter herself, but an attack of

tendinitis prevented her from doing so.
She sends regards.
P.P.S. My belated regrets concerning your
sister's unfortunate jump from the roof.

Gilda imagined Mr. Splinter alternately laughing and weeping as he read the letter. He would rush to write a reply: "By all means; visit at once!" Once she had an actual invitation to San Francisco, Gilda reasoned, her mother would realize that it would be unfair to squelch the idea.

In her mother's tattered address book, Gilda was relieved to find a street address for Lester Splinter on Laguna Street in San Francisco, California. Gilda liked the sound of the word *Laguna*. She pictured herself sitting on the beach, sipping a frothy pink drink garnished with a little paper umbrella and a cherry. She imagined herself riding in a cable car, waving ecstatically to Wendy Choy and her eighth-grade classmates, who were somehow able to view her from their distant and comparatively boring surroundings in Michigan. "You see?" she would say. "I *told* you I was going to San Francisco!"

Gilda took a deep breath and printed the address on the envelope, struggling to make her handwriting appear as adult as possible. Now all she needed was a stamp. She was completely certain that she would soon be on her way to San Francisco.

3

Juliet Splinter

At the same moment Gilda dropped her letter to Mr. Splinter in her mailbox in Michigan, a skinny girl trudged up the steep incline of Laguna Street in San Francisco, struggling to make her way home against an unusually fierce June wind. She was a very pretty thirteen-year-old girl, but she looked more like an eleven-year-old, since she was extremely small. Her long, fine hair was nearly as light as corn silk, and the pallor of her white skin belied her sunny California surroundings. If you looked into her icy gray eyes, you would probably decide right away that this was not a girl you could make friends with easily.

Her name was Juliet Splinter, and she was Lester Splinter's daughter. Juliet's parents had divorced when she was very young, and after living with her mother in San Diego until she was ten years old, Juliet had moved to San Francisco to stay with her father. Because Mr. Splinter had lost contact with virtually all of his relatives, few members of his extended family—including Mrs. Joyce—realized that he had a teenage daughter in his care.

Wearing jeans over a black leotard and clutching a pair of pink ballet slippers, Juliet walked home from a particularly disappointing dance class during which she had stumbled on her pirouettes and left the studio exhausted and defeated. She knew in her heart that it had been her *last* dance class.

Quitting ballet wouldn't be such a bad thing, except for the fact that Juliet had already tried and quickly abandoned virtually every extracurricular activity to which she had been introduced: Girl Scouts, soccer, softball, drama, piano lessons, band . . . The truth was, Juliet didn't want to do much of anything these days except sleep and be left alone.

Although she attended an expensive private school designed both to "inspire" her and to help get her into one of the best colleges, whenever someone asked Juliet if she liked school, she would shrug and stare blankly at some distant corner in the room. This was simply the most honest response Juliet could provide: her elite school was better than going to the dentist, but it wasn't great, either. She earned passing grades, but she couldn't remember the last time she felt genuinely interested in a subject. She knew her lack of academic achievement disappointed her parents, who both believed in solid preparation for an impressive, lucrative career, but the secret truth was that Juliet felt that none of the things she studied in school particularly mattered. *But what in life really does matter?* Juliet often asked herself. She couldn't think of a single thing.

Juliet sat down at the edge of the sidewalk to catch her breath and wish for the thousandth time for a *real* friend. She had acquaintances that called her to go shopping or talk about boys, but there wasn't one kid at school to whom she would ever try to explain how she really felt.

Juliet looked out across a hillside scene of palm trees and colorful houses to the blue water of San Francisco Bay, where white sails moved slowly under a clear sky—a perfect day. All around her, flowers bloomed—gardens filled with pink and yellow roses bobbing in the wind. The whimsical Victorian houses painted in shades of pink, yellow, and blue reminded her of children's drawings. This was supposed to be a happy setting: the beautiful homes of happy rich people, the sunny skies and sparkling water of the bay beckoning to surfers and vacationers, but for some reason, the bright, cheerful surroundings made Juliet feel lonelier than ever. A dark thought seeped into her mind—the idea that she might be better off dead.

Juliet imagined her father glancing up from his *Wall Street Journal* and his tax forms to discover that she had slipped away into darkness. She imagined him rushing to save her, *but it was too late!* "I'm sorry, sir," the paramedic would say. "We did everything we could, but your daughter is gone." When Juliet's mother learned the news of her daughter's death on her cell phone, she would break one of her perfectly manicured pink fingernails and accidentally drive her beloved BMW into a ditch. Suddenly the Louis Vuitton handbag her mother carried and the multimillion-dollar beachfront home she shared with her pharmaceutical-executive husband would seem pointless. "I never appreciated my own daughter!" her mother would sob, hurling her designer purse into the ocean.

Juliet's morbid reverie was broken by the roar of a convertible as it zoomed past, breaking the silence with the lip-glossy music of a Britney Spears song. Inside, four bikini-clad teenage girls sang to the radio, obviously headed for the beach. Juliet stood up and watched them drive down the hill and disappear from sight.

The music from the car faded into the distance, and the atmosphere felt oppressively silent. As Juliet reached the steepest part of the hill where nearly vertical steps led to the front door of the mansion-sized Victorian house she and her father shared, she felt hot. For a brief moment, she thought she might faint—a sensation she sometimes experienced when she reached this spot on the hillside. It was here that Juliet often thought of her aunt Melanie. Ten years ago, Melanie's body had been discovered tangled in the bushes at the foot of the treacherous incline behind the Splinters' enormous house; for some reason, Melanie had jumped from the upper window of the tower at the back of the Victorian mansion.

Only three years old at the time, Juliet remembered virtually nothing about her aunt; she had only ever seen a single photograph of a fair-haired young woman who bore an eerie resemblance to Juliet herself. Whenever Juliet asked either of her parents to explain what had happened to Melanie, they either responded with impatience and anger or became so uncomfortable that Juliet quickly changed the subject. Nevertheless, Juliet still wondered what had really happened to her lost aunt. Why had she decided to end her own life?

Juliet climbed the last of the steep steps leading to her front door and located her house key. Inside, she found the enormous house empty, just as expected. Her father was at work, and Rosa, the housekeeper, was probably shopping for groceries or running other errands.

Juliet was used to being alone, but every now and then, she found herself feeling very aware of the empty rooms that surrounded her. Sometimes she had the strange idea that someone was hiding in the house, watching her. She knew it was a ridiculous notion, but at certain moments, her imagination took flight and she couldn't help wondering: *What if Aunt Melanie is not completely dead after all?*

Of course Juliet, would never dream of sharing this feeling with her father; he would probably send her to a therapist who would prescribe some new antidepressant or antianxiety medication. Either that or he would simply assume that her decision was the product of too many hours of watching television when she should be studying.

Juliet wandered into the kitchen, opened the refrigerator door, stared at the milk, eggs, orange juice, and yogurt sitting on the shelves as if expecting them to entertain her in some way, then slammed the refrigerator shut. On the counter, she noticed a brown plastic container—one of her father's prescriptions for sleeping pills. She picked up the container and stared at the familiar name of the pharmaceutical company where her mother now worked: Alogon. The sleeping pills rarely helped her father's insomnia; he claimed that he stayed awake at night, worrying about the financial problems of his tax clients. Her father also claimed that he hated having dreams, as if dreams were annoying visitors that overstayed their welcome and messed up the house.

Juliet poured three of the white sleeping pills into her palm and imagined herself lying on her bed, wearing a dress of black silk, her blond hair spilling across the pillow like a sad halo. She had no intention of *acting* on her suicidal thoughts at the moment, but she found a kind of poisonous pleasure in contemplating the tragic but beautiful image of her dead self.

Still holding the sleeping pills rather absentmindedly, Juliet trudged upstairs, heading toward her bedroom on the third floor. But when she reached the landing on the second floor, she abruptly dropped the sleeping pills and gasped.

A woman stood silently in the hallway.

Juliet felt she knew this woman—the white-blond hair, the gray eyes very much like her own, the high cheekbones and porcelain complexion. *But her aunt Melanie was dead.*

Juliet turned to run down the stairs, but she took only two steps before her legs weakened underneath her and everything went white. She tumbled down, down the stairs to the floor below.

4

Mrs. Frickle's Wigs

Gilda lay in bed and wondered if today would be the day she would receive a letter from San Francisco, inviting her to visit. More than a week had passed since she'd sent the letter to Mr. Splinter, and she was beginning to feel very impatient.

I have nothing to look forward to, Gilda told herself. She felt a wave of the summer-morning sadness that often followed the euphoria of school ending. Gilda abhorred laziness—in fact, she never let a day go by without pursuing some productive goal or plan associated with her life's "real work"— but today she felt tired as she gazed at her father's old typewriter through half-closed eyes.

Aren't you going to DO something? the typewriter seemed to say.

Gilda looked at her alarm clock. It was nearly 9:00 A.M., and she had a lot to accomplish. Forcing herself to climb out of bed, she shuffled toward her chaotic closet, where she contemplated her clothes and costumes, most of which had fallen from their hangers to the closet floor. Gilda found it unbearably dull to be stuck in the single identity of "Gilda Joyce, thirteen-year-old," and she often wore costumes just to make life more interesting. Her closet was stuffed with hats, scarves, sunglasses, vintage dresses, a very old Girl Scout uniform—even a feather boa and a tutu.

Gilda decided that today she would gather research for a new novel, so she decided to wear her people-watching disguise: fishnet stockings with several holes, a baggy sun-dress, a large floppy hat that covered most of her face, dark 1970s-style sunglasses, pink lipstick, and old tennis shoes. Her goal was to look just eccentric enough that people would instinctively avoid her, assuming she was probably a little crazy, and just unfamiliar enough that none of her neighbors would recognize her and inform her mother that Gilda had been peeking into their windows.

Gilda ran down the stairs and collided with her brother, Stephen, who dropped the bagel he had been munching while reading an issue of *Popular Science.*

Stephen scowled. "Why don'tcha watch where you're going?" Stephen was often in a bad mood in the morning.

"*You're* the one who wasn't looking," said Gilda. "You shouldn't walk up the stairs *and* eat *and* read *Popular Science* all at the same time. It's too much for your brain to handle."

Gilda tried to dart past her brother, but he blocked her escape.

"Where are you going wearing *that?*" he demanded.

"None of your business."

"One of these days, I'm going to tell Mom you spy on people."

There were times when Gilda wished her brother would create a computer program to send himself into a distant galaxy. "One of these days, I'm going to tell Mom you have a stash of Victoria's Secret catalogues in your locker," she threatened.

This comment surprised Stephen enough to give Gilda the opportunity to dart past him and out the front door.

As Gilda walked quickly down the sidewalk, she reflected that it was hard to believe that in the old days, she and her brother had actually been close friends—*real* friends. They used to do things like watch black-and-white horror movies and eat cold pizza and chocolate-chip cookie batter. They used to build snow forts and "tree forts"—little more than a few boards nailed to a tree limb—and then imagine living a life of hardship and struggle in the wilderness while eating licorice and candy corn purchased from Plaid Pants at the Gas Mart.

But after Mr. Joyce fell ill, money was a constant worry to the family, and Stephen began to think that he'd never be able to afford to go to a good college unless he won a big scholarship. He now spent almost all of his time locked in his room, clicking away on his computer and his calculator to make sure he got straight A's (a fact Gilda resented, since her own grades were decidedly less consistent). When Stephen wasn't at school or up in his room doing homework, he worked at Roscoe's Chicken & Fish in an effort to save money to buy a used car. It seemed to Gilda that Stephen was always tired and grouchy these days.

Mrs. Joyce had assured Gilda that her brother was merely going through a sullen phase ("That's called being a teenager!"), and that he was simply under more stress than in the past, but Gilda thought it was possible that his brain had permanently frozen in grouch mode: with the exception of rare moments when Stephen would join Gilda to watch a rerun of *Buffy the Vampire Slayer,* it often seemed that the fun person she used to like being with was gone forever. *I don't care,* Gilda told herself. *I am completely independent, and I don't need Stephen OR Wendy to have adventures.*

Gilda looked up and caught an elderly man staring at her eccentric clothing with a slack-jawed expression that looked both bemused and annoyed. Gilda stopped and curtsied right in front of him, and he quickly turned his attention back to his flower garden.

Turning the corner, Gilda arrived at a brick apartment building. In front of the building there was nothing but a forlorn, plastic structure that had apparently been built for kids, although Gilda had never seen a single child actually play on it.

Gilda walked nonchalantly toward the front entrance of the apartments, then crouched behind some large bushes. There she could peer through a low window into the basement apartment where Mrs. Frickle lived.

Mrs. Frickle and her husband used to own a wig store that had burned down in a fire years ago. Mr. Frickle had apparently died of grief shortly thereafter. "Mr. and Mrs. Frickle *loved* that wig store," Gilda had overheard a gossipy neighbor exclaiming. "It just *killed* him when it was gone— and she's never been the same, either!"

The fascinating thing about Mrs. Frickle was that she still had a passion for wigs.

Each time Gilda peered through Mrs. Frickle's window, she found the tiny, liver-spotted woman slumped in a plaid armchair, wearing a gray bathrobe, watching television, and wearing yet another one of her hundreds of wigs—each in a different color and style. She had long and short wigs, curly and straight wigs. She had wigs with bangs and wigs shaped like large beehives. She had platinum-blond wigs, dark brunette wigs, and fire-engine-red wigs. None of the wigs looked the least bit natural, especially in contrast with the sagging skin and sharp bones of Mrs. Frickle's face, but she wore them anyway.

Never had Gilda seen a more outrageous wig than the one Mrs. Frickle was wearing today, however.

Upon Mrs. Frickle's head was an enormous bouffant—the size of a small poodle or a large bag of cotton candy. The most fantastic aspect of this wig was the color; it was a bright shade of pink. Gilda stared and stared. Thank goodness she hadn't missed visiting Mrs. Frickle today! If only Wendy Choy could see this! If only her father were still alive to hear about this!

Gilda scribbled some notes in the reporter's notebook she carried with her on people-watching expeditions:

Does Mrs. Frickle pretend she's someone else when she wears those wigs? Or do the wigs just remind her of her dead husband and the good ol' days at the wig store? Mrs. Frickle never seems to have any company.
Is she lonely? Is she insane? Will I end up like her someday? After all, I like wigs, too. On the other hand, I would never sit and watch infomercials all day. At the very least, I'd wear my wigs in an exciting setting— like on a yacht or in a really busy shopping mall...

Gilda wished she had her typewriter with her, because the large pink wig had suddenly given her a great plot idea for a novel. She sat on the ground and scribbled furiously:

Plot idea: Mrs. Frickle buys a pink wig that is secretly ALIVE! At first, the wig just amuses itself by playing practical jokes on Mrs. Frickle. But then, when it discovers that Mrs. Frickle is very wealthy, the wig creeps into her bedroom at night and tries to strangle her.

Gilda felt a chill as she looked at Mrs. Frickle's pink wig through the dirty window. Then she stifled an urge to giggle.

I'm freaking myself out again.

The sun had climbed higher in the sky, and Gilda's fishnet stockings and hat were starting to make her very hot. She decided to leave her spying post and head home to work on her novel. She would title the work *A Hairy Situation*.

When Gilda returned home, she checked the mailbox and kicked it hard when she found that it remained stubbornly, mockingly empty. When would Lester Splinter get his act together and invite her to San Francisco? How could he ignore her effervescent letter?

And what about Wendy? Why hadn't *she* written yet? Gilda stubbornly refused to send the first letter to Wendy at camp; she didn't want Wendy to think that she was sitting around with lots of time on her hands. *I'll reply AFTER she writes first,* Gilda thought.

Gilda consoled herself with the memory of Mrs. Frickle's pink wig and her smashing new plot idea for a novel. Without wasting another moment, she ran to her room, turned on the electric fan, and began to type the first chapter of her story.

5

The Invitation

Your daughter is slightly anemic," the earnest young doctor explained to Mr. Splinter. Juliet listened as he told her father that, in addition to having a small fracture in one rib and a severely sprained ankle, she needed to add more iron to her diet. He wrote a prescription for special vitamins. "Anemia might have made her light-headed," the doctor added, handing Mr. Splinter the prescription. "But I don't think this fainting episode indicates a serious problem."

Juliet felt woozy and disoriented. "Doctor . . ." she began, wanting to explain to the physician and her father that it was not simply anemia that had caused the fall, but something far more frightening and mysterious. "I think . . ."

"Yes, Juliet?"

She had *seen* something that had made her fall, hadn't she? A translucent face—*Aunt Melanie's face!*

Juliet felt that there was no possibility of making anyone

understand what had really happened. "Oh, it's nothing," she said. "Never mind."

Back at home, hobbling on crutches and aching where a bandage had been placed around her midriff (but not even a plaster cast on her ankle to dignify her trauma), Juliet felt a wave of shame when her father noticed something lying in the hallway.

"I wonder why I left these *here?*" Mr. Splinter picked up the brown plastic container of sleeping pills that had rolled into a corner. *Must have dropped them,* he told himself. Then he turned to Rosa, the housekeeper, to warn her about the dangers of the slippery steps that had obviously caused his daughter's fall.

Juliet didn't see any point in contradicting her father or trying to explain what had really happened; her desire to create a scene had passed. At the moment, her suicidal fantasies had faded; now she simply wanted to be left alone.

And left alone she would be. After all, it was summertime and there was no school, so nobody could *make* her leave her room.

Mr. Splinter's secretary, Summer, swung her leg impatiently, dangling a sequined flip-flop from her big toe as she spoke on the telephone. "No—no, I'm serious. I can't leave work!" She rolled her eyes.

"Because—*dude*—I've taken like ten days off in the past month, and I'd kind of like to keep *this* job, if you know what I mean. You guys go without me. Okay, I'm hanging up now. Bye!"

Summer slammed down the phone and gazed through the window wistfully at the shimmering water of San Francisco Bay. Then she sighed, pulled a small mirror from her purse, and reapplied her lipstick. A pretty girl in her early twenties, Summer put a great deal of effort into her appearance. Her green eye shadow and toenail polish perfectly matched her tight green T-shirt, upon which the word AQUARIUS glittered in sparkly rhinestones, and her bleached-blond bangs contrasted sharply with the short dark hair on the rest of her head. She wore Capri-cut, hip-hugger stretch pants that revealed a pierced belly button and a taut, suntanned stomach. Sitting amid the filing cabinets, folders, and austere bookcases of Mr. Splinter's home office, she resembled an exotic bird.

During the past hour, several of Summer's friends had called, asking if she could get away from Splinter's office to go to Stinson Beach. Summer was very proud of herself for refusing the invitations.

Summer glanced at her desk calendar. Today was Friday— the day of the week when she worked out of Mr. Splinter's home office rather than his downtown accounting firm, Splinter & Associates. On Fridays, Summer played the radio and sorted through Mr. Splinter's personal mail—a job she particularly enjoyed, since she was somewhat nosy.

Summer couldn't for the life of her figure out what kind of person her boss really was. She found this frustrating, because she considered herself to be extremely intuitive about people. As much as she liked and respected Mr. Splinter as an employer, Summer felt that it was maddening to work for such a private, inscrutable person. For one thing, she had no gossip whatsoever to share with her friends.

Summer sorted through a pile of teen fashion magazines and catalogs for dance camps and ballet costumes, all addressed to Juliet Splinter. She placed a rubber band around Juliet's mail and tossed it aside with a decidedly annoyed turn of the wrist. Although Summer considered herself a "people person," she had to admit that Juliet was exactly the kind of girl she couldn't stand. For one thing, she couldn't imagine why a girl as rich, pretty, and privileged as Juliet was always in such a perpetually sullen mood. She also hated Juliet's habit of correcting other people's grammar by saying things like "You mean, 'you and *me*,' not 'you and *I*.'" Summer took pride in her ability to get along with people of all ages, but despite her repeated attempts to engage Mr. Splinter's daughter in conversation by saying things like "Got any boyfriends?" and "Cool lip gloss, huh?," Juliet's responses remained either monosyllabic or nonexistent.

The last straw came recently, following Juliet's injury in a fall down the stairs: Summer had tried to brighten the girl's day by bringing her a video of the movie *Clueless*.

"You're just trying to suck up to your boss by being nice to me" was Juliet's bitter response. It was all Summer could do to leave the room without giving her employer's daughter a nice hard slap.

Summer spied an envelope addressed to "Mr. Lester Splinter" that sparked her interest. Who in the world was "Gilda Joyce"? Who could Mr. Splinter possibly know in Michigan?

Intrigued, Summer considered whether she could get away with opening the letter from Gilda Joyce. It was true that Mr. Splinter had given her permission to "open and sort" his mail, but this letter looked much more personal than his usual pile of bills, formal letters, and invoices. She contemplated steaming the letter open, but that would require locating an iron. Besides, what if she got caught?

Summer decided to go ahead and open the note and claim that she had opened it by mistake if Mr. Splinter asked her about it later.

As she read the letter, Summer found herself very intrigued by Gilda's situation. *So Mr. Splinter has relatives after all!* And this girl didn't sound the least bit spoiled. In fact, she seemed far more deserving of life in a fabulous San

Francisco mansion than grumpy Juliet. Naturally, Summer was also fascinated by a closing remark about Mr. Splinter's sister and a "jump from the roof." *What in the world could that mean?*

Carrying the opened letter, Summer peeked into the adjacent office, where Mr. Splinter was working at his computer. "Excuse me . . . Mr. Splinter?"

Mr. Splinter mumbled something but didn't turn to look at Summer. He often neglected to look at people when he was absorbed in a financial problem.

"I opened something by mistake from a relative of yours. Her name is Glinda or something? Anyway, she wants to know if she can visit you this summer."

Mr. Splinter continued to type.

"Well, you probably already know all about her, but she sounds totally smart, and she has this hard life in *Michigan,* and her father died, and her mom works in a really yucky hospital or something. Anyway, she sounds like a total genius—really awesome—but she doesn't have much money, so she'd probably need to have you get her a ticket and stuff to fly out here—if it's okay for her to visit. It might be good for Juliet to have some company, you know."

Mr. Splinter didn't look up once while Summer spoke. Although he claimed to be able to focus on two things at once, the truth was that numbers always received his full attention, while the words of human beings were often only partially processed by his brain. What he had just heard Summer say was "totally smart . . . awesome . . . ticket and stuff . . ." and he had automatically filed this in the category of Summer's idle chatter and requests for days off from work. Although he never listened to her very carefully, Mr. Splinter actually enjoyed hearing Summer's voice, which reminded him of the pleasant twittering of a small bird that kept his mind from dark memories he wanted to avoid.

"So what do you think, Mr. Splinter? Is it okay if I go ahead and make the arrangements?"

Mr. Splinter finally looked up. He blinked, noticing Summer's neon-green outfit for the first time that day. It wasn't exactly appropriate office attire, but then, he had hired Summer more for her cheerful, lighthearted demeanor than for her professional skills.

"Oh, certainly. Go ahead, Summer, have a nice time."

Summer stared at him, wondering if he had actually understood her request. What a strange person Mr. Splinter was. She decided to go ahead and invite Gilda before he changed his mind. She went back to her desk and began to type very quickly.

```
Dear Glinda:
   Mr. Splinter has given me permission to re-
spond to your letter. He said you may come to
visit us this summer. I will look into making
```

flight arrangements for you from Michigan to San Francisco.

By the way, you probably remember that Mr. Splinter has a daughter about your age. Her name is Juliet, and I'm sure she could use some intelligent, unspoiled company. Someone like yourself would do her good.

She's recovering from a little accident she had recently, and she doesn't seem to have many friends. She can be a brat sometimes, but I think that's because she's lonely.

Summer thought for a moment, and then decided to delete the last line about Juliet being a brat, just in case Mr. Splinter happened to see the letter.

I hope your mother is keeping a smile on her face, and that your brother's mental condition is improving.

Look forward to meeting you here in San Francisco!

Summer Matthews

Summer Matthews
Executive Assistant

On the third floor of the Splinter mansion, Juliet lay in bed with her foot propped upon a very expensive pillow. Next to her bed, several untouched sandwiches grew stale upon a plate. A large television screen blared a rerun of *The Munsters,* but Juliet did not laugh at the image of Frankenstein-like Herman Munster crashing through a wall as he walked in his sleep; she was reading a letter from her mother, and her facial expression suggested the look one might make while attempting to eat an entire raw onion.

Dear Juliet,

Your father informed me of your unfortunate little spill down the stairs, so just wanted to send you a little "something" to brighten your day! I was going to try to catch a flight up to San Francisco to visit you, but your father tells me you're doing just fine now, although feeling a little "blue." It's so important to stay positive! I just know you'll be up and going in no time! Fresh air will help!! How about calling some girlfriends for a little company? If I were you I would hate to lie in bed all day. Did I ever tell you that I've never taken a single sick day off from work? I always feel much better when I get to the office!

Things are just crazy here at Alogon: our annual Sales & Earnings conference is this week, and Alogon earnings were disappointing this quarter following some

*"adverse reactions" from our new depression/attention deficit
disorder combination-therapy pill. Your mom has
her work cut out for her as Director of Corporate
Communications!*

*I hope it's not too foggy up in San Fran. That city
can be so depressing with that horrible cloudy weather! Get
me to the beach is all I can say!*

Work hard, play hard!

Love,

Mom

Although she knew that her mother only wanted to help,
Juliet hated reading her bright, encouraging notes, because
they always seemed to be yelling at her. This particular letter reminded her of her mother's repeated attempts to encourage a "sunnier disposition" in her daughter through a
program of energetic activities, Rodeo Drive shopping trips
in L.A., and antianxiety medication produced by Alogon—
things Juliet had ultimately rebelled against at the age of
ten, when she begged to move from her mother's beachfront home in San Diego to foggy San Francisco, where her
father lived.

Juliet's parents had gotten divorced when she was four
years old, and Juliet had only the faintest memories of the
early days when her parents lived together in San Francisco.
After spending much of her childhood in San Diego with

her mother and her two giggling, teenage stepsisters, she found her father's dark, quiet house appealing. Her mother's new husband, Chuck, was always starting a game of beach volleyball and yelling at her to "watch the ball!" and Chuck's muscular, tanned daughters had always made Juliet feel like a vampire: her skin blistered in the sun and she was allergic to sunscreen.

Juliet tossed her mother's letter aside, feeling that she now was more firmly determined than ever to enact the exact opposite of her mother's earnest advice: instead of getting some "fresh air," she would stay inside, wearing her dingy bathrobe. Instead of "calling some girlfriends for a little company," she would remain a hermit, residing in her bedroom and rejecting all visitors for the rest of her life.

Every now and then, Juliet's father cautiously poked his head into Juliet's bedroom to say hello or bring her some educational books to read.

"Wouldn't you like to sit outside in the garden and read?" he asked.

"No, thanks. I'd rather watch television."

"I could take you to see a movie—"

"I'd really rather spend some time alone, thank you."

It was better without people, Juliet reasoned. Who in the world could possibly understand how she felt? She was obviously crazy, after all. She had seen her dead aunt's ghost.

6

A Dismal Progress Report

TO: Gilda Joyce
FROM: Gilda Joyce
RE: Careers Progress Report

PROJECT 1--TRIP TO SAN FRANCISCO
PROGRESS: Outstanding letter sent to Mr.
Lester Splinter.
RESULT: I am losing all hope that I will
ever get to San Francisco.

PROJECT 2--NOVEL-IN-PROGRESS--
"A HAIRY SITUATION"
PROGRESS: The novel is in big trouble
due to the use of a pink wig as the main
character. In the story, the wig kills

Mrs. Frickle, after which it jumps on a plane bound for Mexico.

RESULT: This was supposed to be a horror story, but now I see that it's really an absurd cartoon.

PROJECT 3--PLAID PANTS
SURVEILLANCE PROGRAM

PROGRESS: Dismal. An embarrassment. The loss of Wendy Choy was a blow to the Plaid Pants Surveillance Program, and a major pitfall has occurred. The surveillance program must be terminated for the time being, because Plaid Pants has discovered that he's being watched.

Yesterday, I went to observe Plaid Pants at his place of employment--the Gas Mart convenience store. The suspect (Hector Flack) was wearing his usual plaid pants--pants of an enormous size that probably aren't sold in regular stores. (Why plaid? You would think that he would want to call LESS attention to his boat-sized pants. Of course, it's possible that he can't afford to buy new pants. Worst-case scenario: He owns

SEVERAL PAIRS of the SAME plaid pants
because he thinks they look fantastic.)

As usual, the suspect was eating a
Reese's peanut butter cup and pretending
to read a newspaper, which he was using
to conceal a Seventeen magazine. As usual,
Plaid Pants looked annoyed whenever a
customer interrupted his reading to ask
for gum or cigarettes or lottery tickets.

I pretended to examine the ingredients
on a box of Ho Hos while secretly monitoring Plaid Pants, but made the mistake
of remaining in the Gas Mart too long
after other customers left. That's when
Plaid Pants caught me looking at him.

Plaid Pants: Aren't you a little young
for me?

Me: Excuse me?!

Plaid Pants: You seem to be awfully
interested in somethin' in this Gas
Mart. I mean, I've seen you in here,
lookin' at me.

Me: I'm not looking at you. I'm
looking at these Ho Hos.

Plaid Pants: You like Ho Hos?

Me: I don't know. They're okay.

Plaid Pants: I've seen you in here
before, haven't I?

Me: No.

Plaid Pants: You have a friend--a
Japanese girl.

Me: She's Chinese! I mean, she's
American. Anyway, that probably wasn't
even us.

Plaid Pants: So you girls like
convenience stores, huh?

Me: No.

Plaid Pants: Shoplift much?

Me: No!

Plaid Pants: Come on. I know how you
kids are.

Me: I am NOT shoplifting.

Plaid Pants: I'll give you them
cupcakes for free if you want.

Me: No, thank you. I'm just looking.

Plaid Pants: I can get free stuff here.

Me: You mean, you STEAL stuff?

Plaid Pants: Just takin' what's due me.

Me: You mean, you've been stealing
candy. Your boss said so.

Plaid Pants: AHA! See? I knew you've

been watching me. You've got a little crush or somethin'.

Me: Don't make me puke.

Plaid Pants: Well then, see that sign on the door? It says "No Loitering."

Me: I can read, thank you very much.

Plaid Pants: You know what "loitering" means?

Me: Of course I do. (Actually, I thought it meant something like really bad littering, but it just means lurking around a place, doing nothing.)

Plaid Pants: So you'd better get movin'—and leave them Ho Hos behind before I call the cops. Or your mother. You're supposed to be in school. And don't you know it's dangerous to hang around, talkin' to strangers? You don't know what kind of people are around here.

Me: It's summer. We don't have school.

That's when Plaid Pants gave me one of his squinty-eyed serial killer looks, so I thought I'd better get out of there. MISSION ABORTED.

OTHER UNRESOLVED ISSUES

<u>Wendy Choy</u>: Wendy hasn't written a sin-
gle letter yet. When she comes back from
camp, she'll have stories about her new
friends and how they laughed hysterically
every night while making s'mores and
playing their instruments. There are
probably lots of girls just like Wendy
there--musical prodigies with no baby fat
on their stomachs.

The truth is that I miss Wendy, but I
don't want to give her the satisfaction
of knowing that. Maybe I've relied too
much on Wendy in the past. I need to be
more self-sufficient. And maybe she's
right. Maybe I need to grow up and stop
playing these ridiculous games. At my
age, I should be spending my time going
to the swimming pool and staring at
guys. <u>Do</u> I <u>really</u> <u>have</u> <u>careers,</u> <u>or</u> <u>am</u> I
<u>just</u> <u>weird</u>? I never used to care one way
or the other, but now I'm worried that
I'm simply weird.

<u>SUMMARY:</u> PROGRESS IS POOR ON ALL FRONTS!

Gilda reread her progress report with a feeling of disgust. She suddenly felt extremely low.

Whenever Gilda felt extremely low, she did one of two things: (a) she ate a peanut-butter, banana, and chocolate-syrup sandwich, or (b) she sat at her typewriter and typed a FAVORITE MEMORY. If she typed long enough, she could sometimes create the sense that this experience was happening in real life—almost as if she had managed to go back in time.

A FAVORITE MEMORY
BY GILDA JOYCE

I am seven years old, and it's midnight on Christmas Eve. In the living
room, I see the Christmas tree lights
blinking: on, off; on, off. Mom hates
blinking lights because she thinks
they're "tacky" and "too 1970s," but Dad
and I like them because we think they
have more personality than the boring,
plain lights that everybody else uses.
Outside, the world is frozen solid and
covered in snow. In fact, when I look
out the window, everything looks kind of
ghostly.

I tiptoe into the kitchen, and there's Dad, drinking a cup of hot chocolate and eating a doughnut. That's just the kind of thing Dad used to do--drink hot chocolate and eat a doughnut at midnight. I feel like we're in on some big secret as I sit down at the table with him.

Dad: You just missed Santa Claus.

Me: No, I didn't.

Dad: Sorry, kiddo. I got here just in time to meet him, but we decided not to wake you up.

Me: I don't believe you.

Dad: That's okay; you didn't miss much at all.

Me: What happened?

Dad: Let me think. Yes, now I remember: the first thing Santa did was ask if it was okay to let the reindeer come inside to eat some cookies and warm their hooves by the fire. You know, it gets very cold for them when they're flying through the atmosphere up there.

Me: Reindeer don't eat cookies.

Dad: Now, how would you know that?

Reindeer love cookies! Anyway, the next thing we did was watch some television.

Me: What did you watch?

Dad: <u>David</u> <u>Letterman</u>. Oh, I tell you, we laughed!

Me: What about the reindeer?

Dad: Oh, they watched TV, but they didn't get most of the jokes. In fact, what they really wanted was more cookies, but those were all gone.

Me: They ate ALL the cookies?

Dad: Well, you can't expect a team of flying reindeer to have only one cookie apiece, can you? Anyway, Santa began putting his gifts into stockings and under the tree, but the next thing I knew, he and the reindeer were playing with everything he was planning to leave here for you and Stephen. In fact, they were all having so much fun, Santa began to think they might just want to keep everything for themselves. Santa turns to me and says: "These kids of yours—Gilda and Stephen—are they really all that good?"

Me: What did you say to him? You said yes, didn't you?

Dad: I had to think hard, Gilda. Because you can't tell a lie to Santa Claus. So I thought hard, and I scratched my head. I rubbed my eyes and I squinted at the ceiling for a very long time--like this. "Take your time," says Santa Claus. "There's no rush. None at all."

Me: YOU SHOULD HAVE SAID YES!!

Dad: Well, I finally did realize that the truthful answer was yes. "Santa," I said, "I'm not going to lie to you. These kids of mine aren't perfect, and they both need to clean their rooms more often. But I think they deserve the presents, because they're my favorite people in the world."

So Santa says, "I believe you," and he made the reindeer stop playing with the toys.

Gilda's mother returned home from work and found Gilda fast asleep on the purple carpeting of her bedroom floor next to her typewriter—her "progress report" crumpled in one hand.

"Gilda," said Mrs. Joyce, "why are you sleeping on the floor?"

"I'm not," Gilda mumbled, feeling very disoriented. "I was just thinking."

"Well, get into bed."

Gilda climbed into bed without bothering to put on her pajamas.

Mrs. Joyce sighed. "Did you eat dinner?"

"I think so."

"Is everything okay?"

"I was having a good dream," said Gilda.

"What's that in your hand?"

"Nothing," said Gilda, stuffing the crumpled progress report under her pillow. She didn't want her mother to see the details of her failing projects.

"Good night." Mrs. Joyce wedged the covers around her daughter tightly and kissed her forehead. This was the way she used to tuck her in when Gilda was very young.

Just before turning out the light, Mrs. Joyce noticed Gilda's FAVORITE MEMORY in the typewriter. She stood silently reading for a minute, her hand pressed against her cheek. She knew that Gilda was always typing *something* on that typewriter, but she had to admit that she was surprised by the contents of Gilda's "favorite memory." *I didn't realize she still missed Nick this much,* Mrs. Joyce thought.

After closing the door to Gilda's room, she pulled a crumpled tissue from her pocket and pressed it to her eyes with the same pressure she used to stop a headache—as if trying to push one of her own memories far back into her mind.

7

Never Turn Down an Adventure

For years, the black mailbox outside the house had been Gilda's sullen enemy, withholding letters from friends at camp, valentines, invitations to star-studded events, million-dollar checks, and offering only bills and sappy cards from Grandma Joyce. But today, the fickle mailbox was her friend. Today, the U.S. Postal Service had come through with flying colors.

Gilda stared at the letter with SAN FRANCISCO clearly printed on the return address. She tore open the envelope and read the letter, then reread it three more times. Now, simply as a result of a letter she had written, a whole new world had opened up; she was actually going to San Francisco! She allowed herself the indulgence of skipping from the mailbox back to the front door of her house.

After Gilda calmed down a bit, she had to admit that she was just a little concerned about the surprising reference to "a daughter about your age"—Juliet—who had apparently suffered some kind of "accident" and who had no friends.

Gilda pictured herself spending the summer force-feeding mashed carrots to a large, drooling girl who didn't know how to speak or walk properly. This would be God's way of punishing her for the lie about her brother in her letter to Mr. Splinter.

Gilda decided she was willing to take that risk. After all, she would be in San Francisco.

PACKING LIST FOR SAN FRANCISCO TRIP:
typewriter & lots of paper
notebooks & pens
The Master Psychic's Handbook
Ouija board (just in case)
fishnet stockings
pendulum
strand of fake pearls
binoculars
red lipstick
giant handbag
makeup kit (for disguises)
fake fingernails
bug spray
crucifix

```
flashlight
Polaroid camera
suntan lotion
cat's-eye sunglasses
heart-shaped sunglasses
blond wig
dictionary
thesaurus
leopard-print jacket (for evening)
evening gown (for séances)
blue jeans, T-shirts
miscellaneous accessories
bikini
stiletto pumps
giant hoop earrings
underwear (West Coast style)
```

There was only one remaining problem: How would Gilda convince her mother to let her fly across the country to visit a relative she had never met?

Mrs. Joyce sat in her car in the garage, smoking a cigarette. She wanted to forget the hospital before she entered the house, and she felt that one cigarette on the sly would help her do just that. Although she knew better, being a mother and a nurse, Mrs. Joyce still smoked secretly, usually in her car, the bathroom, or outside, behind the garage.

Her shift at work had been particularly draining, because one of her patients was a teenage boy who had lost his foot in a car accident. "But my foot can't be gone!" he kept yelling. "It still HURTS!"

"That's just phantom pain," Mrs. Joyce had said, holding his hand tightly. "It takes time for your brain to understand what happened, but the pain will go away soon."

But getting to that point is excruciating, she thought as she sighed and stubbed out her cigarette.

When she entered the house, she was surprised to find an alarmingly immaculate and silent atmosphere. Neither Gilda nor Stephen was sprawled on the couch watching sitcoms or reruns of *Star Trek*. No one had made pancakes or popcorn for dinner instead of the casserole she had taken the trouble to leave in the refrigerator. Books had been placed back on the bookshelves and photographs had been straightened. The carpet looked fluffier, as if it had been vacuumed. A wonderful aroma filled the air—the smell of Gilda's homemade chocolate-chip cookies. This was an odor that Mrs. Joyce encountered with some trepidation, since it was usually followed by the discovery of cookie dough splattered on the walls and a wreckage of cookie sheets and mixing bowls in the sink.

This time, nothing unpleasant greeted her—just clean countertops and a plate of chocolate-chip cookies. Next to the plate of cookies was an envelope labeled TO MOM.

Uh-oh, thought Mrs. Joyce, bracing herself for some sort of bad news. She opened the envelope.

```
Dearest Mother:

   I just wanted to take the opportunity
to express my appreciation for you.

   Today I was feeling just the teensiest
bit blue when I realized that ALL of
my friends are out of town, pursuing
glamorous adventures of one sort or
another. Who can blame them? It's like
Dad always used to say: "Never turn down
a chance to have an adventure."

   But after vacuuming the living room,
baking cookies, doing the dishes, and
tidying the entire house, I sat down for
a moment to rest, and I said to myself:
"Gilda, how can you ever feel the least
bit sorry for yourself when you have
such a wonderful, beautiful mother who
works so hard?! You should do everything
you can to make her happy."
```

This made me feel much better. I just
wanted to let you know.   .
  Love, Gilda

P.S. I was invited to San Francisco by
your cousin, Lester Splinter, who has
taken the liberty of purchasing an
airplane ticket for me. I'm sure you'll
agree that this is a great opportunity.
I'll be leaving in a week. (Please see
the attached letter from Mr. Splinter's
Executive Assistant.)

Mrs. Joyce snorted. *I should have known Gilda was up to
something,* she thought. *Leave it to her to find a way to get to San
Francisco on her own!*

Mrs. Joyce didn't like the idea of sending Gilda on a
plane to visit a relative she herself scarcely knew. She knew
that there were many reasons why this was a risky plan,
probably not a good idea, and the sort of thing that a responsible mother would never allow. On the other hand,
Gilda usually ended up getting her way through sheer per-
severance, and Mrs. Joyce found it exhausting trying to argue with her once she had her heart set on something.

Mrs. Joyce decided to get to the bottom of this situation
by calling Lester right away. Nibbling on one of Gilda's

cookies, she dialed the Splinter & Associates office number that appeared on the letter from "Summer Matthews, Executive Assistant," thinking that it would still be a reasonable hour to call San Francisco.

"Splinter here." A man's brisk voice answered immediately.

"Oh! Lester?" Mrs. Joyce spoke with a mouth full of crumbs.

"Who is this, please?"

"Lester, this is Patty—your long-lost cousin."

There was a cold silence on the other end of the phone.

"Remember? Patty McDoogle with the braids and freckles?" Mrs. Joyce couldn't imagine why Lester was being so silent and unfriendly, particularly since he had just invited her daughter to visit him. She remembered her cousin as a shy, serious boy—a boy with neatly combed hair who was always polite, but far too quiet.

"Oh, yes. Patty McDoogle," Mr. Splinter finally replied. "Of course I remember you. What can I do for you? In need of some accounting assistance?"

"Accounting assistance? No—I thought you would be expecting my call. It seems that my daughter, Gilda, has somehow invited herself to visit you in San Francisco this summer? I mean, that was very generous of you to offer, but—"

"I'm afraid I don't know what you're talking about, Patty."

"I see." Mrs. Joyce suddenly felt extremely irritated with

both Gilda and her terse cousin. "In that case, it seems that my thirteen-year-old is playing a little joke; she presented me with an invitation written by someone named Summer Matthews, who she claimed was your assistant. She said she was invited to visit you in California!"

"Really? Hmm. Just a moment, please."

Mrs. Joyce ate two more cookies while she waited for her cousin to return to the phone.

"Well, this is quite embarrassing," said Mr. Splinter, a few moments later. "It seems that I accidentally *did* invite Gilda to visit without realizing it; there was a little communication gap between me and my assistant."

"So it was all a mistake."

"Well, yes. But—your daughter is welcome to visit. I must admit I work long hours, so I may not be very entertaining for a young girl. But we certainly have more than enough room in the house. And my own daughter is about that age."

"Oh, I completely forgot! But doesn't she live with her mother in San Diego?"

"Juliet has lived with me for several years now. I've actually been a bit worried about her lately, and—well, I wonder if some company with someone her own age would do her good this summer. Who knows? Maybe Gilda and Juliet would become friends."

"Well, of course they would!"

"Maybe," said Mr. Splinter mysteriously. "But let's not have unreasonable expectations."

"Why would you pack this?" Mrs. Joyce exclaimed, holding up the ratty blond wig that Gilda had packed. "Or this?!" Mrs. Joyce pulled the leopard-print jacket from Gilda's suitcase.

"Mom," said Gilda, "I told you to leave that stuff alone; I might need it."

"For what?"

"It just might come in useful is all."

"This doesn't seem like very practical clothing to take to San Francisco, Gilda. And these stiletto shoes? How are you going to walk around the city wearing *these*?"

"Well, I'm not going to wear them every day. I'm taking my sneakers, too."

Mrs. Joyce sighed as she neatly folded clothes that Gilda had tossed randomly into her suitcase. "Do you have enough underwear?"

"They don't wear underwear in California."

"I beg your pardon?"

"I'm kidding, of course. I have loads of underwear!" Gilda picked up a pile of underwear from her suitcase. "See? Enough panties for the whole city!"

"Very funny, Gilda. I just don't want you to get there and then find out that you forgot something like your toothbrush, or that you have absolutely nothing *practical* to wear. Besides, I'm guessing that my cousin Lester is still a very formal, conservative person, and he may not understand your—your quirks."

"What quirks?"

"You know what I mean." Mrs. Joyce stood up and looked through Gilda's closet. "Why not wear this nice sundress I bought you?"

Gilda watched helplessly as her mother returned to the suitcase and continued to rummage through the luggage Gilda had hastily packed. She knew that her mother had a talent for fitting large amounts of clothing into small spaces and that she should be grateful for the help, but she hoped her mother wouldn't discover the psychic paraphernalia at the bottom of the suitcase.

"What is *this?* You're taking a Ouija board?"

Gilda tried to act nonchalant. "I've read that there are lots of ghosts in San Francisco—in some of those old houses."

"Well, that may well be true," said Mrs. Joyce, "but this is certainly taking up a lot of space in your suitcase." Then Mrs. Joyce picked up *The Master Psychic's Handbook.* "My goodness, you certainly are interested in the paranormal these days!"

"Gilda's always been gullible." Mrs. Joyce and Gilda looked up to see Stephen leaning against the doorway to Gilda's room. He was shirtless and extremely sweaty because he had just been mowing the lawn outside.

"I wouldn't assume that Gilda is merely gullible," said Mrs. Joyce. "After all, my own mother used to claim that she saw ghosts in our kitchen!"

Gilda had always wished she'd gotten a chance to know her grandmother better; it seemed that she might have possessed some psychic abilities. "I bet I could have learned a lot from Grandma McDoogle," said Gilda.

"Grandma McDoogle was nuts," said Stephen. "She was afraid of leprechauns!"

"Leprechauns can be scary things," said Mrs. Joyce. "When I was a little girl, we were all spooked by the idea that they might be lurking around."

Stephen winced as if her superstition actually caused him pain.

"Mom," said Gilda, "if Grandma McDoogle was still alive, do you think she would be able to see Dad's ghost? Or talk to him?"

Stephen abruptly left the room. A quick exit was his usual response when the subject of their deceased father came up.

"I hate when he does that," said Gilda.

"I know, but just be patient with him. Boys don't want to talk about things as much as girls do, and it's difficult for him to see you getting an opportunity to travel while he'll probably be here working all summer."

"Well, I'll buy him a T-shirt," said Gilda, rather unsympathetically. She knew the feeling was wrong, but Gilda couldn't help but enjoy the fleeting sense of superiority that accompanied doing *something* exciting and worthy of others' attention for a change. It seemed to her that Stephen had always been admired for his brains and his work ethic; today it was her turn to be in the spotlight.

"But what do you think about my question?" Gilda asked.

"About whether my mother would be able to see your father's ghost?"

Gilda nodded.

"Gilda, I don't think your father would ever appear as a ghost. I believe he's in heaven, and that means that his soul is at rest. Your grandmother always believed that ghosts are lost souls—people stuck in limbo. She *pitied* them."

"But—don't you ever wish you could *see* Dad, or have a conversation with him?"

Mrs. Joyce's blue eyes crinkled in a way that suggested sadness rather than her usual smile. "Of course I do," she said. "And the truth is, sometimes I still talk to him."

"You do?!" This surprised Gilda; she thought she was the only one in the family who tried to communicate with her father.

"Sometimes I even believe that he hears me," Mrs. Joyce said, "but he can't answer in words."

But I want *him to answer in words,* Gilda thought.

8

The Splinter Mansion

Gilda shivered in the plaid sundress her mother had urged her to wear to San Francisco. Why was California so cold? It was the middle of July, but it felt like November outside the San Francisco airport.

Gilda waved down a cab, and imagined that she was a movie star as she climbed into the taxi and gave the driver the address in the glamorous-sounding neighborhood of Pacific Heights, where Lester Splinter lived. Here she was, all by herself in California! Here she was, riding in a taxi without her mother!

But as the taxi sped over the highway through a land-scape of dry hillsides, Gilda had a strange, wobbly feeling. Nothing seemed to grow on the rocky, red-brown soil. Where were the trees? Where was the sun? What if she had somehow ended up in the wrong state?

"Excuse me," said Gilda to the cabdriver. "Are you sure this is California?"

"You kidding me, right?" the driver replied.

"I thought it was supposed to be sunny here."

"July in San Francisco is fog. And wind." The driver didn't speak much English. He waved his hand as if dismissing the entire concept of summer as an absurd idea.

Gilda gazed through the window at clusters of cube-shaped buildings built into the hillsides. They were small, rickety shacks built almost directly on top of one another.

"Excuse me again," said Gilda, leaning forward and talking into the cabdriver's ear. "Where's the Golden Gate Bridge?"

"Other side of the city." The driver glanced warily at Gilda in the rearview mirror and pointed to a remote spot on the windshield. "But we don't go over Golden Gate from this way."

"Oh." Gilda was disappointed. She had pictured herself driving over the Golden Gate Bridge with sunlight streaming through the windows and her favorite old song, "Hot Child in the City," playing on the radio. *Why is nothing in life EVER the same as in my imagination?* she wondered.

After driving through a dilapidated portion of the city, the cab turned and headed up a steep hill toward a more upscale neighborhood. Mrs. Joyce had told Gilda that the houses of San Francisco were called "painted ladies," and now Gilda could see why: some of them resembled tall women in fancy ball gowns of pink and blue, all sitting coyly along the street, hoping to be admired; others resembled giant wedding cakes frosted with ornate façades of bows, wreaths, and flowers. All along the sidewalk there were stately palm trees and squat trees shaped like umbrellas. Large, bright red flowers hung from their branches like Christmas-tree ornaments.

Gilda dug her fingernails into the leather upholstery of the backseat as the cab ascended a hill that seemed to be as steep as the first incline of an amusement-park roller coaster.

When they reached the top of the hill, the driver squinted through the window at the address of one of the houses. "Is this it?" He looked at Gilda in the rearview mirror.

"I don't know," said Gilda, peering through the window. "I've never been here before."

"This is the address you give me."

"I guess this is it, then."

Gilda hesitated for a moment, hoping that some cheerful adult would emerge from the house to greet her. When nobody appeared, she paid the cabdriver with the money her mother had given her and stepped out of the cab. The taxi drove away, leaving her standing alone at the foot of the huge house.

As Gilda gazed up at the house, she felt as if she were a

peasant approaching the foot of a vast castle. She had never seen anything like *this* in Michigan!

Unlike the other bright, opulent houses on the street, the Splinter mansion showed signs of decay. Parts of the house's façade were crumbling, and the faded pink-and-yellow trim around its doors and windows looked as if it hadn't been painted in ages. One side was rounded with curved bay windows dressed with tattered lace curtains; the other side featured stained-glass decorations in dark shades of red and blue.

Gilda shivered, partly because the wind off the bay carried an icy chill, and partly because she had just noticed something rising from behind the house—a pointed tower shaped like a witch's hat.

Gilda immediately felt a light-headed sensation and an inexplicable tickle in her left ear. She was now certain that there was a reason she had been drawn to San Francisco: she had a gut feeling about this house—the kind of "magnetic attraction" that her *Master Psychic's Handbook* often discussed.

This house has a secret to reveal, Gilda told herself.

Gilda began to climb the steep stairway leading to the front door, lugging her suitcase and backpack. Her suitcase—which had no convenient wheels for pulling it behind her—was extremely heavy because it contained her typewriter. Mrs. Joyce had begged Gilda to leave the heavy machine behind, but Gilda had refused. Even though it weighed a ton, she felt better knowing it would be there with her. In this strange new place, the typewriter was Gilda's only familiar, trusted friend.

Gilda pressed the doorbell, and after several minutes, a short Hispanic woman opened the door and said, "No more Girl Scout cookies today, please." The door clicked shut.

Outraged, Gilda pounded on the door.

The woman cracked the door open and peered at her quizzically.

"I'm not selling cookies," said Gilda indignantly.

The woman stared at her in a way that made Gilda wonder if she was at the wrong house. What if the entire arrangement had been a mistake? "Look," said Gilda, "does Mr. Lester Splinter live here?"

"Mr. Splinter is not here now."

"Well, I'm Gilda Joyce. I'm *related* to him, and he invited me to visit."

The woman frowned. "He invited you?"

Gilda pulled Summer's crumpled letter from her backpack. "See? And Mr. Splinter spoke to my mother just the other day."

Gilda felt worried: what if she was stuck here with nowhere to stay? Her imagination raced through a series of unlikely scenarios as the woman put on her eyeglasses and squinted at the letter skeptically. First, she would steal a shopping cart. She would load her suitcase in it, then wander down to the poor section of town, where she would lose her identity completely. On the other hand, she did have her typewriter with her, which meant that if she could manage to sit on a park bench and quickly type a novel, she might be able to sell it for a million dollars and buy one of these "painted lady" houses for herself . . .

"Okay—you come in, and I will call Mr. Splinter. He never *tell* me what is going on!"

Grateful to get out of the windy air, Gilda entered the dark, brooding house. Always fascinated with the smell of other people's homes, the first thing Gilda noticed inside the Splinter mansion was an antique scent that reminded her of old doilies and stale tea—an elderly, refined smell that evoked a memory of a very tedious historical tour she had once taken. If she hadn't known about Mr. Splinter and his daughter, Gilda would have assumed that she was in the home of a wealthy old woman.

Gilda found herself in a parlor crowded with overstuffed velvet chairs that crouched upon wooden lion's feet. Above her, a crystal chandelier that resembled an enormous ice monster clung to the ceiling. The room seemed to regard visitors with an aged, haughty attitude, and as Gilda surveyed her surroundings, she noticed no evidence whatsoever that a teenage girl lived in the house. Clearly, the inhabitants of the Splinter mansion were very wealthy, but the absence of any books, photographs, or other personal items made it impossible to guess what Mr. Splinter and his daughter would actually be like in person.

Normally Gilda would have wanted to touch every object and inspect every drawer she encountered, but she now had the disturbing sensation that the room itself was observing *her*—as if she were an uninvited guest who had suddenly barged in on a formal party. The chairs actually looked as if they might bite her if she tried to sit on them. Gilda wandered through the room and peered through a large bay window that offered a view of several enormous houses perched at lower levels on the hillside. Farther in the distance, fog drifted across the water of San Francisco Bay.

From the next room, Gilda heard the Hispanic woman, who seemed to be a housekeeper, speaking on the phone: "Her name is Geelda. She has a letter from you. Oh, Mr. Splinter knows? Okay. Okay. That man, he never tell me what is going on!"

The woman returned and picked up Gilda's suitcase. "My name is Rosa," she said. "I am the housekeeper here. Mr. Splinter might not be home until very late this evening, but he will meet you tomorrow."

Rosa lugged the suitcase up a steep flight of stairs that

creaked beneath her feet, and Gilda followed close behind, noticing that she and Rosa were about the same height.

When they reached the top of the first flight of stairs, Rosa put down the suitcase and placed her hands on her hips. "Why is this suitcase so heavy?" she demanded.

"There's a typewriter in it."

"A *typewriter!*" Rosa mumbled something in Spanish. Gilda guessed it was something along the lines of *What kind of lunatic would pack a typewriter in a suitcase?*

"That's okay; I can carry it myself." Gilda dragged the suitcase up another narrow stairway to the third floor. When they reached the top of the stairs, she stopped to catch her breath and gazed down a long, austere hallway lined with several doors—each of them tightly shut. Gilda reflected that there was always something intriguing and ominous about a hallway lined with locked doors.

"What's in these rooms?" she asked.

"I think there is nothing much," Rosa replied. "Mr. Splinter's mother used them when she lived here many years ago, and then Mr. Splinter's wife, Margo, she used to keep her things in those rooms. But now—we keep them closed. I say, thank God for that! Too many rooms to clean!"

Gilda wanted to ask more questions about Mr. Splinter's mother and his ex-wife, Margo, but Rosa turned to the right and walked briskly down the hallway with a businesslike efficiency that silenced Gilda's inquiries for the time being. When she reached the end of the hall, Rosa took a ring choked with about a hundred keys from her pocket. After a few tries, she located the correct key, and the door to the guest room swung open with a creak.

Gilda sneezed.

"It is very dusty," said Rosa. "Tomorrow I will clean."

Inside, there was a canopy bed draped by gauzy curtains, a dressing table, and, to Gilda's delight, a writing table.

"Wow—this is great!" she said, putting down her suitcase and parting the white drapes on the canopy bed. She sat down on the bedspread. "This reminds me of the kind of bed they have in old movies where a vampire creeps into the room at night."

Rosa didn't smile. "I do not think a vampire will come here," she said, very seriously. "But there are ghosts in this house, of course."

Gilda sat up straight. "There are *ghosts* in this house?" she asked eagerly.

"Of course," said Rosa.

"You mean you see them just standing around, or what?"

"Sometimes I see them; sometimes I hear them. The ones in the house here, they don't bother me. They do their thing; I do my thing." Rosa spoke in a matter-of-fact tone, as if she were mentioning some construction workers she had hired for home repairs.

Gilda had the dizzying sensation of wanting to ask a million questions all at once. "But . . . Do you know who these ghosts *are?* What do they *look* like? What do they do?"

Rosa shrugged. "I think they just sit in the chairs and maybe knit and drink tea. Probably same things they do in their life. This is a very old house, and many old ladies have lived here." She began to dust a dresser as she spoke. "But in the tower . . . There is something there that is evil."

Gilda wondered whether Rosa was trying to scare her on purpose. Adults were not supposed to say things like "There is something there that is evil," especially to kids. But Rosa seemed completely serious.

Rosa pointed to a wall at the back of the guest room. "Behind that wall is the tower. You will see it when you are outside in the backyard."

Gilda stared at the wall and remembered the pointy tower that she had seen peeking over the top of the house. "What's *in* it that's evil?" For some reason, Gilda felt the need to whisper.

Rosa also lowered her voice. "Mr. Splinter's sister, Melanie—many years ago she jumped from that tower to her death. Something inside that tower made her turn insane. Since then, Mr. Splinter does not let anybody go into that tower." Rosa shivered. "If he ask me to *clean* that tower—I quit!"

Gilda's mind reeled with two very opposite impulses.

The psychic-investigator part of her couldn't wait to begin snooping to find out what was inside that mysterious tower, but the other part of her mind—the wimpy, fearful, *weak* part that she always made an effort to squelch—simply wanted to get on a plane and return to Michigan, where everything was safe and boring compared with this foggy, ghost-infested place.

Rosa fluffed the pillows on the bed. "The ghost of a suicide—that is very bad luck." She turned to leave. "I go finish my work now, and you come downstairs at six o'clock, and I will make dinner."

"Wait—Rosa?"

"Yes?"

"What about Juliet? Is Mr. Splinter's daughter here?"

"Her room is at the other end of the hallway. She is resting. She took a bad fall and hurt her foot."

Gilda sensed that Rosa was growing weary of her incessant questions, so she refrained from asking exactly how Juliet fell.

"You can go say hello if you wish, but you should know that she is not a person who likes talking."

This didn't sound encouraging. Her mom had warned Gilda that Mr. Splinter was not the warm, friendly sort and that chances were good his mysterious daughter would be similarly aloof.

After Rosa left, Gilda walked to the window and parted

the lace curtains. She gazed down at a small garden of un-kempt rosebushes and tangled lilies that almost completely concealed what appeared to be an angel statue. Beyond that were the flat rooftop terraces and turrets of other enormous houses built on the hillside leading down to San Francisco Bay. Waves of fog now covered the bay like ghostly blankets; the sky seemed to be composed of vapors—steam rising from a witch's cauldron.

Gilda felt another wave of unease, so she turned to the mirror on the dressing table and looked at herself sternly. "Get a grip, Gilda. You're on your own now, so toughen up and stop being a baby. Whoever heard of a psychic investi-gator who's afraid of ghosts?"

Gilda opened her suitcase and placed her trusty Under-wood typewriter on the writing desk. The typewriter al-ways made her feel calmer.

She put a piece of paper in the machine and typed:

Things to investigate:
What is inside that tower? Find a way
to explore it. (I have to admit, I wish
Wendy was here to help with that.)
Ghosts:
Observe as many as possible and try to
communicate with them. Try not to be

```
scared. Remember: ghosts are like
spiders; you might not want to see
them, but most of them can't hurt you.
```

Gilda found this last line very inspiring, and decided to make an effort to use it in conversation sometime soon.

Gilda looked at her watch. It was only 5:00, so she had an hour before dinner at six. She thought of her mother, who would now be working at the hospital. Feeling a momentary twinge of homesickness, Gilda contemplated calling her, but decided instead to take the risk of paying Juliet a visit. Perhaps Mr. Splinter's daughter could tell her more about the story behind the mysterious tower.

9

Meeting Juliet

Gilda hesitated before knocking on Juliet's door at the end of the long hallway. She took a deep breath and rapped lightly on the door.

"Juliet?"

There was no reply. Gilda pressed her ear to the door and heard voices from a television sitcom in the room.

Just as Gilda was about to turn and walk away, the door swung open to reveal a gaunt girl who wore a bathrobe and leaned on a single crutch. Juliet's blond hair was so unclean it looked almost brown, and a large orange-juice stain marked the cashmere bathrobe she had been wearing for the past few weeks. Her room had a musty odor combined with the faint stench of illness.

Juliet gazed at Gilda with blank awe, as if she wasn't sure whether Gilda was real.

"S-sorry to bother you," Gilda stammered, "but I just wanted to introduce myself."

"Who are you?" Juliet spoke with a small voice that was at once soft and icy.

Despite her unkempt appearance, Juliet had a kind of diminutive, prim demeanor that made Gilda feel very large and sloppy, as if she were an enormous puppy with muddy paws that had just been introduced to a tiny French poodle. "I'm a distant relative of your father's," said Gilda. "I mean, my mom is his second cousin or something. Didn't your dad *tell* you he invited me to visit?"

"My father *invited* you to visit?"

"I got a letter from his assistant, Summer—"

"Oh—*her*. I didn't know we had any relatives." Juliet didn't sound particularly excited about the discovery.

"I guess you do," said Gilda, not knowing what else to say.

Juliet eyed Gilda's wrinkled plaid sundress and flip-flops with disapproval. She could tell they were cheap, and not the least bit trendy. Juliet didn't exactly *mean* to be snobbish; this way of thinking was simply second nature to her. Her mother often took her on extravagant shopping trips, and the girls at school were almost all wealthy and well dressed.

Gilda sensed that Juliet was the sort of girl who probably wore designer clothing every day of the week when she wasn't in her bathrobe—the kind of girl who almost certainly would have ignored Gilda if they had happened to go to the same school. Of course, they would never become friends. Gilda now regretted having bothered to introduce herself.

"So what happened to you?" Gilda asked bluntly, staring at the crutch under Juliet's arm.

Juliet closed the door in Gilda's face without another word.

Gilda fumed. *When people are mean-spirited and rude, I pity them,* Gilda's mother sometimes said. For a moment, Gilda tried to feel pity for the obviously unhappy girl who had just dismissed her, but she could only feel rage. She had hoped that she could ask Juliet about the tower and the ghosts, but talking with Juliet was more unpleasant than the notion of facing several demons by herself.

When Gilda was really angry, only her typewriter could help. She returned to her room, and with a flurry of loud, snapping keystrokes, began a story entitled "The World's Most Disgusting Girl":

One morning, Juliet Splinter awoke to discover that her right foot was rotting and that all of her hair had fallen out overnight. Nobody wanted to come near

her because she smelled like a sewer
rat . . .

Gilda felt only slightly better after imagining Juliet's various diseases and misfortunes. Then she noticed that it was just after six o'clock, and that she was very hungry.

Downstairs in the kitchen, Gilda found Rosa flipping a tortilla in a skillet. Gilda's mouth watered at the aroma of melted cheese and sautéed onions.

"What are you making?" Gilda asked.

"Quesadillas. You like Mexican food?"

"I love it!" said Gilda. "My friend Wendy and I go to Taco Bell all the time in Michigan."

Rosa looked disgusted and muttered something in Spanish. She pointed a spatula at Gilda. "That is not real Mexican!" Rosa proceeded to complain that Mr. Splinter and Juliet had no appreciation for Mexican food: "Mr. Splinter, he only wants a vodka tonic after work, and sometimes a steak. Most times he eats out anyway."

"What about Juliet?"

"Don't get me started on that girl! She eats nothing but celery and hard-boiled eggs! And only in her room. She never will come downstairs for dinner."

"She seems kind of . . . different," said Gilda cautiously.

"It is not her fault, but she is a bad seed."

This statement intrigued Gilda, who had always suspected that certain people were simply "born bad."

Rosa deftly sprinkled cheese on a quesadilla while simultaneously flipping several tortillas on the stove. "She never says one nice word. I think she may be *loco* like her dead aunt." She twirled her finger next to her head.

"Did you know Juliet's aunt?"

Rosa shook her head. "Mr. Splinter, he hired me a few years after his sister died."

"So how do you know she was crazy?"

Rosa shrugged. "It is crazy to jump from a tower window, no?"

"I guess."

"You like jalapeños?"

"Who?"

"You like it spicy?"

"I guess so."

"Want a margarita?"

"Okay, I guess."

"Just kidding. You are too young." Rosa seemed more animated when she was cooking—almost giddy.

"Rosa," Gilda ventured, "do you see any ghosts right now?"

Rosa glanced around the room. "Too noisy right now. They like it quiet."

Rosa served quesadillas to Gilda in the dining room, then prepared a tray with celery and hard-boiled eggs to take upstairs to Juliet. "For her majesty," said Rosa, winking at Gilda.

After delivering the tray to Juliet, Rosa wrapped a scarf around her head and placed some of the quesadillas she had made in a basket. "Okay, Geelda. I am leaving now."

"Where are you going? Aren't you going to eat dinner?"

"I will eat at home with my kids."

"I thought you lived here."

Rosa shook her head. "Too many ghosts in this house for me."

"Really?!"

"Just kidding! See you tomorrow."

"Wait—when does Mr. Splinter come home?"

"Tonight, very late. He sometimes works until ten or eleven o'clock."

Gilda sat alone under the massive crystal chandelier, which looked as though it might pull the whole ceiling down at any minute. Through the window, the world outside had been swallowed completely by fog.

Gilda's stomach tightened as she remembered Rosa's comment about how the ghosts in the house "like it quiet." She glanced around the dining room, half expecting to see the chairs suddenly populated with white-haired ladies wearing gauzy dresses and holding teacups. "Hello?" she asked tentatively. "Is anybody here?" A loud, mooing sound, like the mournful call of a giant mechanical cow, was the only reply. Gilda almost jumped out of her seat, but then she realized that the sound was only a foghorn blasting across the bay.

Forcing herself to be brave, Gilda wandered through the parlor and the library. *The ghosts must love this house,* she thought, noticing that all the walls were decorated with peeling wallpaper in faded floral patterns or painted a dusty shade of green. In the dim light, dark pieces of furniture with lion's feet resembled living creatures that had fallen asleep.

Gilda wondered when Mr. Splinter would finally return from work. What if he turned out to be even meaner than Juliet? He certainly didn't seem to be in any hurry to meet his houseguest from Michigan.

Gilda felt something soft brushing against her leg and let out an involuntary shriek. She found herself looking down at a huge gray cat.

"How long have you been here in this room?" Gilda asked.

The cat peered up at her expectantly with topaz eyes, its fluffy tail twitching back and forth like a plume of blue smoke. Gilda was allergic to cat hair, but cats always had a perverse way of seeking her company.

"Excuse me," said Gilda, feeling, for some reason, that it would be rude to walk away from the cat without some explanation.

Deciding that she'd prefer not to meet Mr. Splinter until absolutely necessary, Gilda began to climb the creaking staircases that led to her bedroom on the third floor. As she ascended the stairs, Gilda again had the disturbing feeling that she was being watched. Half expecting to see the cat following her up the stairs, she turned to look behind her, but she was alone in the house.

Except for Juliet.

Now that it was dark, the idea of being alone in this house with her made Gilda feel paranoid. There was something freakish about that frail, haunted-looking girl.

With a burst of frightened energy, Gilda ran the rest of the way up the stairs. Then she noticed a dim glow of light at the end of the hallway.

The light came from Juliet's bedroom; strangely, Juliet had left her door open. There was something odd about this: Gilda distinctly remembered Juliet slamming the door in her face, and it seemed surprising that she would leave her door open on purpose when Gilda was around.

Gilda held her breath and listened. She thought she

heard a faint sound coming from inside the room, like a whispering voice that rose and fell in a cadence of conversation that was too faint to hear clearly. Was Juliet talking to someone? If so—to whom? Weren't the two of them alone in the house? Gilda supposed it was possible that Juliet was talking on the phone, but something about the tone of the voice seemed too whispery and strange to be normal conversation.

Now as curious as she was frightened, Gilda moved slowly toward Juliet's doorway, edging sideways and keeping her back close to the wall in an attempt to conceal herself in the shadows. *Right foot, left foot, right foot, left foot,* until she got close enough to cautiously peek into the room without being seen.

Gilda felt an electric chill when she saw Juliet. Wearing a disheveled white nightgown, the pale girl sat straight up in bed, apparently engaged in conversation with someone Gilda could not see. Juliet's eyes were wide open, staring straight ahead, but they seemed unfocused, like the eyes of a blind girl. She spoke earnestly, but her words were incomprehensibly garbled: some words sounded like regular English, but most of her phrases were complete nonsense. Although Gilda thought she heard the phrase "you will see my eyes" and something that sounded like the "tower," the girl seemed to speak an alien language, as if she were hypnotized—under some kind of spell.

"Juliet?" Gilda whispered, feeling bewildered and wondering whether she should try to do something to help. Was it possible that Juliet was speaking to one of the ghosts that Rosa claimed to see? "Juliet, who are you talking to?"

Juliet didn't respond. She couldn't hear or see Gilda.

Gilda boldly stepped directly into Juliet's room, but Juliet remained in her trance, completely oblivious to Gilda's presence.

As she observed with horrified fascination, Gilda reflected that something about Juliet's demeanor reminded her of a kid she had known at Girl Scout camp who used to talk in her sleep. Sometimes the girl would even climb out of her bunk bed in the middle of the night and walk around the cabin. This had been a source of great amusement to her fellow campers, since she would sometimes blurt embarrassing nonsensical phrases from her dreams like "Butts ahoy!" and "Aren't you wearing panties?"

After that experience, Gilda had taken a brief interest in sleepwalking and sleep-talking, and had read about a man who once woke up waist-deep in a lagoon, surrounded by alligators, and a woman who awoke from a deep sleep to find herself in her car, driving down the highway. Clearly, there were people who did all kinds of strange things in their sleep.

Juliet had now lowered her voice to a faint whisper, but her blank eyes remained focused on the same spot on the wall. Gilda reflected that even if Juliet wasn't speaking to a ghost, there was something decidedly *spooky* about her entranced state of mind.

Worried that Juliet might suddenly awaken, Gilda quietly retreated, closing the door behind her. She walked as fast as she could down the dark hallway leading to her own bedroom.

Once safely back in the guest room, Gilda turned on the light and sat down in front of the typewriter. She typed one of her favorite quotations:

```
"The only thing we have to fear is
fear itself."
```

The familiar *click! clack! clack!* of the typewriter was immediately comforting. In an attempt to distract herself from her own racing imagination, Gilda decided to write a letter to Wendy Choy. After all, she wanted Wendy to know that she had made good on her promise to get herself to San Francisco.

```
Dear Wendy,
    I hate to interrupt the campfire
debutante ball or whatever it is you're
```

doing, but just thought I'd write to say hello.

You may be interested to know that I'm writing to you from San Francisco, from a haunted Victorian mansion. I'm getting great experience for my new business, Psychic Investigations Inc.

The current inhabitants of the house are myself (dressed very stylishly); a Mexican housekeeper named Rosa (who makes the best margarita this side of Tijuana); an anorexic sociopath named Juliet who is either a sleep-talker or under a witch's spell (it's hard to say exactly how old she is); and Mr. Lester Splinter, who is so mysterious, he seems to be invisible. (I haven't even met him yet.)

Lester Splinter had a sister who killed herself about ten years ago by jumping out the window of a tower that's attached to the house. Apparently it's just on the other side of the wall of the room I'm staying in. There are rumors of something evil lurking in this

```
tower, so in the event you never hear
from me again, please try to get my
novels published when you come home
from camp. They're in my bedroom closet.
Thanks.
    To be honest, I wish you were here; it
would be more fun.
    Miss you,
    Gilda


P.S. Remind me to tell you about a
fiasco involving Plaid Pants.
```

A door slammed shut downstairs. Gilda froze. She heard footsteps moving from room to room. For a moment, Gilda panicked, then decided the intruder had to be Mr. Splinter, returning from work.

Not wanting to face an awkward introduction and a series of questions, Gilda quickly pulled on a nightshirt, turned off the light, and jumped into bed. She drew the gauzy drapes around her bed and curled up in a ball under the covers. She heard Mr. Splinter's quick footsteps moving upstairs and into a room on the second floor, then the sad mooing of the foghorn across the bay. Gilda squeezed her eyes shut and hoped to fall asleep quickly.

10

The Footsteps Behind the Wall

At two o'clock in the morning, Gilda awoke to the sound of something moving behind her bedroom wall. She listened: *thump, thump, thump, thump, thump . . .* The sound grew louder, then softer, then louder again. Could it be the sounds of a small animal? Tree branches bumping against the house? No—these definitely sounded like *footsteps* pacing back and forth.

Gilda remembered Rosa's warning about the tower: *There is something there that is evil.*

Gilda pulled the covers over her head, but it seemed that the sounds of nervous, pacing footsteps only grew louder. *Thump, thump, thump, thump, thump!*

I'm supposed to be a Psychic Investigator! Gilda chided herself. *Would a real psychic investigator lie in bed, quaking with fear? No! She would get up and do her job!*

With a surge of courage, Gilda threw off her covers and

ran to switch on the lamp perched on the writing desk. Flooded with light, the room suddenly fell eerily silent.

Gilda rummaged in her suitcase until she found her small silver crucifix. *Just in case it IS an evil spirit,* she told herself. Clutching the cross, she pressed her ear against the wall and listened. The sounds of footsteps seemed to recede, as if they might be heading down a staircase behind the wall. Moving her hands over the floral wallpaper, Gilda half expected to push open a secret entranceway into the tower.

"Hello?" she said hesitantly.

SLAM! Somewhere on the other side of the wall, a door closed with violent force.

Startled, Gilda stumbled backward into the writing table. The lamp crashed to the floor with a loud clatter. The lightbulb broke with a dull popping noise, leaving her in darkness.

Gilda groped her way through the room in search of a light switch. Stubbing her toe in the process, she let out a shriek of pain before finally locating the doorknob and bursting into the hallway.

A man's voice called out from the floor below. "Juliet? Juliet, are you okay?" Gilda heard purposeful footsteps heading up the stairs.

"It's just me," Gilda called out in a small voice. "I—I knocked over a lamp . . ."

Light spilled up the stairway and Mr. Splinter appeared on the landing below, tying a maroon bathrobe over his matching pajamas. He was tall and silver-haired, with the same thin-lipped mouth as his daughter. Even in his pajamas, he had the look of a serious man—a man of business. Gilda couldn't help but notice that this man was the exact opposite of her own father, who used to sleep in his underwear and a torn T-shirt that advertised GREAT CARS AND BARS OF THE MOTOR CITY! In the morning, her father's curly hair had always stuck up in clumps and spikes that seemed to defy gravity.

A fleeting expression of horror, followed by blank confusion, crossed Mr. Splinter's face when he saw Gilda standing at the top of the stairs wearing nothing but an oversized General Motors T-shirt that had once belonged to her father. He squinted, trying to see Gilda more clearly without his glasses.

The terror Gilda had experienced just a moment before now turned to embarrassment. "Hi, I'm Gilda," she said awkwardly.

"Oh, you're Patty's daughter," said Mr. Splinter, sounding relieved. "Now I remember—Summer said you would be arriving today."

Gilda felt as if she were a young child who had wandered into the wrong house by mistake. Mr. Splinter made no move to ascend the stairs, to shake her hand or give her a perfunctory hug as a long-lost, distant relative. It was impossible to tell whether he was mildly pleased, irritated, or secretly angry to see Gilda. He simply looked up at her from the landing below, as if expecting her to explain herself further. Gilda wondered if this was because she had essentially invited herself to visit.

"Thanks for letting me visit," she said.

"I hope you'll enjoy your stay here," said Mr. Splinter.

He sounds like a hotel manager, Gilda thought. Was this cool, formal politeness simply the way rich people talked to one another?

"How is your mother?" Mr. Splinter asked, more out of politeness than genuine curiosity.

"She's very well, thank you," said Gilda, attempting to mirror Mr. Splinter's terse, formal manner.

"And your father?"

Was Mr. Splinter kidding? "Well, he's *dead,* but otherwise fine," said Gilda.

Mr. Splinter looked confused and embarrassed. "Oh— I'm sorry. Perhaps I did hear something, but . . . I haven't seen Patty in so long. I'm terribly sorry."

Gilda didn't know what to say. When people said "I'm sorry" about her father's death, she was supposed to say "That's okay" to make them feel better. But it wasn't okay. There couldn't ever be enough "sorries" to make it "okay," so instead she remained silent.

"Well, I heard something fall, and I wanted to see if anyone was hurt." Mr. Splinter glanced up in the direction of his daughter's bedroom door, then turned to leave.

"Wait—" Gilda blurted. "Something was making a strange noise near my room."

"You know how these old houses can be," said Mr. Splinter dismissively.

"But I'm sure I heard *footsteps* coming from the other side of the wall. There's somebody—or *something*—in that tower!"

Mr. Splinter's shoulders stiffened, and his face contorted for just a split second, resembling the lopsided grimace one makes when avoiding tears. "Well, I know Rosa claims that we have some ghosts in the house, but I myself am not superstitious."

"Maybe it isn't a ghost," said Gilda impatiently, "but there's *something* moving around in there!" Gilda realized that her tone had become shrill, but she couldn't stand it when adults tried to dismiss something that was real. She had once had a lengthy argument with a biology teacher who had refused to believe that the starfish she was dissecting had moved on her tray, when Gilda was certain that it had.

"There couldn't be anything in that tower because it has been locked and completely sealed for the last ten years!" Mr. Splinter retorted, showing his irritation openly. "Now, if you'll excuse me, I have to get up early in the morning. Good night, Gilda. I'll have Rosa see about the lamp in your room tomorrow."

"But—"

Mr. Splinter disappeared down the stairs, leaving Gilda standing alone in the dim light.

A door creaked open down the hall, and Gilda turned, breathless, to see Juliet peering at her.

"I heard it, too," said Juliet.

11

Melanie's Ghost

So I'm *not* crazy," said Juliet, sitting on her bed with her arms wrapped around her legs, chin resting on bony knees. "You heard it, too."

The purplish hollows under Juliet's eyes and cheekbones made her face look almost bruised in the gloomy light of her bedroom; she looked as if she hadn't slept in weeks.

A pile of dirty dishes and a plate covered with eggshells cluttered the night table next to Juliet's bed, and a pair of pink ballet slippers hung sadly from a chair that also propped up a pair of crutches. In one corner, there was a television set that was much larger than any TV Gilda had ever seen in a kid's bedroom. There were no random piles of books or clothes; there were no posters of celebrities or photographs of friends. Aside from the ballet shoes, something about the environment reminded Gilda of an elderly person's bedroom in a nursing home.

"I definitely heard *something*," Gilda replied. "It sounded like footsteps coming from behind the wall in my room."

"I've heard noises coming from that tower for years," said Juliet. "But my father always tells me I'm imagining things."

Gilda stared at Juliet, wanting to ask her about the unusual scene she had witnessed earlier that evening. "Do you ever *talk* to ghosts?" Gilda blurted.

"No!" said Juliet, surprisingly offended by the question.

"I only asked because I heard you talking to yourself in here earlier this evening. I mean, you seemed to be having a whole *conversation* with some invisible person! I just assumed you were talking in your sleep, but after hearing those footsteps, I wondered if it might be something else."

Juliet bit her fingernail. "I didn't know I still did that," she said. "When I was little, my nannies used to tell me that I said all kinds of nonsense in my sleep, but I haven't done that in years, as far as I know." Juliet glanced around the room nervously, as if wondering what other things she had done in her sleep.

"I think you might have said the word *tower*," said Gilda.

"You mean you stood here and *listened* to me?"

"Well, your door was open."

"Even if it was, I still think that was an invasion of privacy."

"Listen, I could hear you blabbing all the way down the hall," said Gilda, exaggerating the truth.

"Well, it doesn't mean anything," Juliet insisted, as if trying to convince herself more than Gilda. "It's just gibberish."

"Maybe," said Gilda. "Anyway, I still think your father's wrong if he says there aren't ghosts in the house. Rosa told me that she thinks there's something in the tower, so we're not the only ones who have heard things."

"Rosa sees ghosts in her *coffee*." Juliet rolled her eyes. "You know how superstitious housekeepers are."

"Oh sure," Gilda replied, thinking that there was something annoyingly snobbish about this statement, but not wanting to admit that she didn't know a single person who actually *had* a housekeeper. "We used to have a housekeeper who was *really* superstitious," Gilda lied. "She was convinced there was a ghost in the freezer who kept eating all the ice cream."

"Really?"

"Well—it was actually something that my brother and I made up," Gilda admitted, "but then my mother started believing it, which was kind of funny."

"You have a brother? That's so *lucky!*"

"You wouldn't say that if you got to know him."

"I wish I had a brother," said Juliet, suddenly wistful.

"No—I wish I had a couple of brothers. Then I'd never be scared because I wouldn't have to be here by myself. There would always be someone at home."

Gilda snorted, thinking that Juliet was very naive. "I'd rather have a sister," she said.

Juliet wrinkled her nose. "I *have* two stepsisters, and I can't stand them. When my parents got divorced, I moved down to San Diego with my mom, but then she married Chuck and that meant living with his two airhead daughters. All they ever talked about was getting tans and shopping and which boys on the beach were 'hotties' and how much money their dad was going to give them for a new car. They sure hated having *me* around."

"Oh," said Gilda, not knowing what to say. Juliet's family situation sounded far more complicated than her own.

"Anyway, when I was ten, I begged my mom to let me move here to live with my father. It's better here than with her, but sometimes I almost miss those bimbos. I mean, even if they drove me crazy, I'd be less lonely."

Gilda felt a wave of sympathy at Juliet's honest admission of loneliness, but she still felt exasperated. Why did only-children always pine for siblings? Gilda had little patience with people who needed other people to entertain them. She was sure that if she herself were an only child, she would be perfectly happy pursuing her various projects. On the other hand, she had always had Stephen around, so she guessed she didn't really *know* what it felt like to spend days completely alone in an enormous house, just as Juliet had no idea what it was like to have someone slip ice cubes down your shirt when you weren't expecting it, or sneak a spider under the sheets of your bed—a spider that bit you *several times* during the night. Still, Gilda reflected that it was possible that being all alone in a big house would be more terrifying than she realized.

"I wish she would just leave me alone!" Juliet blurted.

"Who?"

Juliet's gray eyes looked unusually dark. "Aunt Melanie, of course. My dad's dead sister. I *saw* her the other day," she whispered. Her voice grew quivery, and the pupils of her gray eyes were now two black wells.

Gilda felt a prickly sensation all over her skin. This was the first time she had met anyone who had been face-to-face with a real ghost.

"She was standing right in the hallway on the second floor," Juliet continued, leaning closer to Gilda. "That's when I fell and twisted my ankle."

"What did she *look* like?"

Juliet closed her eyes, trying to visualize the phantom in her memory. "It's hard to explain," she said. "I'm not sure why, but I just knew it was her. She looked like a real person, but somehow she wasn't completely *there;* I just knew I was looking at a dead person's face."

Gilda could hardly contain her excitement at finding herself with a real psychic phenomenon to investigate. "Are you *sure* it was your aunt Melanie?" she asked, remembering that her psychic handbook advised against jumping to hasty conclusions about a ghost's identity. "Rosa thinks the house is full of ghosts; she said a bunch of old ladies used to live here."

Instead of answering, Juliet flopped onto her stomach. Hanging halfway off her mattress, she searched for something underneath the bed and pulled out a small, dusty jewelry box. When she opened it, the room filled with the awkward, antique chimes of a music box, and a tiny ballerina stuck on a metal pole came to life, pirouetting jerkily upon stiff plastic legs.

The music box contained nothing but a faded snapshot of a woman whose slight frame and pale coloring bore a close resemblance to Juliet's. The woman, squinting into the sun, stood on a bluff overlooking the ocean. Her straight blond hair blew behind her, as did the long silk scarf she wore loosely around her neck. There was something blurry and uncertain about the picture; it was difficult to see the woman's face clearly enough to determine exactly what she would look like in person.

"This is the only belonging of hers I've ever found in the house," said Juliet. "I don't think my dad kept any of her clothes or *anything*."

Gilda realized that she hadn't seen a single picture of Aunt Melanie displayed anywhere in the house. It was the opposite of her own home in Michigan, where her mother kept the mantel over the fireplace devoted to memories of her father, and even a closet where some of his favorite clothes still hung.

"I was just a little kid when she died, so I don't really remember anything about her." Juliet stared at the faded picture of her aunt. "When I was younger, I used to ask both of my parents lots of questions about Aunt Melanie, but it seemed to make them both so angry—especially my father—that I just stopped asking. It seems like they both want to pretend she never existed in the first place."

"Very interesting," said Gilda, standing up to hold the picture closer to Juliet's bedside lamp, but not quite sure what she was hoping to see. "But tell me one thing."

"What?"

"Why do you think your aunt is haunting *you?*"

"I have no idea," said Juliet. "I just wish she'd stop."

Gilda nodded. "Listen," she said matter-of-factly, "I happen to be a part-time psychic investigator, and I think I could help you communicate with your aunt's ghost. She's probably trying to tell you something."

"You're a *psychic investigator?*"

"It's one of my careers," said Gilda, trying to convey more self-confidence than she actually felt.

111

"You have careers?"

"Of course. Don't you?"

"How old are you, anyway?"

"I'll be fourteen next month."

"Oh. I thought you were younger than me, but I guess we're about the same age. I'll be fourteen in September."

"Well, I assumed you were about twelve," said Gilda, eyeing Juliet's skinny arms.

"Same to you," said Juliet. "You kind of act younger than your age."

"Well, you act *snottier* than your age."

"Excuse me?! You can't talk to me that way, Gilda. For one thing, nobody even invited you to be here!"

Gilda didn't see how this had anything to do with whether or not she could perform a psychic investigation. "Well, do you want me to help you or not?"

"No, I don't want you to help me."

"Why not?"

"First of all, I don't see how you could be a real psychic investigator, and secondly, what makes you think I even *want* to communicate with Aunt Melanie?! It's not like I miss her! I never even knew her!"

"Suit yourself," said Gilda, feeling miffed. "No wonder you don't have any friends."

"How would you know?"

"Just guessing," said Gilda, abruptly walking out of the room and closing the door behind her.

It was dark in the hallway—so dark that Gilda almost turned around and went right back into Juliet's room, but instead, she groped her way down the hallway until she reached the doorway to her room. What a strange kid Juliet was: one minute you felt sorry for her, and the next minute you wanted to strangle her.

Holding her breath and peering through squinted eyes, Gilda stumbled blindly into her bedroom and tripped over the lamp on the floor. "Ow!" she yelled for the second time that night.

This time, nobody in the house stirred in reply. Gilda fell onto her bed and threw the covers over her head.

Downstairs, the grandfather clock chimed three times. For some reason Gilda thought of her father. *Dad,* she whispered to herself, *I wish you hadn't died. But at least you didn't jump out a window.*

Gilda fell asleep quickly and slept so soundly she didn't hear the restless sounds of a haunted house awakening in the night—the clinking of antique china and the soft shuffling of footsteps wandering from room to room.

12

The Hidden Truth

Juliet couldn't sleep. She sat up in bed and wondered if Gilda might be right. Was it possible that Aunt Melanie's ghost wanted to tell her something?

Juliet had always tried to ignore the sounds of clinking china, rustling curtains, and footsteps that she sometimes heard echoing through the house—sounds that kept her awake, leaving her exhausted when it was time to go to school.

Juliet had learned at an early age that she must never tell anyone about the "haunted house" in which she lived; they would assume she was delusional or merely imagining things.

But now this strange girl—Gilda—believed that there really *was* a ghost. Gilda wanted to help her. So why had she pushed her away? True, Gilda was not the sort of girl Juliet would expect to befriend. For one thing, Gilda was terribly blunt—almost rude. Besides, she lived in a very unfashionable Midwestern city and wore bizarre clothes. But Juliet had to admit that she admired something about her. Gilda had a kind of brash courage; she was *brave*.

I can see why you don't have friends, Gilda had said. Juliet was surprised that this comment had stung like a hard slap even though she had decided some time ago not to care about friends.

She thought about the clique of girls at school that had included her when she first moved to San Francisco. On the surface, they had seemed very much like herself—girls who lived in large houses and had wealthy, divorced parents. But Juliet had let the loose ends of her friendships unravel. She had become an observer rather than a participant in the activities of her peers: she watched as the girls around her passed notes to one another in class; she watched as boys and girls flirted in the hallways. The margins of her notebooks were filled with nervous sketches of her classmates' faces.

When did I become such an outsider? Juliet wondered.

The question led her to a memory—the morning of her eleventh birthday. She had stood next to her father, looking at the sailboats in the marina. The water glistened in the morning sun, and the two of them had just eaten an enormous breakfast of pancakes at Juliet's favorite restaurant. Juliet knew that she was supposed to feel happy, but instead she felt awkward. There was an uncomfortable silence.

"Well, how's school going these days?" her father asked.

It was the second time he had asked the question that morning. "It's okay," Juliet replied, feeling more annoyed than usual by the predictable conversation. Aside from the fact that she didn't want to think about school on her birthday, it often seemed to Juliet that when her father spoke to her, he might as well be addressing a stranger—someone he had just met. True, she preferred her father's cool politeness to her mother's forced, pushy cheerfulness, but on her birthday she was painfully aware of the wall of silence between herself and her father—a wall that grew thicker as the two of them stared at the boats bobbing on the sparkling waves.

"Are you enjoying math?" her father asked with a hopeful note in his voice.

"I'm only getting a B in math this time." Juliet knew that her father would be disappointed by this response.

"Well, I'm sure you'll get an A next semester. That's one thing your mother and I agree about—the importance of good grades and a great education. You have wonderful opportunities ahead of you if you just work hard and stay competitive."

Juliet sighed.

"If you set goals and stick to them, you'll really go places."

Juliet nodded dutifully. She knew that her parents had

invested a lot of money in her private school and that she was supposed to take her education very seriously—so how could she explain to her father that she didn't *have* any goals that excited her?

"Dad . . ." Juliet ventured, wanting to change the subject completely and break through some invisible barrier. "Why exactly did you and Mom get divorced?" The question came out spontaneously, like an unexpected belch.

Mr. Splinter's eyebrows shot up, but instead of answering he tilted his head and looked thoughtfully at the ground, as if expecting to find an explanation written there. "I suppose your mother and I just grew apart," he said. "It was such a long time ago."

Juliet waited for him to continue.

"Of course," he added, "you know that our divorce had nothing to do with us caring about you."

"I know." Juliet wasn't sure what she had expected to discover. She already knew that her parents had been a mismatched couple, and that her mother had met her new husband at a marketing conference while she was still married to Juliet's father—an obvious trigger for the separation. Still, Juliet felt she wanted to explore *something*—some mystery about her family that was buried in the past. The problem was that she didn't even know where to begin digging.

"A long time ago—when I was really little and you and

Mother lived here in San Francisco together—Aunt Melanie lived in the house with you, right?"

"Yes, that's right. My mother left the two of us the house when she died, and we decided to stay here."

Juliet nodded. "Did Mom and Aunt Melanie get along?"

Her father turned away from her and started walking along the path. His steps were slow, as if he had to remind the muscles in his legs to work. Juliet followed close behind.

"Melanie and your mother didn't always see eye to eye," Mr. Splinter replied haltingly, "but they certainly got along. We all got along just *fine* living in the house where Melanie and I grew up. Melanie was my sister, and I cared for her very much!"

"Okay," said Juliet, taken aback by her father's sudden outburst. She looked at him expectantly, waiting for him to explain further, but he obviously wished that she would simply change the subject. Normally she would have, but something made her push ahead. "How exactly did Melanie die?" Juliet blurted.

"Juliet, you *know* the answer to that question," said Mr. Splinter impatiently. "You've asked me that before."

"I guess I forgot the answer." This was a lie; the truth was that something had always seemed *wrong* with her father's answer. It always seemed that he was concealing something.

"I told you," Mr. Splinter said. "Your aunt fell."

"So she just fell from the window in the tower."

"That's why I've always told you not to play there; it's dangerous."

"I still don't see how a person could just fall out a window."

"She—I suppose she was looking out at the bay and she leaned out the window too far. She wasn't being careful enough."

"But why—"

"Don't you want to think about more pleasant things on your birthday?"

Juliet fell silent, but her mind churned with questions. *Why didn't her father want to talk about his sister? What kind of person was her aunt Melanie? What was she doing in the tower on the day she fell to her death?*

"You must be excited about your party!" Mr. Splinter declared brusquely.

"Sure," said Juliet, feeling an inexplicable sense of dread.

Juliet had invited her four "best friends" from school over to celebrate her eleventh birthday with a slumber party: Emily, a freckled, sporty girl who had an infectious laugh; Liz, an extremely outgoing, boy-crazy girl who had bouncy brunette hair and braces on her teeth; Meghan, who was known for her sense of humor; and quiet, refined Jenna.

Each of these girls wore her hair in long layers with sunny highlights in shades of platinum or honey. Each wore pale pink nail polish and took ballet lessons and occasionally vacationed with one of their estranged parents in Hawaii.

"This is an awesome house!" Liz peered at the carved lion's feet beneath one of the chairs in the parlor. "Can we see the rest of it?"

Juliet showed her guests the narrow stairways that ascended three floors, the antique velvet furniture, the library stuffed with books, her own pink bedroom with the giant television, the curved windows that offered a view of the foggy bay far below the hill. Although she saw her four friends regularly at school, at ballet lessons, and at their houses for parties, Juliet had never actually invited them to her own house before. This was partly because her father didn't encourage houseguests and partly because Juliet herself felt uneasy about the prospect of bringing friends into the darkened, aged atmosphere of her home—as if they might discover some truth about her that was better kept hidden.

"Wow! This place is so cool!" they exclaimed.

So far, so good, Juliet thought.

"What's in that tower behind the house?" Liz asked, peering through an upstairs window at the pointy turret that rose from the house's rooftop. "Can we go in there and take a look?"

"It's locked," said Juliet, feeling uneasy. "I'm not allowed to go in there."

"Why not?"

"My father says I can't." Juliet didn't feel like explaining to her friends how her aunt Melanie had fallen from the tower, and how it had been locked ever since because her father insisted that it was "too dangerous." She thought she saw Emily nudge Liz with her elbow, as if trying to shut her up, but perhaps she was just being paranoid.

"It looks like something out of a fairy tale," said Liz wistfully.

"I think it looks kind of spooky," said Jenna. "I think it would be scary to be alone in this house."

"I'd pee my pants if I had to stay here alone!" said Emily. Then they all looked at Juliet.

"Well, I'm *not* alone here," she protested. "There's my father, and the nanny, and the housekeeper comes a couple times a week."

"Still," said Jenna. "It must be kind of spooky sometimes."

"Sounds like it's time for a ghost story," said Liz.

The girls sat on their sleeping bags in Juliet's bedroom. Liz knew lots of ghost stories, and she was the type of girl who stayed calm and unruffled while everyone else grew hysterical. She told the story of Bloody Mary ("if you say her name three times while looking in the mirror, she appears behind you"). Then she told a "true story" about a man who had married a beautiful woman who always refused to remove the red silk scarf that she kept tied around her neck—even on her wedding day and wedding night. Years passed, and still the scarf remained around the woman's neck. Finally, her husband had had enough of the scarf, and while his wife was asleep, he untied the material that was tightly bound around her throat. When he whisked the scarf away, he watched in horror as her head rolled away from her neck, down the pillow, and onto the floor with a heavy thud.

Juliet was appalled. "Did that *really* happen?"

"Of course it did," said Liz. "I just *told* you it happened."

"That's the most horrible thing I've ever heard!" Juliet exclaimed.

The other girls laughed. "You mean you've never heard that one before?" said Emily

Juliet shook her head.

"You're an innocent one, Juliet," said Meghan.

"That's why she's a good audience for ghost stories," Liz said.

"Can we talk about something else?" Jenna exclaimed. "It's so scary talking about this stuff in this house!"

"What do you mean?" Juliet was growing weary of hearing about how spooky her home supposedly was.

"It reminds me of a house in a horror movie," said Jenna.

"It's not *that* scary," said Juliet defensively.

"Not to mention the fact that that lady who used to live here *killed* herself and everything," Liz blurted.

The girls collectively caught their breath. Suddenly there was not quite enough oxygen in the room. "You mean my aunt. But she didn't kill herself," Juliet explained, feeling for some reason as if she had just been punched in the stomach. "She *fell.*"

"You're kidding," said Liz unsympathetically. "You mean you didn't know she committed suicide?"

"It was an accident," Juliet insisted.

The other girls stared at the floor.

"She jumped on purpose," Liz said. "Everybody knows that. My mother told me; she said she read about it in the newspaper years ago."

"I think my own father would know what happened—"

"Your father is lying if he says it didn't happen that way. My mom told me she jumped!"

Juliet felt a bleakness spreading through her body. They were right. Juliet had never fully believed her father's weak explanation for Aunt Melanie's death. At some unconscious level, she *had* known; perhaps that was why she continued to ask her father: *How did she die?*

Juliet nevertheless felt an inexplicable desire to defend her father's version of the story. "My father told me the truth," she insisted.

"Why don't you go *ask* your father right now if you don't believe me?" Liz persisted.

"Liz," said the ever-diplomatic Emily, "it sounds like Juliet's dad didn't *want* her to know that her aunt committed suicide right here in her house. You can't blame him."

"He told me she fell," Juliet repeated coldly. She suddenly heard her own voice as a hollow thing—something lost in the internal desert that seemed to be spreading like dry sand in the wind, taking her very far away from her four houseguests.

"Listen, I can see why he told you it was an accident," said Liz, backpedaling a bit now that she had been chastised by Emily. "It's all very freaky."

Juliet sensed that something inside each of her friends was pulling away from her just as an animal might back away after catching the faint whiff of poison in a plant or a disease in a fellow creature. *They think I'm a freak,* she told herself. *Now they'll reject me in order to protect themselves.*

"I—I never really knew my aunt," Juliet said weakly, sensing that in order to keep herself connected to her friends—to the world of the living—she should try to distance herself from the crazy woman who had jumped from the tower window years ago. "She must have been pretty weird."

All four girls looked at Juliet. With pity? Horror? Contempt? Juliet could no longer read their emotions, but she sensed that she herself had become transparent.

"I know!" said Liz. "Let's have a séance and talk to your aunt!"

"No—too creepy," Jenna protested.

"I don't think that's a good idea." Juliet thought of the footsteps she sometimes heard in the house in the middle of the night.

"Liz, the thing about you is that you don't know when to stop," said Meghan.

Liz jumped to her feet. "Don't be a bunch of chickens. Let's do it!"

"Where are you going?"

"Outside, of course. We'll do the séance inside the tower!"

"We can't go inside the tower," said Juliet. "It's locked."

"Then let's unlock it."

"I don't know where the key is—or if there even is a key anymore."

"Okay. Then we'll do the séance right *next* to the tower. We should get as close as possible to the place your aunt died."

Unable to stifle their nervous giggles, the girls tiptoed down the stairs, then out the back door. Outside, the wind blew more fiercely than usual.

"It's cold out here!" Jenna complained.

Standing on the patio behind the house, the girls gazed down the steep hill at the tops of palm trees and the lights of houses and restaurants clustered by the dark water below. Juliet crept along behind the others, past the angel statue that seemed to regard the girls mournfully and toward the overgrown vines and flowers surrounding the base of the tower.

"Come on!" Liz whispered loudly, beckoning to the other girls.

Juliet had never been outside in her own backyard at night. She had never looked up at the tower with its boarded windows like bandaged eyes and sinister, pointy tower that looked like a witch's hat in the moonlight. Juliet had expected to feel terrified, but instead she merely felt that it was now much easier to imagine someone falling—or *jumping*—from the tower window in the soft darkness, down toward the colorful, twinkling lights and black water far below. In the night wind, it seemed that if you jumped, the sky might pick you up and carry you as if you were a weightless leaf or a witch perched upon a magic broom. Perhaps that's exactly what had happened. Perhaps, on a night like this, Aunt Melanie had momentarily thought that she might actually be able to turn herself into an owl or a bat and fly over the bay.

"Let's sit in a circle next to the tower," said Liz.

"It's freezing out here!" Jenna complained again.

"Maybe if you wore normal pajamas instead of a baby-doll nightgown, you wouldn't be so cold!" Liz snapped.

"Are you sure you know how to do a séance?" Juliet asked in a small voice as she sat down on the ground and took Liz's hand.

"*Not* knowing how wouldn't stop her," said Meghan.

"Of course I know how to do a séance," said Liz. "I've done about *ten* at slumber parties. First, we join hands like this, and then—all together—we chant something."

"What do we chant?"

"Something like: 'Dark forces of the spirit world, grant me the power to speak to Juliet's aunt!' Wait—what's your aunt's name again, Juliet?"

"M-Melanie." It sounded strange to Juliet to hear her own voice say the name aloud. *Melanie* suddenly struck her as a very lonely word.

"You know what?" said Jenna, standing up and breaking the circle. "This is just too creepy. I'm going inside."

"Suit yourself, but if this were a horror movie, you'd be the one who'd be killed first—because you went back inside *by yourself.*"

Jenna sat back down.

"Let's begin," said Liz quietly.

"Dark forces of the spirit world, grant me the power to speak to Melanie Splinter, who jumped from this tower to her death. Dark forces of the spirit world, grant me the power . . ."

The girls' whispering voices vibrated in the air. Juliet felt a wave of dizziness. For a moment, she thought she might faint.

Juliet sensed someone approaching. She opened her eyes and saw a slim shadow moving quickly toward the group. She gasped, causing the other girls to open their eyes.

Screams erupted from all five girls.

Their shrieks were quickly followed by relieved laughter, however, when they realized that it was only Mr. Splinter walking toward them. "Omigod!" Liz sputtered. "I almost peed my pants!"

Emily and Meghan rolled on the ground, giggling. Jenna and Juliet looked as if they might cry.

Mr. Splinter rubbed his eyes and then pressed the palms of his hands to his forehead as if trying to stop a migraine headache. Wearing his pajamas, he looked exhausted.

"Sorry we woke you up," said Liz, collecting herself. "We were trying to be quiet."

Juliet stood up. She knew her father would be angry to discover her outside, sitting right next to the entranceway to the tower, but she suddenly didn't care. She felt a surge of rage. Her father was probably planning to reprimand her. But wasn't it *his* fault that she had been humiliated—left to discover the truth about her dead aunt from her friends?

"What kind of shenanigans are going on out here?" said Mr. Splinter, causing Juliet's friends to stifle giggles at his use of the word *shenanigans*. Mr. Splinter glared at them. "Juliet," he continued, "you know you aren't supposed to be outside in the middle of the night. You also know that you are not supposed to play near that tower. You should have explained to your friends that it's strictly off-limits."

"It's my fault," said Liz. "Juliet told us not to, but—"

"We were having a séance," said Juliet defiantly.

Mr. Splinter pursed his lips. "I don't think you should be outside in the middle of the night. Time for you girls to get back to bed."

"You're a liar," said Juliet in a clear, hollow voice that suddenly cut the air like a piece of broken glass.

Mr. Splinter blinked, unable to respond for a moment. "Juliet, I don't know what you're talking about."

"You lied about how Aunt Melanie died."

"I most certainly did not—"

"She killed herself on purpose, and you never told me that!" said Juliet coldly. "Apparently everybody knows that except me. You *lied.*"

Liz, Emily, Meghan, and Jenna watched nervously. This exchange was fascinating, but nearly as scary as the séance. There was something frightening about the icy rage in Juliet's voice.

For a moment, Mr. Splinter's mouth moved as if he was trying to find words that wouldn't come to him. He looked as if he would like to pick up something and break it. Then he turned his attention to Juliet's friends, who stared at him with blank, stricken faces. "I hope you're happy," he said. "Look how you've upset my daughter!"

"Don't blame *them*," said Juliet.

The girls remained silent, glancing at one another nervously. There was something mortifying about being reprimanded by someone else's parent, and they had no idea how to respond. "We're sorry," Emily offered in a small voice.

"It isn't your fault," said Juliet.

"I think this slumber party has come to an end," said Mr. Splinter, turning his attention back to Juliet. "I'll drive your friends home."

Eyes downcast, Juliet's friends stared at their manicures.

"But I want them to stay!" Juliet suddenly shouted, her voice echoing over the hillside. "I'm sick of being alone in this haunted house!"

Juliet suddenly felt as if she were falling into a deep crevice in which all of her problems had become cold hands that grabbed at her clothes and hair: her slipping grades, the stepsisters she hated, her father's secretiveness, and now the probable loss of her friends. . . . *Stop it!* she tried to tell herself, but it was too late: she had lost control. Juliet covered her face with her hands, unable to stop herself from sobbing.

The girls stared. Juliet's outburst was like a tantrum that a much younger girl might throw if she didn't get the present she wanted on her birthday—a seizure of tears.

Emily, Liz, Meghan, and Jenna watched as Mr. Splinter put his arm around his daughter's shoulders and led her back inside the house.

At school the next week, the girls had treated Juliet with distant politeness, the way adults might act after witnessing an embarrassing incident that each would rather forget. Juliet wasn't surprised or even particularly disappointed; the feeling was mutual. *Perhaps it's simpler to have acquaintances rather than bothering with real friends,* she thought.

Every now and then, Juliet thought she glimpsed a brief look of sympathy—or was it merely curiosity?—from Jenna or Emily. Every now and then, Liz or Meghan would call to see if she wanted to join them for a shopping spree. Juliet herself did not dare to extend invitations to any of the four girls; she was not one to risk another failure.

I'm not *alone,* she had told the four girls on her birthday.

But she was. And she guessed she would just have to learn to live that way.

13

The Locked Door

Gilda climbed out of bed and peered out the window. A foggy haze hovered over the neighborhood. At the base of the steep hill behind the house, the bay resembled a giant cauldron of white smoke. *Here I am in San Francisco,* Gilda told herself, *in a house with a real ghost!*

In the morning light, the memory of the ghost in the tower and the conversation in Juliet's room seemed like events she might have dreamed or imagined. But there, lying on the floor, was the lamp she had knocked over the night before—a small piece of evidence that it had all really happened.

Gilda put on a pair of jeans, a sweatshirt that declared SAY NICE THINGS ABOUT DETROIT!, and her sunglasses shaped like cat's eyes. She clumped downstairs.

On the second floor, Gilda heard the sound of a young woman's voice coming from one of the rooms. She peeked through the doorway. A suntanned woman in her early twenties, surrounded by piles of unopened mail, waved to her enthusiastically and hung up the phone. "Hey! You must be Glinda!"

"My name's actually *Gilda.*"

"I'm Summer—the one who replied to your letter, remember? I can't believe you're only twelve; you're such a good writer! I wish I could write that well."

"Thanks," said Gilda. "But I'm almost fourteen." Summer's gushy, extroverted personality made her feel slightly shy.

"So did your mom find someone to take care of your brother while you're here?"

"What? Oh . . . I think so."

"Is he doing any better?"

"Well, he's still having some trouble with potty training, but otherwise great."

Summer bared her teeth in a look of sympathetic terror at this comment. "That's so tough," she said. "He's lucky to have a sister like you."

Struggling not to laugh, Gilda pretended to have a sudden coughing fit. *Good thing Wendy isn't here, or I'd really lose it,* she thought.

"Uh-oh," said Summer. "I hope you didn't pick up some kind of cold on the plane. The air in those planes is so *germy!*"

Summer and Gilda suddenly fell silent because Mr. Splinter entered the room. In his expensive gray suit, he had the crisp, generic look of a brand-new office building.

"Lester," said Summer, "this is Gilda."

"Yes, we've met," said Mr. Splinter, who offered a stiff smile.

Maybe he doesn't like being called Lester, Gilda thought.

Mr. Splinter began to rummage through some forms on Summer's desk. "Good morning, Gilda," he said. "Just let us know if there's anything we can do to make your stay more comfortable." He spoke with the articulate formality of a gentleman in an old black-and-white movie.

"Sorry about waking you up last night," said Gilda. "I didn't mean to knock over the lamp—"

"That's quite all right," said Mr. Splinter absently, flipping through a document.

Gilda observed him for a moment. *He's a secretive person,* she thought. Gilda had an urge to interrogate him ruthlessly, like a detective on a television crime show, but she sensed that this would prove futile. "Mr. Splinter," she ventured cautiously, "I still think I heard something strange coming from the tower." She tried to refrain from blurting several prying questions all at once. "Have you ever noticed anything out of the ordinary in this house?"

"Well, I know Rosa claims that we have some ghosts, but as I said last night, I myself am not superstitious."

"Oh, *I* am," Summer interjected. "I totally believe in ghosts. Wait—there's a *ghost* in here?!"

"I believe there is," said Gilda, attempting to speak in her most assertive psychic-investigator voice.

Mr. Splinter looked up from his papers, surprised by Gilda's authoritative tone.

"I mean," Gilda added, now feeling slightly ridiculous as she met Mr. Splinter's steady gaze, "I'm positive that I *did* hear something moving around inside the tower. And if it's been locked for years like you said, that's rather odd, don't you think?"

"Gilda, one of the rules in this house is that the tower is strictly off-limits," Mr. Splinter explained. "That goes for everyone."

"Okay," said Gilda, watching as Mr. Splinter turned to head back to his desk. "But—may I ask *why* it's off-limits?"

Gilda knew that this question was rude and that her mother would have been appalled if she had been present. At the moment, Gilda didn't care; she wanted to see how much information she could get secretive Mr. Splinter to reveal. She had a gut feeling that he was hiding something sinister.

Summer's mouth hung open as if she were watching a particularly juicy soap opera.

Mr. Splinter's back seemed to bristle. "I don't feel that the tower is a suitable place for Juliet to play," he said, ignoring Gilda's question, "and I expect her friends to abide by the rule as well. Understand?"

Gilda nodded, secretly thinking that she was now more curious than ever to find out what lurked inside that tower. *There's something very strange about Mr. Splinter,* she thought. *He's definitely hiding something!*

"Wow," Summer whispered to Gilda when Mr. Splinter was back in his office and out of earshot. "You ask some really good questions! It sounds like you know more about Lester than I've been able to figure out in an entire year!"

"That's because I have a part-time job as an investigator," Gilda whispered. "A psychic investigator, to be specific."

Summer laughed, which was not the response Gilda wanted. She knew that the job "psychic investigator" sounded unrealistic to most adults—like a child's imaginary game rather than a real career. Would she have to be sixty years old before she could tell someone she was a psychic investigator without eliciting chuckles?

"Sorry!" said Summer, perceiving Gilda's disappointment, but nevertheless unable to completely stifle a few more giggles. "So—you can read minds and stuff?"

"Well, I'm working on that," said Gilda, "but it's more like being a detective of the supernatural."

"Like on *The X-Files?*"

"I'm not looking for *aliens,*" said Gilda, annoyed that Summer seemed to think she was mimicking a television show.

"Hey," said Summer, "you should take a look at a fortune-cookie message I just got last night." Digging in her messy purse, she began to chat about a psychic she had recently seen who "seemed to know everything" about her current boyfriend. "Here it is!" she said, handing Gilda a tiny, crumpled piece of fortune-cookie paper.

The fortune said: *You will meet a stimulating younger person.*

"That must be you!" said Summer, smiling. "Hey, I know! I'll take you to Chinatown this afternoon! Would you like that?"

Gilda supposed that she would. After all, it was unlikely that Juliet was going to be much of a companion for exploring the city.

"I'm sure Lester will let me take you this afternoon, as soon as I finish my work here. Now—why don't you ask Rosa to give you some breakfast?"

As Gilda made her way toward the aroma of coffee coming from the kitchen, she felt someone pinch the back of her arm.

"Ow!" She turned to find Juliet grinning at her impishly. "Oh, it's *you.*"

Wearing black pants that hung loosely from her bony hips and a jean jacket over a T-shirt, Juliet leaned on her crutches. With her translucent skin and pale hair, she looked out of place—like someone visiting California from a very winterish country, or a patient who had just emerged from the hospital following treatment for some wasting disease.

"Wow—you actually left your room!" said Gilda, thinking that it was strange to see Juliet outside her bedroom, wearing something other than her bathrobe. She also appeared to have washed her hair.

"I changed my mind," said Juliet, who looked more animated than usual.

"Changed your mind about what?"

"You know," said Juliet. "What we talked about last night. You said you would help me."

"Help you with *what?*" Sadistically pushing a person by forcing her to beg was a technique Gilda had learned from her brother.

"Never mind," said Juliet.

"I'm just giving you a hard time. Of course I'll help you. In fact, I was just asking your father about the tower."

"You *were?*"

"He definitely knows something that he's not telling."

Juliet's small mouth twisted into a mischievous smile. "Look." She pulled something shiny from a pocket in her jacket. It was a large ring of keys—about a hundred keys of all shapes and sizes. She shook them triumphantly. "Rosa's key chain," she said proudly.

"You took Rosa's keys?"

"Rosa was so surprised to see me downstairs asking for breakfast, she started talking to herself in Spanish, and she didn't even notice when I grabbed her keys. She's in there making pancakes or something right now, so we have some time to go see if any of these will open the tower!"

"You really think your father would let Rosa have a key to the tower?"

Juliet shrugged. "This key ring is supposed to hold all the keys to the entire house, and besides, everyone knows that Rosa wouldn't go in there even if she did have a key."

"Let's try it," said Gilda.

Juliet led Gilda through the small garden behind the house, where an overgrowth of lilacs and rosebushes nearly concealed a brick path.

"But what if your father sees us back here?" Gilda asked, untangling a thorny branch from her hair. "He seemed pretty strict when he told me to stay away from the tower this morning."

"You can't see this part of the garden from his office window," said Juliet nonchalantly. "Besides, I think he avoids looking at anything behind the house. He certainly doesn't seem to care that the garden is so overgrown."

"When they reached the center of the garden, Gilda saw the empty marble pool with a large statue of an angel at the center.

"This is supposed to be a fountain, but the water hasn't been turned on in ages," Juliet explained.

Gilda peered up at the house—three floors, then the attic. There was the tower: the lower half was almost completely concealed by lilac bushes and several trees, but when she looked up, she saw that it peaked like the Gothic turret of a castle, its pointy roof a bit higher than the rest of the house.

The windows of the tower were covered with boards, and its walls were cloaked in the creeping vines and flowers of wisteria. Peeking through the vines was something bronze—a glimpse of a rusted doorknob.

"Well, let's see if any of those keys unlocks the door," said Gilda.

It was difficult to find the rusted lock on the door within the tangled vines—vines that seemed to want to protect the entrance to the tower like thorns around a sleeping kingdom.

Juliet stood guard just in case her father or Rosa decided to come outside unexpectedly while Gilda hurriedly tried every key on the ring. There were keys of every shape and size—old rusty keys that looked like they had been made a hundred years ago, and tiny keys that must have been used for locked jewelry boxes and desk drawers.

"Any luck?" Juliet whispered.

Gilda shook her head. None of the keys worked.

Standing in front of the tower door, Gilda suddenly felt cold. Once again, she had the distinct feeling that the house was observing *her*. She gazed up at the tower looming above, then turned to look behind her, where, just beyond the angel fountain, the hill plunged down at a steep incline. She imagined a woman falling from the upper window, then crashing down—down into the tropical plants with pointed leaves and low-growing shrubs that covered the hillside. For a moment, Gilda wondered if Mr. Splinter's decision to keep the tower locked might make some sense: perhaps it was wrong to open it after something so terrible had happened.

"I feel like somebody's watching us," said Juliet. "Maybe we should go."

"Someone is," said Gilda, who had just noticed a shadow creeping out from under a rosebush into the sunlight.

It was the gray cat.

"That's Phantom," said Juliet. "He's lived with my father since before I was born; we don't even know how old he is."

The cat jumped up on the edge of the fountain and walked toward Juliet on tiptoe, moving as stealthily as a dark cloud.

Purring, Phantom jumped down into the empty fountain, curled up, and blinked lazily at the two girls, as if inviting them to join him for a nap.

"Rosa's probably made breakfast by now," said Juliet. "We should go."

Back in the house, Rosa thrust an enormous burrito in front of Juliet's nose. "You sit down and eat now!"

"Okay, okay!" said Juliet, who began to pick at a corner of the burrito daintily with a fork.

Rosa handed the telephone to Gilda. "Your mother, she has just called."

"Hello? Mom?"

"Hey, sunshine! How's San Francisco?"

"It's okay."

"Having fun?"

"Sure."

"Behaving yourself?"

"In a manner of speaking."

"Gilda, I want you to have fun, but just keep in mind what we talked about before you left, okay?"

"What did we talk about? Leprechauns? Sundresses?"

"No—I don't want you to ask too many prying questions, okay? I know you're curious about Lester, but please remember that he's a very private person, and it was very generous of him to let you visit."

"When do I ever ask prying questions?" Did her mother have ESP, or had Mr. Splinter called to complain about the questions she had asked that morning?

"Frequently. You frequently ask rude questions about personal subjects."

"Name one."

"I don't like your tone, Gilda Joyce. All I know is that I've *heard* you blurt out some very personal questions to people you hardly know when they aren't expecting it."

Gilda rolled her eyes. "I don't really know what you're talking about, but fine."

"Please be considerate of others, Gilda. And please don't go wandering in bad neighborhoods, okay?"

"Well, I was just about to put on my bikini and go visit all the bad neighborhoods, so that kind of ruins my plans."

"Very funny, Gilda. How's the weather?"

"Foggy."

"It's sunny here—very hot. Your brother's a little jealous of your trip, you know, so I'll tell him that at least he has sunnier weather here in Michigan!"

"No—I *want* him to be jealous!"

"Honestly, Gilda!" Mrs. Joyce sighed. "I have to go to work now. Miss you!"

"You, too."

"Love you!"

"Okay."

"Bye, sweetie!"

"Bye!"

Gilda hung up the phone and caught Juliet staring at her intently. "She's so irritating," Gilda said, trying to sound like someone who had little need of phone calls from her mother.

"At least your mom asks you how you're doing. Whenever my mother calls me, she spends the whole time talking about sales-and-earnings reports or the new car she just bought. Then, after she's talked about herself for ages, she'll say, 'Got any boyfriends yet, Juliet?'"

"Just tell her you're dating one of your teachers at school," Gilda suggested. "That'll shut her up!"

Juliet let out a strange yelp of laughter.

"I'm serious," said Gilda. "My grandmother used to ask that question every time she saw me, but after I told her I was having an affair with the school principal, she got the point and stopped bringing up the subject."

"You didn't!"

"Did, too," said Gilda. "I mean, it's none of her *business*."

Juliet smiled. "Maybe I'll try that one next time my mother calls."

"Juliet's coming with us to Chinatown," Gilda announced as Summer emerged from Mr. Splinter's office.

"You're kidding!" Summer forced a smile.

"My ankle doesn't hurt as much now," said Juliet.

"Are you sure?"

"I can almost walk using just one crutch."

"She's been faking the whole time, anyway," said Gilda.

"I have *not* been faking," said Juliet.

"Well, this will be fun," said Summer, trying to sound cheerful. "As long as Juliet will be okay, walking with the crutches and everything. Let's go!"

14

Chinatown

On the crowded cable bus that lumbered down San Francisco's sloping hills, Gilda stared at three elderly Chinese women whose faces were as puffy and lined as old apples. They gazed wearily through the windows behind Gilda at the elaborate "painted lady" houses. Soon the bus became extremely crowded, and the driver yelled grumpily at a long line of people who wanted to climb aboard: "I take no more people on this bus. *No more people!*"

"Ugh," said Juliet, glaring at an old man who accidentally kicked her ankle as he staggered past her, attempting to find a seat. "Now I remember why I hate riding the bus."

"I like riding the bus," said Gilda, who enjoyed all kinds of crowds, since they provided opportunities for observing strange people at close range. She was torn between wanting to listen to the conversation in Chinese between the old women (which she couldn't understand) and listening to Summer, who talked more than anyone Gilda had ever met. With Summer, there was no need to ask prying personal questions: unlike most people Gilda knew, Summer was a transparent window, revealing everything about herself. Summer explained that she had grown up in Marin County, just across the bay, and that she was currently dating a college student who spoke fluent French and worked in a pastry shop. Deep down, Summer wanted to be a hairdresser, "but that would mean being on my feet all day, you know?" She was currently attending community college part-time to learn accounting, and she had worked for Lester Splinter's accounting firm for almost a year. Then Summer explained how, shortly after she had first begun working for him, she had made the mistake of attempting to fix Lester up on a date with a very attractive older woman who owned the apartment building in which Summer lived.

Gilda's ears perked up at this piece of information.

Juliet looked horrified. "You did *what?!*"

"As you can probably imagine, that led to a totally embarrassing moment," said Summer.

Gilda pictured Mr. Splinter and a mysterious woman with white hair meeting each other in a restaurant and holding hands across the table. To Gilda, Mr. Splinter seemed ancient—way too old for dates. "What *happened?*" she asked.

"Well, first of all, Lester said, 'Thank you very much, Summer, but my personal life is not your concern.'"

Juliet snorted. "My father on a date. That's a laugh!"

"But your father is a fairly attractive man for his age, don't you think?"

Gilda and Juliet wrinkled their noses. Neither would have used the word *attractive* to describe Juliet's father.

"I mean," Summer continued, "it's been ages since Lester got divorced, and I think it's kind of sad that he hasn't found a companion to share his life with."

"What about *me?*" Juliet demanded. "He *has* someone to share his life with—his daughter."

"Oh, I meant an *adult* companion," said Summer patiently, as if attempting to make something clear to a very small child.

"She meant that he needs someone *pleasant* to share his life with," Gilda joked.

Summer giggled, but quickly clapped a hand over her mouth.

"I knew I should have stayed at home," said Juliet. Secretly, she admired Gilda's ability to make cutting remarks in a deadpan voice that somehow didn't make you want to hate her for the rest of the day. It was different from the more hurtful put-downs she had sometimes endured from her stepsisters during her childhood: they had called her names like "Miss Anorexia" and "albino" when she went to the beach. *Gilda is blunt, but she isn't mean-spirited,* Juliet thought.

Gilda was thinking that Mr. Splinter's apparent lack of a social life only confirmed her suspicion that he was hiding something. *Maybe he avoids having a real girlfriend because she might discover his secret,* she thought.

"What about your mom, Gilda?" Summer asked, attempting to change the subject.

"My mom? What about her?"

"Well, you told me she's a single parent too, right? Does she have a boyfriend?"

"Of course not!" said Gilda, appalled that Summer would ask such a question. "She's practically *forty!*"

"That's not old, silly," said Summer.

Gilda felt that the idea of her mother going on a date— or even being considered attractive by any man—was ludicrous. Still, she had to admit that she had not yet considered this question: Would her mother be going on dates soon? Her father had been gone for more than two years. Would she eventually have to get used to an entirely new father living in her house? Gilda pictured herself pretending to laugh at her new stepfather's jokes at the breakfast table. The jokes wouldn't be funny, but she would have to *pretend* to laugh. The new father would wear ugly ties and aftershave that smelled like old cheese, but she would have to tell him that he looked nice and smelled pleasant, even though she secretly hated him. Stephen would never go along with it; he would almost certainly run away. Gilda decided that she was lucky that her mother hadn't started dating anyone yet. On the other hand, what if her new stepfather turned out to be rich? What if her mother married a doctor or a lawyer or something? After all, it wouldn't be so bad to have a swimming pool and vacations to Disney World. . . .

"Come on, Gilda," said Summer, interrupting Gilda's reverie. "We're here!"

The streets of Chinatown seemed to shout and dance with red-and-green flags and signs waving both American brands and Chinese characters. The air bloomed with the smell of woody, pungent spices and dried mushrooms from the restaurants and open markets. In the shop windows, Gilda glimpsed bananas hanging from ceilings, giant silver fish on ice in display windows, butchers slicing chicken and pork, jars of unusual candies. On the crowded sidewalks, small elderly people moved slowly under awnings, maneuvering carefully around crates of tangerines and cabbages and lingering in front of displays of dead piglets and dragon masks. After the brooding silence of the Splinter mansion, the pulse of Chinatown was almost overwhelming. All the elements of life seemed intermingled in a lively stew—past and present, old and young, reality and fantasy, life and death.

Gilda suddenly wished that her father were alive so that

he could be there with her to see it all. *He'd probably buy something bizarre here,* Gilda thought, *giant melons or fish heads or something—and then he'd tell me they were magic.*

Juliet and Gilda followed Summer into a series of whimsical, chaotic shops crammed with hand-carved bamboo figurines and silk kites and jade jewelry and copies of ancient paintings.

"Hey," said Juliet, "my armpits are killing me from these crutches."

"Then let's take a break," said Summer. "I'll get us a snack." She walked up to a small outdoor counter and bought spring rolls, and they sat down at a table on the sidewalk to eat.

Gilda watched what appeared to be the oldest woman in the world crossing the street. It seemed to take her an hour; the light changed at least twice before she made it from one corner to the other. Cars darted around her as she moved with tiny, shuffling baby steps, using a cane. *It probably takes her an entire day to do a single errand,* Gilda thought.

"Look, Juliet," she said. "There's someone who's even slower than you."

"You're hilarious," said Juliet drily, "you know that?"

"Don't you just love people-watching?" said Summer.

"It's one of my favorite things," said Gilda.

"People are just so *interesting,*" Summer gushed.

Gilda suddenly felt inexplicably sad as she watched the

woman reach the curb and begin to turn the corner to head slowly down the sidewalk. She watched her approach the entranceway of a building. "Where do you think that old lady is going?" she asked.

"That's a Chinese temple," said Summer.

The old lady made her way inside the building.

Then Gilda noticed the familiar ticklish sensation in her ear. "Let's follow her," she said impulsively.

"You've got to be kidding," said Juliet. "Why would we want to do that?"

"Just to see what she's up to," said Gilda. "And I want to see what's inside that temple."

When Summer, Juliet, and Gilda entered the silence of the worship space, they immediately felt awkward. Their loud curiosity was out of place in the contemplative environment.

The temple was empty except for the old woman they had followed; she lit some incense in front of a small altar that was adorned with the picture of a young girl.

"That must be one of her dead relatives," Summer whispered.

The woman took a piece of paper and a fountain pen from her bag. With painstaking slowness, she began to draw Chinese characters.

"What's she writing?" Gilda whispered.

Summer shrugged. "Maybe it's a message to that little girl."

Then Gilda remembered that Wendy Choy had once told her that Mrs. Choy believed it was possible to send messages—and even money—to dead people. Maybe the Chinese had a knack for getting letters delivered to the dead. It was worth a try, at any rate. Gilda started walking toward the old woman.

"Gilda!" Summer whispered loudly. "What are you *doing?*"

"I want to find out what she's writing."

"You can't disturb someone in a church or temple or whatever just because you're curious," Juliet whispered frantically. "Don't you have any manners?"

"I'm just going to *ask* her what she's writing!" Gilda blurted this in a regular speaking voice that echoed through the temple. The woman looked behind her, but decided that the trio must be tourists and turned back to her pen and paper. When she had finished writing, she burned her paper in a flame and lowered her head to pray.

Juliet and Summer pretended to examine the ornate sculpture of a Chinese goddess as the woman exited the temple with excruciating slowness, but Gilda stared directly at her.

"Excuse me," said Gilda, "what were you writing?"

The woman shook her head as if to say, *No, no; I can't help you.*

"I don't think she speaks English," said Summer.

"I think she was writing a letter to her granddaughter," said Gilda, after the woman had left.

"How would you know that?" said Juliet. "You have no idea what she was writing."

"I just have a *feeling* that her granddaughter was sick and died, and that's what she was doing."

Gilda turned to Juliet. "Hey—why don't you write a letter to your aunt Melanie?"

"No thanks," said Juliet, shaking her head. "I don't know what I'd say."

"You could ask her if she has something she wants to tell you."

"Oh, good idea!" Summer exclaimed. "I'm going to write one to my cat who died. It was so sad; I had to put her to sleep."

Juliet rolled her eyes as Summer dug around in her purse for a scrap of paper.

Gilda suddenly knew that she wanted to write a letter to her father. Maybe there was something about writing a letter to a dead person in a Chinese temple that actually gave the letter more power. She took out the small notebook she kept in her pocket and began to write quickly.

Hi, Dad. I hate to ask for favors when you're supposed to be having eternal rest, but if you bump into Juliet's aunt up there (her name is Melanie Splinter), could you ask her what the deal is? Her niece is trying to figure out what happened to her.

I also wanted to let you know that I'm doing fine. I haven't stopped missing you, though. Write to me if you can.

Love, Gilda

Gilda suspected that she didn't have the right kind of paper to send to a spirit, and she obviously didn't have a special altar in the temple for her father (who wasn't the least bit Chinese). Still—she felt that it was worth a try.

Juliet and Summer watched as Gilda burned her letter in the small flame of a candle, just as the old woman had done.

"Who were you writing to?" Summer asked as they emerged from the temple into the bright afternoon sunlight.

"My father," said Gilda, without further explanation.

Summer and Juliet fell silent, unsure whether to offer a sympathetic comment or simply leave Gilda alone.

"Well, I bet his spirit is reading your letter right at this moment," said Summer, attempting to say something helpful.

"It's worth a try," said Gilda matter-of-factly.

Juliet observed Gilda, who seemed more subdued than usual. Juliet hadn't realized that Gilda had lost a parent, but now she glimpsed a different side of her cousin—a hidden side that might secretly be more hurt and sad than she acted. *Maybe that's why she's so interested in contacting the dead,* Juliet thought. *It's because she lost someone, too.*

15

A Disturbing Theory

Sitting on the floor in Juliet's room, Gilda and Juliet stuffed handfuls of popcorn into their mouths while watching a true-crime television show called *The Criminals Amongst Us.* It was a rerun of one of Gilda's favorite episodes: the featured criminal was a trusted doctor well loved by his community because he was one of the last physicians in the country still willing to make house calls in the middle of the night. "But they were DEADLY house calls!" the television narrator warned. "WHY were there so many unexplained deaths? WHY so many mysterious illnesses?"

Gilda already knew the outcome of the case: the "deadly doctor" killed an elderly woman by giving her a lethal dose of a drug and then forging a suicide note to cover up the crime. Because the woman's family simply couldn't believe that their "sweet Grandma Jones" would actually commit suicide, they kept pushing the local police to investigate further until the truth was finally revealed: the doctor was, in fact, a murderer!

As she watched the show, Gilda once again felt the ticklish sensation in her left ear. Was it a special sign that this particular episode of *The Criminals Amongst Us* happened to be on at just this moment? An idea that had been simmering in her mind began to boil. She stood up and began to pace back and forth.

"I think *7th Heaven* is on now," said Juliet, her mouth full of popcorn. She observed Gilda, who was still pacing. "What are you doing?"

Gilda abruptly walked over to the television and turned it off.

"Hey! It might be polite to *ask* the other person in the room before just turning off the television—"

"Juliet," said Gilda, "what if—just *what if*—your aunt Melanie didn't commit suicide after all?"

"But she *did* commit suicide."

Gilda resumed her pacing, her hands clasped behind her back.

"Why are you walking that way?" Juliet asked. "Nobody our age walks like that."

"Let's consider all the facts," said Gilda, ignoring Juliet's comment. "First of all, we know that Melanie's ghost has been trying to communicate with you for some reason."

"Well, I don't know if we can consider that a fact," said Juliet, "but I agree it *might* be true."

"Melanie's ghost must have *something* she wants to explain to us," Gilda continued, "and I know from my research that ghosts normally appear as a result of a traumatic death. The spirit wants us to fix some kind of injustice or resolve something that was left unfinished."

"Suicide *is* a traumatic death."

"That's true," said Gilda. "But—and this is just an idea—*what if* Melanie's death was not a suicide at all, but a *murder?* That would be REALLY traumatic! What if the message she's trying to communicate is that someone pushed her out that window and made it *look* like a suicide?!"

Juliet stared at Gilda. "You've definitely watched too much television."

"Have I? Or have I watched just *enough* television?"

"What are you talking about?"

"I have a sneaking suspicion that your father knows *a lot* more than he's telling about your aunt's death."

"But that doesn't mean that Melanie was murdered!"

"Juliet, are you aware that in most murder cases, the victim was killed by a close friend or relative: a spouse, a boyfriend or girlfriend, or even—a *sibling?*" Gilda had learned this on an episode of *America's Most Wanted.*

Juliet regarded Gilda with a cold stare. "So you actually believe my father is a murderer?!"

"Well, it's just a theory at the moment."

Juliet picked up the remote and turned the television back on, dismissing Gilda's theory with a single contemptuous gesture. "I bet you'd be pretty angry if I suddenly called *your* father a murderer."

Gilda realized that Juliet was right: she hadn't even considered the possibility that her cousin might actually feel offended by her murder theory, because the relationship between Mr. Splinter and his daughter seemed so formal and distant. *Sometimes you offend people without realizing it,* Gilda's mother had warned on numerous occasions.

"I'm sorry," Gilda offered lamely. "When I get these hunches, I just have to follow them."

Juliet glowered at the television screen.

"But what if I'm right?" Gilda added hopefully.

Juliet didn't reply, so Gilda simply closed the door behind her. She wondered, for a moment, if she should go back into Juliet's room and apologize for everything she had said. *But if I can't follow my hunches where they lead me, I'll never be a real psychic investigator,* Gilda thought. One of the rules in her *Psychic's Handbook* was:

Make it your policy to tell the truth you perceive — even when it's not what people want to hear.

Of course, she had no way of being sure that her murder theory *was* true. Gilda decided that she had better get right to work to test her hunch.

• • •

Back in her room, Gilda opened her *Master Psychic's Handbook* and turned to a chapter entitled "Automatic Writing." "This writing technique is like being a ventriloquist for the dead," Balthazar Frobenius commented, rather eerily. "Handwriting is simply another means of accessing a voice from beyond!" Whereas Balthazar wrote by hand, using a tablet of paper made from a very rare type of tree, Gilda used her typewriter. She decided to begin with a short note to her father, whom she hoped might function as a type of spiritual medium to help her contact Melanie.

```
Hi, Dad,
   Hope you're doing well in heaven or
wherever you are.
   I'm working on a psychic investigation
right now, so help me if you can!
   Okay--here goes....
```

Gilda closed her eyes and did her best to focus all of her mental energy on accessing the voice of a ghost. She typed MELANIE SPLINTER at the top of the page. Then she waited and listened, her hands poised over the typewriter keyboard.

No words came to her; she perceived nothing but a prickly, late-afternoon silence. After a minute had passed, Gilda opened her eyes and stared at the round letters of her typewriter keyboard, feeling extremely disappointed.

When she turned back to her *Psychic's Handbook,* her eyes rested on the "Principle of Amplification": "Get an object that is closely connected to the person you are trying to contact," Balthazar advised. "This will *intensify* your psychic link with that individual."

Maybe that's the problem, Gilda thought. *I need something more closely connected with Melanie if I'm hoping to access her voice.* This meant going back to Juliet's bedroom and asking if she could borrow the photograph of Melanie—a prospect Gilda dreaded.

Nevertheless, Gilda took a deep breath and marched back down the long hallway toward Juliet's bedroom. She rapped on the door.

"What do you want?" Juliet yelled, without getting up to open the door.

Gilda cautiously cracked open the door and found Juliet still sitting in the same position on her bed, watching an episode of *7th Heaven.* Juliet glanced in Gilda's direction and then quickly turned back to the television. Despite the unfriendly reception, Gilda thought she detected a glimmer of hope in Juliet's face.

"I was wondering if I could borrow that photograph you showed me—the picture of your aunt Melanie."

"What for?"

"I'm doing some automatic writing."

"You can't write on that photograph."

"I wasn't going to *write* on it; automatic writing is just a way of channeling a spirit. It helps to have an object connected with the person you're trying to contact."

"Why should I help you incriminate my father?"

"Juliet, I'm not trying to incriminate anyone; I'm just trying to figure out what happened to your aunt."

Juliet sighed. "You know," she said, making a rather big production of standing up and rummaging under her bed to find the jewelry box, "between the two of us, you'd think that *you* were the one who lived in California."

"Because I'm the cool one?"

"No, because of all your talk of channeling and spirits and everything," said Juliet, holding out the small photograph for Gilda.

"Don't forget that you're the one who's actually seen a real ghost," said Gilda, closing the door behind her.

After Gilda left with the photograph, Juliet tried to recall the vision of the face she had seen at the top of the staircase. Why had she felt so certain that she was looking at her dead aunt Melanie?

Don't forget that you're the one who's actually seen a real ghost. . . .

Juliet chewed her lower lip for a moment, then stood up, turned off the television, and surveyed the contents of her bedroom as if she were searching for something that had been hidden among someone else's belongings. On impulse, she opened the bottom drawer of a dresser that contained a wealth of neatly folded Ralph Lauren T-shirts. Buried beneath her clothes, Juliet found a pile of papers— sketches of kids and teachers at school she had doodled while she was supposed to be paying attention in class. There were also a few unflattering caricatures of her step-sisters with giant biceps and toothy grins. *Why do I keep these dumb things?* she wondered.

Juliet frowned when she came to the last sketch in the pile—a drawing she had created with crayons when she was a very young girl. A stick-figure child gazed out of the pic-ture with oversize blue eyes. Filling the entire sky, an enor-mous angel composed of a triangle-shaped gown and two awkward, waxy blue wings reached down with a clawlike hand to touch the stick figure's balloon head. Juliet had no memory of actually creating the drawing, but something about it now seemed both significant and disturbing.

She stuffed the drawing back under her T-shirts, then rummaged through a desk drawer until she found a piece of paper and a pencil. Sitting down on the floor and lean-ing against the foot of her bed, she tried to recall her vision of Melanie's ghost. She began to sketch a gaunt face that closely resembled her own.

• • •

Back in her room, Gilda looked at the seaside photo of pale, ethereal Melanie. *It almost looks like a picture of a ghost,* she thought. She closed her eyes and began to type.

```
MELANIE: WHAT DO YOU WANT TO TELL US?
   Juliet is my niece. I am Lester's
sister. I have blond hair.
```

The response felt forced, and it was disappointedly obvious—hardly information requiring psychic skills. But at least it was a start. Gilda typed another, more probing question:

```
HOW DID YOU DIE?
   I'm not dead!
```

The immediate response seemed to come from Gilda's fingers rather than her mind—"a sign that you may have made contact," her *Psychic's Handbook* had explained.

Gilda was so surprised, she sat back and stared, awestruck, at the letters she had just typed. It was hard to know what to make of this. Was it possible that Melanie was actually alive but missing—or *hidden* somewhere?

Gilda pictured a frail, prematurely aging woman locked inside the tower like a medieval princess, her ankles bound by iron chains. Every now and then, Mr. Splinter would stick some bread crusts and water through a crack under the door. Perhaps he would occasionally leave a bit of roast turkey with gravy or some chocolate cake—just far enough out of reach to cruelly taunt his starving victim.

Gilda found this idea intriguingly horrible, but then she felt silly when she remembered one of Balthazar Frobenius's rules: "Don't ever use the word *dead* when communicating with a spirit," he advised. "The spirit probably does not think of herself as dead! Instead, use the phrase *pass over to the other side.*"

Gilda attempted another question:

```
MELANIE: HOW DID YOU PASS OVER TO THE
OTHER SIDE?
    WHAT HAPPENED TO YOU IN THE TOWER??
```

Gilda waited for a response. For a moment, she heard nothing but a heavy gust of wind that caused loose boards on the house to creak.

"Is anybody there?" she asked, her fingers still poised over the typewriter keyboard. She thought she heard a soft *thump.*

I sense a presence! Gilda thought.

Gilda peeked through half-closed eyelids and nearly fell off her chair when she discovered a pair of yellow eyes peering back at her.

Phantom, Juliet's smoke-colored cat, had entered the room and jumped up onto the desk with scarcely a sound. Like an enormous furry owl, he was perched right next to Gilda's typewriter and quietly observed her with his sleepy eyes. *There's something uncanny about the way this cat always seems to appear unexpectedly, like the Cheshire cat in* Alice in Wonderland, *Gilda thought.* The cat stretched his mouth wide open in a massive yawn, as if he were a boa constrictor about to ingest a large animal.

Gilda sneezed, causing Phantom to jump down from the table and exit the room, his tail twitching with disdain.

Gilda sighed and again turned back to her *Psychic's Handbook* to see if Balthazar Frobenius had any other ideas.

Many inexperienced psychics have difficulty sufficiently clearing their minds in order to "hear" the spirit voices that call out to them. These individuals may find more success with an ancient divination technique using the written word. When a text with strong magical vibrations is opened randomly in response to a specific question, the first word that appears to the seeker is a message that must be interpreted: it may be an omen of events yet to happen in the future or a clue to explain a secret of the past. The ancients used this psychic technique by turning to the works of Homer or Virgil, whereas Christians in the Middle Ages flipped through the pages of the Bible. Of course, the accuracy of this method is linked to the interpretive abilities of the psychic who uses it.

Gilda thought this method sounded appealingly simple. Instead of using writing, perhaps Melanie's spirit could more easily send her a clue through the words in a book!

Gilda couldn't remember seeing a Bible or any books by Homer or Virgil in the Splinter mansion, but she did remember noticing a dusty, clothbound dictionary stashed in the bottom drawer of the writing desk.

Deciding that the dictionary was "magical" enough, Gilda lifted the heavy book out of the drawer, brushed away some dust bunnies, placed her hands on its cover, and closed her eyes.

"Melanie," she asked again, "what happened to you in the tower?"

Keeping her eyes tightly shut, Gilda thrust open the dictionary and then jabbed her finger at a page.

Her finger pointed to the word *maffle,* which meant "to cause to become confused or baffled." Gilda was delighted by this word, but she was yet more intrigued by the word just below her finger—the word *Mafia:*

Mafia *n* 1. a secret organization of criminals who control illegal activities, often using violence to achieve goals; of Italian origin, but also active in the United States.
2. any of various similar criminal organizations.

Gilda leaned back and chewed a lock of her hair as she contemplated the significance of this clue. *If only Mr. Splinter were Italian!* Gilda knew that he was nothing like the Mafia bosses she had seen on television.

Then she remembered an episode of *The Criminals Amongst Us* in which a Mafia boss had found an accountant to help him conceal illegal sources of income. With a new burst of energy, Gilda began to type:

<u>HYPOTHESIS:</u>

A group of organized criminals (the Mafia!) hired Mr. Splinter to help them cheat on their taxes. They probably paid him thousands of dollars to help keep their illegal income a secret and the government off their backs.

But Melanie became suspicious of her brother's expensive tastes and his paranoid behavior. She started snooping around and soon discovered what Lester was up to. When she threatened to blow the whistle on the operation, the Mafia bosses forced Mr. Splinter to get rid of his sister and make her murder look like an accident. . . .

Here was an intriguing motive to support her murder theory! What if Melanie was silenced because she discovered that Mr. Splinter was involved in some sort of criminal activity?

As Gilda considered what she hoped was a real clue in response to her questions, she had to admit that her confidence in her ability to channel Melanie's spirit was tempered by a feeling of doubt. *Am I* really *developing psychic skills,* Gilda wondered, *or am I simply making things up?* She had to admit that it was a little difficult to imagine Mr. Splinter himself pushing his own sister out a window. But what if a hired hit man had done the dirty work, and he had simply been an accomplice by keeping the crime secret for all these years?

"Trust your instincts," Balthazar Frobenius had written.

Gilda decided that starting the very next day, she would investigate Mr. Splinter to find out whether his accounting business had any criminal connections.

16

Going Undercover

That's the most ludicrous idea I've ever heard." Juliet watched with obvious disapproval as Gilda calmly dumped six teaspoons of sugar into the cup of coffee that Rosa had reluctantly poured.

"What's so ludicrous about it?" Gilda stirred her coffee calmly. She had just finished explaining her theory about Melanie's death.

"For starters—everything about it is ridiculous. My father isn't a murderer!"

"I'm not saying that he necessarily committed the murder himself. But what if he knows who did it, but just can't say anything? Maybe he's afraid for your safety."

"It's still pretty far-fetched."

"Well, my plan is to go downtown to your father's office to see if I can find any evidence to support my theory. You can come with me and distract the receptionist, and I'll—"

"No way," Juliet interrupted. "You're on your own with this scheme."

"Come on. It'll be fun!"

"Nope."

Gilda stared fiercely at Juliet, trying to use mental telepathy to force her to change her mind. It didn't work. "Well," Gilda sighed, "will you at least show me where your father's office is?"

Juliet poked her half-eaten hard-boiled egg with a fork as if it had offended her in some way. "I guess. But don't blame me if you completely embarrass yourself."

"Juliet, if I wasted time worrying about embarrassing myself I would never get anywhere as a psychic investigator."

"No comment."

"Now, if you'll excuse me, I have to go put on my disguise."

Waiting together at the bus stop, Gilda and Juliet were a strikingly mismatched pair: Juliet carried an elegant leather handbag and wore the "distressed" designer jeans that were a fashion requirement among the girls at her school. Gilda wore an elaborate disguise composed of vintage clothing purchased from obscure flea markets and garage sales.

"So how do I look?" Gilda asked, making her voice low and hoarse in an attempt to mimic an aging smoker. "You haven't even commented on my disguise."

Juliet squinted at Gilda, as if trying to shield her eyes from an unpleasant source of light. "Terrible," she said. "You look absolutely terrible. You sound terrible, too."

Gilda's wig was obviously synthetic: originally designed as a bob with flirty bangs, the hairstyle now featured brassy, disheveled clumps. Along with the wig, Gilda wore a bright shade of magenta lipstick, beige foundation makeup, a cheap set of metallic gold fingernails, a strand of fake pearls, her leopard-print jacket, an oversize purse, and a pair of stiletto pumps with pointy toes. The shoes hurt her feet, but Gilda was willing to endure the torture of her high heels because the pain forced her to walk with a pigeon-toed gait, and that was part of the disguise. Gilda had read somewhere that being recognized had as much to do with a familiar walk as it did with one's face, body, and clothing. Before leaving the house, she had practiced slouching forward and limping slightly with each step.

"But would you *recognize* me?" Gilda persisted.

"No—I don't think so." Juliet wrinkled her nose as she surveyed Gilda's attire. "I mean, if I didn't already know it was you and I saw you on the street, I'd just assume you were one of the freaks who hangs out downtown."

"Then the disguise works," said Gilda, secretly disappointed with Juliet's unimpressed response. "I'm supposed to be a rich, eccentric woman who has some connections with organized crime."

Juliet snorted. "That wig looks like rats have been nesting in it."

"Well, this woman doesn't waste money on her hair."

The bus crept up the hill toward them and groaned to a halt. Gilda put on a pair of sunglasses as she and Juliet climbed aboard.

To Gilda's surprise, people on the crowded bus took little notice of her unusual clothing. *Back in Michigan, people would have stared like Cub Scouts in the girls' locker room if I got on the bus wearing this getup,* Gilda thought.

Gilda and Juliet found a seat together. "So," said Juliet as the bus inched its way up a steep hill, "what, exactly, are you planning to do once you get to my father's office?"

Gilda opened a tiny powder compact, peered in the mirror, and rubbed off some lipstick that had collected on her teeth. "I need to figure out whether Splinter & Associates is open to helping clients who are involved in organized crime, so I'm going in there disguised as a potential client who wants to hide some money from the government."

"I sincerely doubt you're going to discover anything." Juliet wasn't quite sure why she was even willing to help Gilda find her way to her father's office. Was it the nagging feeling that since her father was so secretive, there just might be some kernel of truth in Gilda's far-fetched ideas? Besides, ever since Gilda has been around, Juliet had felt different. At least something *interesting* was happening for a change.

The bus reached the busy financial district of the city. "This is our stop," said Juliet.

Wind blasted between tall buildings, and Gilda had to hold her wig down with one hand to keep it from flying away like a large, blond pigeon. Juliet led the way through crowds of people: tourists, office workers on their lunch breaks, homeless people wearing layers of clothing, merchants selling jewelry in the street, a sinewy contortionist who had attracted a small crowd of spectators.

Juliet stopped in front of a tall office building. "My father's office is on the fifth floor."

Gilda felt a stab of stage fright at the idea of actually walking into the building to carry out her risky scheme. "Well," she said, "I guess this is it."

"So what are you waiting for?"

"Don't rush me." Gilda tried to steady her nerves and put herself in the mind-set of an undercover detective.

"I knew you'd chicken out."

"Well, you were wrong." Gilda adjusted her wig. Taking a deep breath, she walked into the building, breezily passed the security guards, and boarded the elevator.

At the entrance to Splinter & Associates, Gilda faced an imposing reception desk where a woman looked up at her with a quizzical, annoyed expression.

"May I help you?"

"I'm here to see Mr. Splinter," said Gilda, willing herself to act confident and reminding herself to disguise her voice.

"Do you have an appointment?"

"Yes," Gilda lied.

"Your name?"

Gilda suddenly realized that despite all the attention she had given to her disguise, she had completely forgotten to invent a false name for herself.

"My name is . . . Sophia. It's Sophia Lasagna."

"What an unusual name," said the receptionist, looking at her appointment calendar. "I think I would have remembered that one! I'm sorry; I don't see your name here."

"That's impossible!" Gilda did her best to convey genuine outrage. "There must be some mistake! I *told* my assistant to make the appointment for today. I simply must speak with Mr. Splinter immediately!"

"I'm sorry, Ms. Lasagna, but Mr. Splinter is very busy—"

"Perhaps you could ask him to squeeze me in. I have a lot of money that needs accounting!" Gilda realized that there was something idiotic about her last comment, but the receptionist had already picked up the phone to call Mr. Splinter, so perhaps she hadn't noticed.

"Mr. Splinter, I have Sophia Lasagna here who says she needs to speak with you urgently."

The receptionist hung up the phone and regarded Gilda primly. "You're in luck. He just had a lunch cancellation, so he's willing to see you."

"I should hope so," said Gilda.

"This is unusually lucky, you know. Mr. Splinter keeps a very tight schedule."

"As do I."

The receptionist looked grim. She was obviously irritated that Gilda had succeeded in getting an appointment. "His office is down the hallway to your left."

There were no decorations of any sort in Mr. Splinter's office—just gleaming white surfaces under fluorescent lights. Gilda immediately wished that the atmosphere were darker and more mysterious: she was confident that she could carry off her disguise in a dim, smoky restaurant, but harsh office lighting was another matter. She decided to leave her sunglasses on to prevent Mr. Splinter from recognizing her eyes.

As Gilda walked in, Mr. Splinter was busy writing something in a leather day planner. Sitting in his work environment, he looked grayer than usual.

"Yes, have a seat please; be right with you," he said without even looking in Gilda's direction.

Gilda sat down, crossed her legs, and adjusted her wig.

When Mr. Splinter finally glanced up, he seemed startled. He frowned at Gilda, who felt a wave of panic: Did he recognize her?

The truth was that although Gilda had succeeded in making herself largely unrecognizable, she had not quite managed to avoid looking as if she were wearing a deliberate disguise. For one thing, she was still wearing her dark sunglasses.

In an effort to obscure Mr. Splinter's view of her face, Gilda opened her large purse and began to rummage through the contents. Inside, she discovered a package of Virginia Slims that she had removed from one of her mother's hiding places shortly before leaving Michigan. Trying to stay in character as Mr. Splinter scrutinized her, Gilda took the package out of her purse and attempted to extract a cigarette from the box with a shaking hand. In the process of fumbling through her purse, one of Gilda's false nails fell off and lay at her feet accusingly.

"I'm sorry, Ms. Lasagna, smoking isn't allowed here," said Mr. Splinter.

"Oh dear," said Gilda, feigning a hacking cough. "I can't go more than fifteen minutes without my ciggies!"

"So what can I help you with, Ms. Lasagna?" Mr. Splinter asked, already opening another client file and flipping through its contents impatiently. "My receptionist said you needed some urgent assistance."

"I'll get right to the point," said Gilda, still holding an unlit cigarette. "I'm interested in tax evasion."

Mr. Splinter raised his eyebrows. "I beg your pardon?"

"What I mean is that I don't want to pay taxes. I have money—a lot of money. I have money that needs to be 'swept under the rug,' so to speak. You know what I'm talking about, don't you, Mr. Splinter?"

Mr. Splinter leaned back in his chair and folded his arms across his chest. "I think you've come to the wrong place, Ms. Lasagna."

"Are you *sure?*" Gilda pressed. "That's not the word on the street."

"I beg your pardon?"

"Word is—you've helped some pretty shady characters 'cook the books.'" As Gilda gestured nervously, the cigarette flipped out of her fingers and landed on Mr. Splinter's desk.

Mr. Splinter picked up the cigarette with the disgusted gesture one might use to pick up a night crawler. He dropped it into his wastebasket. "Listen," he said, "none of my clients are criminals, if that's what you're suggesting."

"Of course not," said Gilda. "They're simply 'in the business.'"

"I don't follow you."

"Ever hear of a little organization called the Mafia?"

The expression on Mr. Splinter's face changed, as if he

had just realized that he might be having a conversation with an individual who was completely insane. "Are you saying that you're connected with the Mafia, Ms. Lasagna?"

"Let's just say I'm a client in need of some very *special* tax assistance."

"Ms. Lasagna, I think this conversation is over," said Mr. Splinter. "I'm trying to run a serious business here, and I don't know where on earth you got the idea that I'm running some sort of tax-evasion program for the Mafia."

"We have ways of *convincing* people to help us, you know."

"Good day, Ms. Lasagna."

Perceiving that she wasn't getting anywhere, Gilda sighed and stood up to leave. At just that moment, Summer entered Mr. Splinter's office. "Hey, Lester—want me to pick up a coffee from Starbucks for you? Oh, hi there, Gilda! A little early for Halloween, isn't it?"

Panicked, Gilda sought a quick escape, but Summer was blocking the doorway.

"Gilda?!" Mr. Splinter looked shocked.

"That is Gilda, isn't it?" Summer asked. "Sure it is! I'd recognize that freckled button nose anywhere—right, kiddo?"

It was over. Gilda slowly removed her dark glasses and sank down into her chair, trying not to meet Mr. Splinter's cold, silvery gaze.

Mr. Splinter couldn't help but feel nearly as annoyed

with himself as he was with Gilda. How could he have failed to recognize a thirteen-year-old in his office? Perhaps his ex-wife had been right years ago: "You never really *see* the people around you," she had said on more than one occasion.

"Summer," said Mr. Splinter, "will you excuse Gilda and me for a moment?"

"Okay," said Summer, giving Gilda a sympathetic wink and closing the door behind her.

"Well," said Mr. Splinter, folding his hands and facing Gilda with what he hoped was an authoritative demeanor, "I suppose you think this was a hilarious prank."

"Not really." Gilda stared at her metallic gold fingernails. She had dropped the smoker's voice and now felt that she was playing a more familiar role—the part of the kid sitting in the school principal's office, waiting to be reprimanded.

"Care to explain yourself?" Mr. Splinter asked.

What could she say? Obviously, Gilda couldn't admit that her disguise had been part of an attempt to secretly investigate Mr. Splinter's business practices. She also couldn't tell him of her suspicions that his sister was murdered and that he himself might have been responsible in some way.

"It was just a game," Gilda said. For once, she felt unable to come up with a more creative fib at the spur of the moment.

"A game? This is a place of business, Gilda."

"I know. It was just a silly game of Truth or Dare, and I got a dare to put on a disguise and come in here with a crazy story. I'm sorry."

"I think I'll need to speak with your mother about this."

"Okay, but just so you know—the whole thing was Juliet's idea." Gilda immediately felt terrible. It was one thing to deceive Juliet's father, but pinning the blame on Juliet herself was far worse than one of Gilda's whimsical, spontaneous lies. *I'm a horrible person,* she thought. *Juliet will hate me now, and he's probably going to send me home anyway.*

But to Gilda's surprise, Mr. Splinter's face actually brightened at the suggestion that Juliet was behind the scheme. "Really?" he said. "I've never known Juliet to do something like this. I mean, I'm glad to hear that the two of you are having some fun—I really am—but I just don't think it's appropriate to come into my office and waste my time."

"I completely agree," said Gilda.

"Time is money in business," Mr. Splinter added.

"I think Juliet just thought you might need a laugh because you've been working so hard. You know, a little joke."

"She *did?*" The hope in Mr. Splinter's voice was undeniable. He obviously liked the idea that his daughter had thought of brightening his day. "I mean, I don't approve, but I admit I'm glad to hear that she's having some fun for a change. I know Juliet has had a difficult time lately." For a moment, Mr. Splinter looked at Gilda with a more open expression that usual—something close to appreciation.

"Oh, Juliet is a barrel of laughs once you get to know her," said Gilda, warming to her audience.

Mr. Splinter hesitated. "I'll let this slide this time, but I trust that you girls can find some other ways of entertaining yourselves from now on?"

"Absolutely," said Gilda. "It won't happen again."

Gilda left Mr. Splinter's office feeling relieved. She couldn't believe her luck; one of the lamest excuses she had ever concocted had actually succeeded not only in getting her off the hook but in making Mr. Splinter feel happy.

On the other hand, she felt a little deflated by her failure to find any evidence whatsoever to support her Mafia cover-up theory about Melanie's death. Perhaps her automatic writing had been wrong; was it possible that she had misjudged Mr. Splinter? If so, then why his secrecy about the tower?

Gilda found Juliet outside Mr. Splinter's office building, propped on her crutches like a sullen scarecrow. "He recognized you, didn't he?" she said.

"Well, yes," Gilda admitted, "but only after Summer saw me and called me by name. You'd be surprised how close I came to pulling it off!"

The two girls made their way down the crowded street toward the bus stop. "But you have to admit that your Mafia murder theory is crazy," said Juliet.

"Maybe it is and maybe it isn't," said Gilda. "I'll need to do a little more investigative work before tossing the whole theory out the window."

The city bus pulled up to the curb with a belch of exhaust. A crowd of people climbed aboard, but Juliet remained motionless, staring at Gilda. "You are so weird, you know that? Do kids at your school think you're weird?"

"No." Gilda thought that Juliet had no business talking, since her status as the resident of a haunted house rendered her well outside the norm. "Kids at my school think I'm fabulous." In truth, Gilda was aware of a group of girls who had made it clear that they regarded her as strange, but since she found this particular clique tedious, she had decided their opinion didn't count. "I don't really care what other people think of me anyway," she added.

"Come on," said Juliet as she boarded the bus. "Everybody cares what other people think!"

"Not me. People who don't like me now will probably be asking for my autograph in the future."

"Must be nice to be so confident in yourself," said Juliet under her breath.

"What was that?"

"Nothing."

Gilda and Juliet found seats in the back of the bus. This time, Gilda noticed that people viewed her with mild curiosity.

"By the way," said Juliet, "your wig is falling off."

Gilda pulled off the wig, which aroused yet more interest from the people around her. "Oh, that reminds me," she said, "after your father recognized me, I had to tell him that I was playing a game of Truth or Dare and that my disguise was all your idea." Gilda spoke quickly, as if the speed of her words might make them sound more agreeable to Juliet. She knew that she had to warn Juliet about her impulsive lie, because Mr. Splinter would almost certainly mention something to Juliet about the supposed game of Truth or Dare.

"You'd better be kidding me," said Juliet.

"Unfortunately, I'm totally serious."

Juliet curled her upper lip in an expression of exasperation and disdain. "Then I guess I'll just have to explain to him that I had nothing to do with your dumb game."

"Come on, Juliet—I'll be in so much trouble if you tell him. What if your dad tells my mom? I'll probably be sent home tomorrow."

"Too bad." Juliet turned away from Gilda and pretended to be very engrossed in the scenery out the window.

Gilda stared very intently at the side of Juliet's head,

once again trying to use the power of her own thought waves to change Juliet's mind. "If I leave," she said, "I bet you'll never find out what really happened to your aunt."

Juliet shrugged.

"You'll have to spend the whole summer alone in a haunted house," Gilda added.

"So? I've already spent most of my time alone in that house!"

Gilda had to admit that Juliet had a point. She attempted another angle of persuasion. "Then at least consider your father's feelings," she said. "You should have seen his face light up when I told him what a great sense of humor you have!"

"I suppose you're attempting to be ironic," said Juliet.

"Well, if you can't take a compliment, it's not my fault."

Juliet rolled her eyes, but Gilda noticed that she also blushed slightly. *She won't get me in trouble,* Gilda thought. *She doesn't want to admit it, but she doesn't want me to leave.*

17

The Psychic Pendulum

Searching through her *Psychic's Handbook* for another investigative technique, Gilda turned to a chapter entitled "The Mysteries of the Pendulum." Balthazar Frobenius wrote:

> Of all the psychic methods I've used, the pendulum is perhaps the most efficacious technique for "reading" objects connected with an individual. I've found numerous missing persons and also located the bodies of murder victims this way.

This sounds promising, Gilda thought.

Balthazar explained that his pendulum had been a gift from his grandmother, who was also a psychic. It was made of a rare crystal sphere that hung from "a very old piece of twine." The author claimed that the twine had been used to hang an innocent man during the nineteenth century. Using this object, Balthazar was able to "detect wrongful deaths." When dangled over a street map of Detroit, for example, Balthazar's pendulum helped him pinpoint the exact location of a body hidden in a Dumpster. When it was waved over the photograph of a missing person, hidden symbols emerged, providing clues that revealed whether the individual was alive or dead, and where he or she might be found.

Gilda also owned a pendulum, but hers had been created rather hastily from an enormous blue jawbreaker—an "Ever-lasting Gobstopper"—that her father had once given to her. The jawbreaker had been affixed to a lengthy piece of pink yarn that Gilda had swiped from the knitting basket of Grandmother McDoogle. Since psychic pendulums were supposed to detect things that were "wrong," Gilda had attempted to use hers to detect errors in her math home-work on several occasions. The results had been disap-pointing.

Gilda searched through her luggage until she located her pendulum stuffed inside a sock in the corner of the suit-case. Sitting cross-legged on the bed, she dangled the Ever-lasting Gobstopper over the photograph of Juliet's aunt. The goal, Balthazar Frobenius said, was to allow the pen-dulum to respond to "unconscious psychic vibrations" that reveal psychic information. "Do your best to avoid *forcing* it to swing one way or another," he advised.

Suspended from Gilda's fingers, the makeshift pendulum

swung steadily back and forth over Melanie's image. Gilda regarded this as an encouraging sign: "Circular motion means the person is alive, whereas side-to-side swinging means that he or she is dead," the *Psychic's Handbook* said. As the pendulum swung side to side in a straight line, Gilda examined the photograph of Juliet's aunt Melanie more closely.

The image seemed darker, moodier than it had before. Melanie stood at the edge of a seaside cliff: her silky white scarf billowed behind her, and she seemed fascinated by something in the distance. Behind Melanie, there were the shadows of trees shrouded by mist. In the distance, a lone, sharp church steeple pierced the fog like a sword.

As the pendulum swung back and forth hypnotically, Gilda's eyes were drawn to the texture of the porous, mossy cliff upon which Melanie stood. In the slippery, stone contours Gilda thought she detected a face—a face with chiseled features, a narrow mouth, and watchful eyes. Was it possible, or was she imagining things?

She felt certain that she saw Mr. Splinter's face peering out of the photograph.

"Mr. Splinter would like to have dinner with you and Juliet at eight o'clock," said Rosa, peering into Gilda's bedroom.

"Really?" said Gilda excitedly, quickly hiding the pendulum and the photograph beneath a pillow. "That's great!"

"Why so happy?" Rosa asked.

"Oh, no reason." Gilda's enthusiasm about dining with Mr. Splinter was linked to the occasion it provided to ask him a few more questions. Perhaps, in a more relaxed setting, she could actually get him to reveal some information.

"I suppose I should get dressed for dinner," said Gilda.

Rosa shrugged. "What's wrong with the clothes you're wearing?"

"Doesn't Mr. Splinter expect the ladies of the house to dress for dinner?" Gilda had read about "dressing for dinner" in novels, and the Splinter mansion struck her as exactly the sort of place where one should descend the staircase wearing an evening gown.

"I don't see any ladies around here," Rosa joked.

"Very funny."

"Dinner will be served at eight," Rosa said. "I have to cook now."

For a moment, Gilda actually considered wearing the vintage evening gown that was stuffed into her suitcase, but she changed her mind in favor of her plaid sundress.

A plan was percolating in Gilda's mind: she would lull Mr. Splinter into relaxed conversation with her demure sundress and friendly, girlish chatter. Then, right when his guard was down, she would use one of the oldest tricks in the book—the element of surprise. Gilda knew that detectives sometimes inserted unexpected questions and probing insinuations into casual conversations. This made the criminal suspect nervous, tricking him into revealing himself unintentionally.

Gilda dabbed on some bubble-gum-flavored lip gloss and what she hoped was an innocent-looking smile. On her way out the door, she hesitated for a moment, then went back and slipped the photograph of Melanie into a pocket of her dress.

In the parlor, Gilda found Mr. Splinter sitting in a leather armchair sipping a martini. Juliet reclined on a velvet sofa, twirling a lock of her hair. Gilda noticed that Juliet had made no effort whatsoever to dress for dinner: she wore the same jeans that she had worn all day, and her hair looked stringy and uncombed.

"I didn't see anything I liked at Saks," Juliet was saying to her father.

Mr. Splinter stood up with a gesture of formal politeness as Gilda entered the room. "Good evening, Gilda," he said.

"Good evening," said Gilda, wondering why using good manners always felt so very odd to her. She suspected that it was because her own family never did *anything* in a formal way. Gilda and Stephen usually ate dinner in front of the television, and the Joyces often conversed by yelling at one another from various rooms in the house. In fact, it was only on rare occasions that they were able to sit down together to have a conversation or a meal.

"Nice to see you out of costume," said Mr. Splinter.

"And you as well," said Gilda, realizing too late that Mr. Splinter's comment had been a joke.

Rosa appeared with a tray of hors d'oeuvres. "Something to drink for you?" she asked Gilda.

"I'll have a sidecar." Gilda wasn't sure what a sidecar contained, but she had always wanted to ask for one; it sounded like an appropriate cocktail for an attractive young sleuth.

"Coming right up," said Rosa, in a serious voice that made Gilda wonder if she was actually going to go make one.

"Nothing like a sidecar at the end of a long day," said Mr. Splinter in a surprisingly jovial tone of voice.

Rosa returned with a Coke. "Here is your sidecar," she said.

"So what grade are you in, Gilda?" Mr. Splinter asked.

"I'll be in ninth grade next year," said Gilda, immediately wishing that they could get back to the more interesting subject of sidecars.

"Oh, just like Juliet!" Mr. Splinter glanced at his daughter, who looked as if she was trying to appear as bored as possible.

Gilda already knew what Mr. Splinter's next question would be.

"Do you like school?" he asked.

"Of course," said Gilda. "Without education, where would we be?"

Mr. Splinter raised his eyebrows in surprise; this was an unexpected comment from a thirteen-year-old. "That's what I keep telling Juliet! Just pick a direction, work hard, don't lose sight of your goal—get good grades, of course—and the world's your oyster."

Juliet was now examining a lock of her hair with furious intensity—as if she had just realized for the first time that she actually had hair growing out of her head. With her knees tucked up to her chest, she also seemed to be trying to make herself as small as possible.

"I agree completely," said Gilda, relieved to find any subject that Mr. Splinter wanted to talk about so enthusiastically. Perhaps his martini was loosening him up. "So many young people today squander their opportunities," Gilda continued, "but personally, I will do just about *anything* to achieve my goals."

Juliet glared at Gilda from behind her hair.

"That's admirable," said Mr. Splinter. "And what's your favorite subject at school?"

"It's accounting," said Gilda, trying a little too hard to get Mr. Splinter on her side.

"I doubt they teach accounting at your school," Juliet blurted.

"How would *you* know?" Gilda retorted, losing her poise.

"Well, I think that's wonderful," said Mr. Splinter tactfully. "I assume you enjoy math?"

"Can't get enough," said Gilda, lying with as much sincerity as she could muster. "Just give me a trigonometry problem and a bag of Chee·tos, and I'm in heaven!"

Mr. Splinter's mouth twitched as if he wanted to laugh but wasn't sure whether it would be rude to do so.

"Oh, please," said Juliet.

"I'm serious," Gilda continued, thinking that now might be the time to steer the conversation toward the subject of criminal activity, since she had Mr. Splinter's full attention. "I think accounting is just fascinating."

"I'm probably one of the few people who will agree with you on that subject," said Mr. Splinter.

Gilda leaned forward eagerly. "And you must meet so many interesting people in your accounting firm."

"I do meet all types." Mr. Splinter seemed bewildered but extremely pleased by Gilda's apparent interest in his profession.

"I imagine some of your clients tell you some pretty juicy secrets."

Mr. Splinter frowned. "Well, I don't know how 'juicy' their secrets are. Sometimes there are situations that require some tact."

"You mean, situations that need to be covered up?"

"I beg your pardon?" Mr. Splinter looked as if he had lost track of the actual topic of conversation. Gilda scrutinized him closely, watching for what her *Psychic's Handbook* called "the telltale signs of lying and concealment: twitching hands, touching of the face, clenched fists, fleeting facial expressions that last only a split second but which betray a person's *true* feelings or intentions." So far, Mr. Splinter looked more confused than guilty.

"I mean," Gilda continued, "I'm sure there's been at least *one* situation where you had to compromise your own morals in order to help a client."

"Gilda, why don't you just shut up for once?"

Both Gilda and Mr. Splinter turned to stare at Juliet.

Gilda tried to feign innocence. "I'm sorry, Juliet—did I say something that offended you?"

"Yes, actually. The idiotic things you've been saying have offended me."

"Juliet!" Mr. Splinter snapped at his daughter with the voice one might use to yell at a muddy dog that had just trotted across a white carpet. "That's no way to speak to a guest."

"But Dad, she knows why I said it."

"Gilda, I apologize on my daughter's behalf."

"That's okay." Gilda felt uncomfortable that Mr. Splinter was taking her side against his daughter, but she nevertheless took the opportunity to tease Juliet with a patronizing smile. "Juliet didn't get her nap today, so she's probably a little cranky."

"That's the last straw!" Juliet pushed her hair from her eyes impatiently. "Dad, if you haven't noticed, Gilda has some pretty funny ideas about you."

"Oh? What sort of ideas?"

Now it was Gilda's turn to send a glare in Juliet's direction. What was Juliet doing? This was going to ruin her entire plan.

"For one thing, Gilda thinks you're connected with the *Mafia* or something," Juliet continued, glancing nervously in Gilda's direction.

To Gilda's annoyance, Mr. Splinter's face broke into a shy grin. He let out a surprisingly high-pitched giggle. "Most of my colleagues assume that I would never do anything so daring as eat sushi, let alone get involved in organized crime."

Oh, he's clever, Gilda thought. *He's a better liar than I am.*

"See?" Juliet turned to Gilda. "I told you it was a dumb idea."

"*The Godfather* has always been one of my favorite movies," Mr. Splinter said to Gilda, "so I must admit that I'm almost flattered. But what in the world would make you imagine such a thing about me?"

Gilda turned red. She had prepared herself for the possibility of getting in some kind of trouble, but she had not expected to be a source of amusement for Mr. Splinter. She slipped her hand into the pocket of her dress and touched the picture of Melanie. Remembering the eerie image of Mr. Splinter's face she had perceived while using the pendulum, Gilda gathered her courage and decided to seize the moment—to provoke Mr. Splinter into revealing the true cause of his sister's death.

With one swift, bold movement, Gilda pulled the photograph of Melanie from her pocket and placed it on the coffee table directly in front of Mr. Splinter.

It was as if Gilda had released a toxic agent into the atmosphere: the air in the room turned instantly brittle. Juliet gasped, and Mr. Splinter's face grew pale at the sight of the black-and-white image of Melanie. *The look on his face must be what writers mean when they say someone "blanched,"* Gilda thought.

"To be honest," said Gilda, doing her best to respond to Mr. Splinter's question with a detective's false nonchalance, "I'm a little bit psychic, and when I saw this picture, there was something about it that gave me a strange feeling." Gilda scrutinized Mr. Splinter closely as she spoke. "I guess you could say it gave me some funny ideas."

Mr. Splinter attempted to put his drink down on a coaster, but his hand shook, causing his martini to slosh upon the carpet. He covered his mouth with his other hand, as if he were overcome by a wave of nausea. "I have no idea what you're talking about, Gilda," he said.

Taken aback for a moment by the emotion that cracked the stony elegance of Mr. Splinter's face, Gilda felt almost guilty about revealing the picture of his deceased sister. On the other hand, she also noticed Mr. Splinter's hand sneakily covering his mouth as he spoke—"a possible sign that someone is hiding something," according to her *Psychic's Handbook*.

Collecting himself, Mr. Splinter stood up and folded his arms across his chest. "I realize you girls have been having some fun at my expense today, but this is where my sense of humor comes to an end. Juliet, I don't know where you and Gilda found this picture, but I think you know that I do not wish to speak of your aunt Melanie!"

"Why are you blaming me?! Gilda's the one—"

"I'm sure Gilda wouldn't have found this picture without your help," snapped Mr. Splinter. "And Gilda—I'm afraid I'll have to call your mother and arrange for your visit to come to an end if there are any further high jinks."

The palpable tension in the room combined with Mr. Splinter's prim use of the word *high jinks* made Gilda want to giggle nervously. She struggled, unsuccessfully, to stifle the urge.

"This isn't funny," said Mr. Splinter. "If there are any more prants that disrupt my business or seem disrespectful, that's the end."

"Yes, sir," said Gilda, biting her lip in an attempt to squelch any further giggles. "No more high jinks," she added. She sensed Juliet's searing glare from across the room.

"All right then," said Mr. Splinter, dusting off a shirt-sleeve irritably, as if attempting to brush away the unpleasant conversation like some lint. "I think Rosa must be ready for us in the dining room. I don't know about you girls, but I have quite an appetite."

Mr. Splinter exited, taking the remains of his martini with him.

Immediately after her father left the parlor, Juliet hobbled across the room and grabbed Gilda's arm with the tightest grip her thin fingers could manage.

"Ow!" Gilda yelled. "You're pinching me!"

"Thanks a lot for showing my father that picture," Juliet hissed.

"Well, you have to admit he acted pretty suspicious, spilling his drink and everything! I mean, it proves that he's definitely hiding something—"

"I don't care!" Juliet spit the words in a hoarse whisper. "Now my father probably hates me, and it's all your fault!"

Gilda realized that she hadn't expected Juliet to become quite this upset. She wondered if this situation was going to erupt into a lengthy fight like one she had had with Wendy Choy following an overenthusiastic game of water-balloon tag. "I'm really sorry I showed him the picture without asking you first," Gilda said, softening her voice and doing her best to sound sincere. "Sometimes I just get a little carried away."

"That's an understatement."

"On the bright side, I think we're on the right track with the investigation."

"*We* aren't on any 'track.' In fact, I want you to stop this stupid investigation."

"But you said you wanted me to help you figure out what really happened to Melanie! Don't you want to find out what's in the tower?"

"I've changed my mind," said Juliet icily. "Please just leave me and my father alone."

18

A Suicide Gene

Juliet stood facing the entranceway to the tower. She put both hands on the doorknob and tried to turn it. As expected, it was locked.

"Try using this," said Gilda, handing her a crowbar.

Juliet took the crowbar, wedged it between the door and the wall, and with one great burst of strength, she pried the door open.

She realized something at that moment—a secret about herself that had either been concealed or forgotten. She had power. She could open locked doors.

The open door released a sickening odor—stale air combined with the scent of something rotting. Perhaps it had been a mistake to open the tower. Nevertheless, Juliet walked through the doorway. She felt a wave of nausea as her eyes adjusted to the dim light.

"Gilda?"

Juliet glanced behind, but Gilda had disappeared. She was by herself in the tower.

"Help me."

Then Juliet saw her: a woman crouching in the corner—so thin she was a mere skeleton. She wore decaying rags. Dirt streaked her face, and her blond hair had turned gray. Next to her, there was a plate on the floor—a few crusts of bread and a bowl of filthy water. Despite her deteriorated body, the woman's eyes were fierce—speckled with multicolored flecks of light.

Juliet realized that she had walked into a prison: it was like a dungeon in a fairy tale with a princess chained to the wall.

"Aunt Melanie? Is that you?"

"He locked me in here," the woman said. "He keeps me alive as a prisoner." She pointed to the heavy chains around her ankles and shook them: *clink, clank, clank, clank!* "Your father has the key," she said.

"But he hides things," said Juliet.

"Yes," said the chained woman. "He hides things."

Juliet awoke suddenly, and earlier than usual. She had the disturbing, *changed* feeling that one gets after awakening from a vivid dream. Although she couldn't remember the details, she knew that she had dreamed something about the tower and her aunt Melanie. She also sensed that it was not the first time she had had this dream.

Your aunt Melanie's ghost may be trying to tell you something.

Juliet sat up and reached for her bathrobe. She noticed that, for the first time in weeks, she didn't feel a stab of pain in her midriff as she used her stomach muscles to sit up in bed. She stood up and found that her ankle barely hurt when she walked without her crutches. *Maybe this is a sign,* she thought. She decided to go see Gilda.

"I've changed my mind," said Juliet. She found Gilda sitting up in bed, reading her *Master Psychic's Handbook.*

"Again?" Gilda was growing weary of Juliet's ambivalence; it seemed to her that one moment, Juliet would say she wanted to investigate Melanie's death; the next, she would get angry and say she wanted nothing more to do with it.

"But I don't want to question my father any more about it," Juliet said. "I just want to find out what's inside the tower."

Mr. Splinter's bedroom reminded Gilda of the elegant but impersonal atmosphere of a nice hotel room or a furniture-store display. There were no clothes strewn about, no socks on the floor, no rumpled sheets, no stacks of books and papers. It was hard to believe that a person actually slept in the bed each night.

Juliet lingered in the doorway, watching as Gilda surveyed Mr. Splinter's bedroom. As much as she wanted to find a key to the tower—or at least some clue about what might be hidden there—she also felt paralyzed by the thought of violating her father's personal belongings. She rarely spent time in his wing of the house, and she had the uncomfortable sensation of trespassing in a stranger's room. Gilda, on the other hand, seemed unperturbed by any moral conflict associated with snooping through someone else's room; she had a long history of spying, and now she simply viewed herself as an investigator with a mystery to solve. Besides, she knew Mr. Splinter had left for work and that Rosa had the day off. She and Juliet had hours of investigative time.

Gilda opened the drawer of a mahogany dresser.

"Be careful with his stuff," said Juliet. "He has a specific place for everything. If you move something, you have to put it back exactly where you found it."

"Don't worry," said Gilda, noting that Mr. Splinter's underwear and pajamas were folded neatly and grouped in color categories. She also noticed that the only personal possession lying out in the open was a single book on the nightstand; its title was *The Death Tax Reconsidered*.

Gilda picked up the book. "Hey," she said, "this looks like a clue!"

"That's just an accounting thing," Juliet explained. "When people die, their estates get taxed, and then their kids don't get to inherit much. My father helps people find loopholes."

"Oh," said Gilda, thinking that it must be nice for the kids who inherited lots of money. She remembered how her mother had panicked when she discovered how many of her father's experimental medical treatments had not been covered by insurance and how much her father's funeral would actually cost. As a result, her mother had warned both Stephen and Gilda that there was "no guarantee" that she would be able to pay for college in the future. Gilda knew that her father had left behind debt, not an estate.

She opened Mr. Splinter's closet and found perfectly pressed shirts, pants, and suit jackets hanging in neat rows. "There's nothing here," she said after checking the pockets of several jackets just in case Mr. Splinter might use them as a hiding place. "Let's look in his bathroom."

With Juliet trailing close behind, Gilda entered Mr. Splinter's bathroom, which was similarly spartan and clean. The mirror and sink gleamed spotlessly. A bathrobe hung on a hook from the door. Inside the medicine cabinet, a shiny razor, shaving cream, a toothbrush, and soap were very tidily arranged. The only intriguing objects were a bottle of aspirin and several containers of prescription sleeping pills.

"Interesting," said Gilda, picking up one of the clear plastic containers of sleeping pills and examining it.

"What's so interesting about it?" said Juliet. She remembered, with a small wave of self-loathing, the day she had toyed with the idea of taking an overdose of sleeping pills and how she had imagined her parents' devastated reactions. "My father has insomnia."

"Could it be that the sounds of a ghost keep him awake at night, too?"

"I guess it's *possible,*" said Juliet. "But then why would he always tell me that he doesn't believe in ghosts?" As she said the words, Juliet remembered how her father had concealed the fact of Aunt Melanie's suicide until she had discovered the truth for herself. He hadn't exactly *lied,* but he was obviously capable of hiding the truth. What if, secretly, he knew that there was a ghost in the tower?

"Okay," said Gilda brusquely. "Let's check out his office next."

"I don't know," Juliet said. "He's pretty picky about his office, and I don't think he'd want us rummaging around in there."

"Exactly the reason we need to search it. It's more likely to be a place he hides things."

An enormous oak desk and a leather chair confronted the girls accusingly as they entered Mr. Splinter's home office.

"You look through the desk drawers, and I'll look in these file cabinets," said Gilda.

"You know," said Juliet, "you're being kind of bossy if you consider the fact that this isn't even your house."

Gilda threw herself down in the chair behind Mr. Splinter's desk and put her feet up like a self-satisfied executive. "Okay," she said, "why don't you tell *me* what to do for a change?"

"Well," said Juliet, "what about checking the computer?"

Gilda had to admit that this was a good idea. "Okay— you go ahead and check his computer files."

"But I'm pretty sure I'll need his password to get into his files, and I have no idea what it is."

"You're his daughter. I'm sure you can guess some words he *might* use." Gilda turned her attention to the row of wooden file cabinets that lined one wall of the office.

Juliet sighed and tried to ignore a stab of anxiety in her stomach as she began attempting to log into her father's computer. Meanwhile, Gilda opened the first drawer of the file cabinet and searched through one folder at a time. Most of the files were organized by what appeared to be names of Mr. Splinter's clients: *Allen, Ashton, Applegate, Billingsley, Borden* . . . Gilda peeked into a few of them, but they only contained records of letters, bank statements, boring financial documents that didn't mean much to her. After fifteen minutes of staring at numbers, Gilda had to admit she had no idea what she was looking for.

"I can't get into his files," said Juliet.

"Try typing in *Juliet,*" said Gilda.

"I already tried that."

"How about . . . *Melanie?*"

"I tried that, too; it doesn't work. For all I know, his password could be a series of numbers. I doubt he'd pick something easy to guess."

The mention of Melanie's name gave Gilda a sudden impulse; she jumped ahead to the file drawer labeled *L–N* and began to finger through the *M* folders.

Gilda's mind was ablaze; she felt, for a moment, that she must be a genius. She also couldn't believe her luck; there was actually a plastic file folder labeled *Melanie.* "I think I actually found something!" She sat down on the floor in front of the file cabinet and opened the folder.

The file contained several pieces of paper. The first was simply titled "Final Expenses," and it seemed to be a list of costs associated with Melanie's death:

```
Casket (closed casket service):    $3,000
Flowers:                           $2,000
Minister:                          $900
Funeral catering services:         $1,000
Organist:                          $400
Contractor (windows sealed, etc.): $3,000
Locksmith:                         $400
```

"What is it?" Juliet asked.

"Looks like after your aunt died, your father got right to work on locking up that tower," said Gilda, noting the fees for "contractor" and "locksmith." She felt that there was something cold and begrudging about the list of expenses.

"Let me see that," said Juliet.

Gilda handed Juliet the document and continued to look through the file.

Beneath Mr. Splinter's terse list of itemized expenses was a yellowed newspaper clipping from the *San Francisco Chronicle*, dated Monday, June 21.

Suicide Casts a Pall over Neighborhood Party

Residents of affluent Pacific Heights were shocked when twenty-seven-year-old Melanie Splinter plummeted to her death from an upper window of her house at approximately midnight Saturday.

"We were just partying, and then I looked up and saw a woman climb out of a window and stand up on the window ledge. Then, before I could do anything to help, she jumped!" said neighbor Mick Young, who was hosting a late-night gathering on his patio when he saw Ms. Splinter fall to her death from her home. "We all rushed next door to see if we could do anything to help, but of course it was too late."

Survivors of the deceased include Ms. Splinter's brother, Lester Splinter, who owns the accounting firm Splinter & Associates, and her three-year-old niece, Juliet.

Mr. Splinter received the horrifying news of his sister's death when police woke him with a request to identify the body. "I'm shocked," was Mr. Splinter's only comment. "We're all shocked."

The Victorian home on Laguna

Street where Lester Splinter and his sister, Melanie, had lived their entire lives is widely considered a landmark in the Pacific Heights neighborhood for its many architectural features such as the tower in back of the house, from which Ms. Splinter fell.

A graveside funeral service for the deceased will be held at Sunshine Cemetery on Friday, June 25, at 3 p.m.

So it really was a suicide, Gilda thought. Her elation at finding an actual piece of information about Melanie's death was tinged with some disappointment that her murder theory and psychic investigation had apparently led her astray: after all, here was evidence that an eyewitness had *seen* Melanie jump from the window. Gilda also hated seeing a person's life and death summed up in a few brief sentences on a piece of aging newsprint. She remembered the feeling of revulsion she had experienced when she had first read her father's obituary in *The Detroit News.* The words were tiny helium balloons that blithely carried away her father's entire existence.

Nicholas Joyce—1959–2002
Joyce was born in Brighton, Michigan. He was an employee of American Engines for twenty years. Survived by his wife, Patricia, and two children, Stephen and Gilda.

In response to her father's disappointing obituary, Gilda had written an angry letter to *The Detroit News:*

Dear _Detroit_ _News_ Obituary Writer:

I suggest that you cut down on the gin-and-tonics during work hours and start attending some writing classes in your spare time to supplement the degree you apparently purchased at Walt Disney World.

I am the daughter of Nick Joyce, whose pathetic obituary recently appeared in the paper I am now embarrassed to call _The_ _Detroit_ _News_.

In order to help you do the job for which you are clearly overpaid, I have rewritten Nick Joyce's obituary for you to reprint as follows:

Nick _Joyce_ _Makes_ _It_ _Into_ _Heaven!_

After a life of brave struggles, Nicholas Joyce III has made his way into the Kingdom of God.

Mr. Joyce died of a mysterious form of blood cancer. He battled this disease for more than a year with the valor of a knight fighting a dragon in a fairy tale.

During his life, Mr. Joyce worked as an automotive artisan for the great company American Engines, where he was well loved. "We laughed our butts off!" is the memorial chant of his admiring and ample-bottomed coworkers.

But Nicholas Joyce's true love was the art of writing: he wrote like a madman, documenting his dark moods and sudden inspirations, his hopelessness and hope. His story (once discovered) will likely become a future source of English-paper topics and SAT questions.

Mr. Joyce is survived by his stylish daughter, Gilda, a promising young writer who possesses psychic abilities. To Gilda, Mr. Joyce bequeathed his most cherished possession--his typewriter.

Nicholas Joyce is also survived by his wife, Patricia, a hospital nurse who has been called "the Florence Nightingale of the new millennium"; and by a son, Stephen, who has rudimentary computer skills.

Gilda had sent her revised obituary to the newspaper, but, not surprisingly, there was no apology from the obituary writer who had attempted to erase Gilda's father in two tiny sentences.

"What's the matter?" Juliet asked, noticing that Gilda looked uncharacteristically glum. "What are you looking at?"

"Well, it looks like your father isn't a murderer, at any rate," said Gilda, doing her best to disguise the disappointment in her voice as she handed the newspaper article about Melanie's death to Juliet. "Sounds like your aunt really did commit suicide."

"Well, I'll spare you the irritation of hearing me say 'I told you so,'" said Juliet.

"That's big of you."

"But you have to admit, I told you so." Juliet frowned and twirled a lock of her white-gold hair as she read the news article.

There was one more item in the file for Gilda to investigate: a large white envelope. Gilda opened it and found copies of several medical bills for psychotherapy sessions— all for Melanie Splinter. There was also a glossy brochure from a place called Lilyvale Residential Facility. "Cutting-Edge Treatment in a Beautiful Setting," the cover of the brochure announced. Inside the brochure, Gilda found a letter:

Dear Mr. Splinter:

   This letter confirms registration of Melanie Splinter for in-patient treatment at Lilyvale

Residential Facility. We enjoyed meeting with you and your wife, Margo, recently, and feel certain that the psychiatric expertise and safe but comfortable environment we offer here at Lilyvale will be beneficial for your sister.

Here at Lilyvale, women with a range of psychiatric disorders live in an environment where they have access to outstanding medical professionals, a caring staff, and supervised recreational activities—all within the beautiful surroundings of Mendocino County in Northern California. Whether your family member's illness is mild or severe, we feel certain that choosing Lilyvale is a decision you can feel comfortable with; we provide the close monitoring our patients require and the reassurance and peace of mind their families want.

We look forward to Melanie Splinter's arrival on June 20, and to admitting her into our residential program. Please forward all medical records in advance of your arrival.

Note: New patients are welcome to bring

personal belongings, but these will necessarily be subject to search. Our furnished rooms meet the needs of most of our patients.

   If you have any questions, please don't hesitate to give me a call.

Regards,

Shirley Monroe

Shirley Monroe
Director of Residential Services
Lilyvale Residential Facility

"Juliet," said Gilda. "What's the date on that newspaper article about the suicide?"

"June twenty-first. Why?"

"*Very* interesting," said Gilda. "Do you know what that means? It means that Melanie committed suicide *the night before she was supposed to go to Lilyvale.*"

"Lilyvale? What are you talking about?"

"Here—take a look at this. It sounds like your parents were planning to send Melanie to some kind of fancy mental institution up north, but she never made it there. She killed herself the night before she was supposed to go!"

Juliet chewed a thumbnail as she read the letter from the Lilyvale Facility. She had known for some time that her aunt Melanie must have been experiencing emotional trauma at the moment she committed suicide, but now she began to wonder about the nature of her aunt's illness. Just how disturbed had she been?

"I don't see why your parents couldn't just *tell* you that," said Gilda. "I mean, why should having a mental illness be such a big secret for all these years?"

"I don't know. Maybe they were ashamed of her."

Juliet suddenly remembered an evening in San Diego when she was sitting on the beach next to her mother. As the sun set over the ocean, the two of them watched Juliet's stepfather play volleyball with his two athletic daughters. Something about the roar of the ocean and the fuchsia color of the sun had made Juliet feel very melancholy.

"Don't you want to play volleyball?" Juliet's mother asked.

"No," said Juliet. "I hate games."

"What do you mean, 'I hate games'? You can't possibly hate *all* games."

"Yes, I can. Games are so—so futile."

Her mother stared at her. "Well, *futile* is an impressive vocabulary word to use, but having that attitude is going to get you exactly nowhere, young lady."

"Where, exactly, am I trying to get?"

Her mother sighed. "I don't know," she said. "Some-where!"

The two of them watched the game of volleyball as the sun descended, turning the water shades of purple and rose.

"What a lovely sunset," said Juliet's mother.

"I don't think I've ever seen the sun that color before," said Juliet. "It looks like a swollen pink eyeball."

Juliet's mother regarded her daughter with a disturbed expression. "I hate to say it," she said, "but you're begin-ning to remind me of your father's sister, Melanie."

"The one who fell from the tower?"

Her mother nodded. "You're even starting to *look* like her."

"What do you mean? What was wrong with her?"

"Never mind," said Juliet's mother. "I'm sure it's just a phase you're going through."

Juliet had already been feeling inexplicably morose, but something about her mother's words made her feel com-pletely worthless. Clearly, her mother viewed *any* resem-blance to Aunt Melanie as a negative thing, although it was unclear exactly why. All Juliet knew about her aunt was that she had died a tragic death at a young age. *What if I resemble Melanie in that way, too?* Juliet thought. *What if I'm destined to die young?*

"I wonder if *I'm* going to end up like Aunt Melanie," said Juliet as she flipped through the Lilyvale brochure's hope-

ful images of patients eating breakfast and strolling in a garden outside the clinic.

"Why would you end up like Melanie?" Gilda asked.

"Well, I *look* like her, for one thing. For another thing, I
saw her ghost. What if that was just some kind of halluci-
nation, and I'm really in the early stages of going insane?"

"You *aren't* crazy," said Gilda. "There's been plenty of evidence that there's a real ghost in this house. And besides—
the ability to see a ghost is a gift. In fact, I'm jealous!"

Juliet shook her head. "There's something I didn't tell
you about the day I saw my aunt's ghost."

"What?"

Juliet hesitated. Why was she sharing this with Gilda,
who couldn't possibly understand? Still, she wanted to tell
somebody how she had really felt on that day. "I wasn't
really going to do anything—but I was *thinking* about what it
would be like if I took a bunch of my father's sleeping pills,"
she said quietly. "I was imagining how bad my parents would
feel after I was dead. . . . And then I saw Melanie—or something I *thought* was her—and I just fainted." Juliet looked
up at Gilda defiantly, as if daring her to say that this episode
was *not* evidence of imminent insanity.

Gilda knew that she should say something sensitive and
encouraging, but she couldn't think of anything. The truth
was, she couldn't understand why a rich, pretty girl like
Juliet would even contemplate suicide.

"Well," said Gilda, after a few moments had passed, "I admit I don't really understand why you would think of committing suicide, but I do know what it's like to feel completely rotten." She remembered the bland, wobbly feeling she had experienced for months after her father died. "What helps me when I get that feeling is either imagining I'm someone else who's got a much better life or writing a letter to my father."

Juliet seemed intrigued with this piece of information. "Does your father write back?"

"Of course not."

"Oh. Well, I just thought since you're supposed to be a psychic investigator and all—"

"I mean, I don't get a stamped letter in the *mailbox,* but I think he responds in other ways." Gilda wasn't actually sure that this was true. She had been on the lookout for signs of a response from her father for the past two years, and aside from the facts that Charlene Duzco (a girl at school whom she loathed) had recently chipped a tooth, that Mrs. Frickle had a new pink wig, and, of course, that she had gotten herself to San Francisco, Gilda hadn't seen much evidence of anything that could be considered a direct reply from her father. Nevertheless, she somehow felt that he was *listening* while she typed.

"Well, suicide can be hereditary," Juliet pointed out.

"Really? Like being short?"

"Sometimes all the kids in one family will commit suicide. I've read about cases like that!"

"I see," said Gilda, now squinting at Juliet as if she were a strange creature in a biology lab. "So you think you may have inherited a suicide *gene* from your aunt?"

"I don't know." Juliet stared at one of her tennis shoes as if she had never seen it before in her life. "I guess it's something that worries me."

Gilda felt that Juliet was wallowing in self-pity, and this suddenly annoyed her. "Cancer is hereditary, too," she blurted, "but do you see me giving up and smoking four packs of cigarettes a day? Do you see me eating lard sandwiches and smoking crack, and crying about how I'm going to die young?"

"You have *cancer?*"

"My father died of cancer." Gilda always hated saying the nasal, mediocre-sounding word *cancer.*

"Oh," said Juliet. "You never told me how he died."

"It happened a couple of years ago." Gilda was annoyed to find that she was surprisingly close to tears. She dug her fingernails into her arm in an attempt to replace a wave of sadness with physical pain.

"I'm sorry," said Juliet, who sounded genuinely sympathetic.

Gilda didn't want sympathy; sympathy was dangerous

because it had a way of making her want to weep. "My point was that lots of things are hereditary," said Gilda, attempting to shift the focus back to Juliet's problem. "Getting bad grades, being poor, being unhappy—I bet you could argue that they're all hereditary!"

"But—that's just *my* point," said Juliet. "What if I'm destined to end up like my aunt? What if *that's* the message her ghost is trying to send me?"

Gilda thought for a moment. "Even if that is true, it doesn't mean you should give up and assume you have no choice. Besides, did you ever consider the fact that your aunt Melanie's ghost might have *saved your life?* You saw her ghost, and instead of taking the sleeping pills, you fell! What if she's not just haunting you; what if she wants to *help* you?"

"That's a nice idea," said Juliet after a moment. "I don't know how plausible it is, but it's a nice idea."

"Listen," said Gilda, lowering her voice. "Now that we know a little more about Melanie, I think tonight's the big night."

"For what?"

"We should have a séance tonight."

"I don't like séances," Juliet said quickly. "But I guess we could try."

"There's nothing to be afraid of," said Gilda.

A door slammed shut downstairs.

"My father's home," said Juliet. "Quick! Put the file back!"

"But—I thought he was supposed to be downtown all day!" Gilda hurriedly wedged the file back in the drawer.

"I thought he was, too," Juliet whispered. "We've got to get out of here. You have no idea how angry he'll be if he sees us in here!"

Breathless, the girls hurried out of Mr. Splinter's office, down the hallway, up the staircase, and down another hallway to Juliet's room.

Juliet closed her bedroom door, sank to her knees, and rubbed her ankle, which now ached from running down the hallway and up the stairs.

"Are you okay?"

Juliet appeared to be hyperventilating. Then Gilda realized that she was actually convulsed by a fit of laughter.

"What's so funny?" Gilda demanded.

"I don't know . . ." Juliet gasped. "The look on your face when you heard the door slam was like . . ." Juliet attempted to imitate Gilda's bug-eyed face. "And then the way you ran up the stairs was just so funny!"

"I'm glad you find me amusing," said Gilda drily. "Your gimp leg is also hilarious."

Gripped by a seizure of giggles, Juliet doubled over and rolled around on her bedroom floor.

"Juliet, have you been taking drugs or what?"

"I just—I don't even know why I'm laughing."

"You're hysterical," said Gilda, wondering if Juliet might be crazy after all.

Juliet could only giggle in reply.

"You know, if you laugh like this during the séance tonight, it won't *work*," said Gilda, speaking from experience.

"I won't laugh. I promise." Juliet mimed crossing her heart solemnly, then collapsed into another fit of giggles. She had never laughed so hard in her life. She felt that she had let go of something that had been weighing her down, and for the moment, all her feelings of despair, fear, and irritation had suddenly mutated into a wonderful sensation of silliness.

19

Contacting Melanie

Mrs. Joyce applied pink lipstick and pressed her lips to-gether. She gazed at her reflection in the mirror critically, wondering when her face had become a desert of fine lines and freckles. When she had been married, she had rarely worried about her appearance, but now that she was going on an actual date, looks suddenly mattered again. Her friend Lucy had recently treated her to a makeover, telling her that she needed "to define her features," but Patty Joyce had never really understood how to wear makeup. She was the opposite of her daughter, who loved trying on different faces and personas. And Gilda's father had also loved artifice and costumes—but no, she could not let her-self think about Nick right now.

"I'm just not ready for a boyfriend!" Mrs. Joyce had protested when Lucy had mentioned that her own boy-friend "had a friend" whom she might enjoy meeting.

"Who said anything about a boyfriend? Just a little male attention is all. A night out, for goodness' sake. You deserve to enjoy life a little!"

The telephone rang just as Mrs. Joyce was attempting to apply eyeliner. *Uh-oh,* she thought, eyeing Gilda's cellphone number on her caller ID. Maybe Gilda had run out of money. Either that, or someone was hurt.

"Gilda! Is everything okay?"

"Hi, Mom. Everything's fine—"

"Oh, good. Honey, I'm really sorry, but I can't talk long right now. I'm getting ready to go out."

"But you never go anywhere," said Gilda.

"Well, I'm going somewhere now."

"Where are you going?"

"To meet some friends." Mrs. Joyce cradled the telephone under her chin while gazing into the mirror as she attempted to apply mascara with her free hand.

"Friends? You don't have friends."

"I most certainly do have friends. I'm going out with my friend Lucy. You've met her before." Mrs. Joyce sneezed and left a black splotch of mascara under her eyebrow. "Rats! Why do I even bother with mascara?!"

"Are you going on a *date?*" Gilda blurted suspiciously.

"What?! No. I mean, not really. I'm just meeting some friends." *The kid should become a detective,* Mrs. Joyce thought. *Or an FBI agent.*

Gilda reflected that her mother's response reminded her of her own evasive answer when she had been asked point-blank whether she had flushed cigarettes down the toilet several weeks ago. "Well no," Gilda had stammered. "I mean, not intentionally. . . ." There was no question about it; her mother was lying. "YOU ARE GOING ON A DATE, AREN'T YOU?!" Gilda practically shouted.

"Gilda, please calm down. It's nothing—just a friendly drink."

"Well, I'm just a little *surprised,* that's all. I mean, you never said you had a boyfriend, and just when I turn my back, you're out carousing around the town."

"Gilda—I don't have a boyfriend, okay?"

"Just don't ask me to call him 'Dad,' because I won't do it!"

Mrs. Joyce sighed. "You're way ahead of the game. I said I don't have a boyfriend. In fact, I don't even know how to put on lipstick and mascara, so this may be the only date I'll get."

"Well, you need to curl your eyelashes first," said Gilda. "If I was there, I could have told you that. You probably need to wear false eyelashes anyway. And maybe a wig." She suddenly felt guilty. It was true that her mother never went anywhere fun, so she knew she shouldn't begrudge her a night out; nevertheless, she couldn't help worrying about the potential ramifications of a mother who was now actually going on a *date*.

"I will *not* be wearing false eyelashes," said Mrs. Joyce, wiping off all of her makeup with a tissue. "Or a wig, for that matter."

She opened her closet door and stared at rows of shapeless hospital garments and stacks of blue jeans and sweatshirts. She realized that she didn't have a thing to wear.

"I'm sorry, Gilda," said Mrs. Joyce, looking at the clock, "but I'll have to call you back later." She was supposed to be at the restaurant in fifteen minutes.

"Don't do anything I wouldn't do," said Gilda.

"Same to you, young lady."

Gilda turned off her cell phone. She knew that she should be happy for her mother, but instead she felt betrayed. Who knew where this new development would lead? Gilda had initially called to ask whether her mom had ever heard of Lilyvale Residential Facility and whether she remembered anything else about Juliet's aunt Melanie, but the revelation of her mother's date had taken the wind out of her psychic-investigation sails for the moment. It was frustrating to Gilda to discover that her mother was going on a date without being there to witness, supervise, and, ideally, spy on the event.

Attempting to distract herself from imagining her

mother's behavior on a date, Gilda decided to prepare for her séance. She turned to a chapter entitled "Reasons Ghosts Appear" in her *Psychic's Handbook:*

> Some spirits become trapped in the material world due to unresolved trauma or extreme emotion at the time of death — rage, lost love, regret. These spirits may appear as "ghosts" — phantom fragments of a personality, often trapped in an endless cycle of repetition of the events or feelings that preceded their death.
>
> In rare instances, a spirit may appear with a specific message or warning for a relative. It is unclear whether such spirits have the ability to perceive events in the present and react to them, or whether they are actually a projection of the relative's mind — a kind of psychic connection with the past that may surface at a time of danger or distress.

Gilda reread the passage, noting that it sounded as if Melanie had appeared to Juliet at such a moment of "distress." She also couldn't help but reflect that part of what made ghosts scary was the idea that a bad *feeling* could continue long after the body had disappeared.

Gilda removed her Ouija board from her suitcase and then changed out of her jeans and into the crumpled vintage evening gown she had discovered at a thrift shop. The *Psychic's Handbook* said that it was important to treat a séance as a serious ritual and to dress appropriately for the occasion of speaking to a ghost.

Gilda had tried several séances in the past—most of them attempts to communicate with her father after his death—but the truth was that none of them had really worked. While Gilda's mother believed that this was because Mr. Joyce's spirit was completely at rest—far beyond the realm of the living—Gilda blamed Wendy Choy and her brother for her failure to "make contact." She suspected that it was Wendy who kept making the planchette slide across the letters on the Ouija board to spell the word *buttmunch*—although it was possible that this was a joke from her father's spirit. *After all,* Gilda reasoned, *it was the kind of thing he might do.*

The mournful blast of the foghorn echoed over San Francisco Bay and a gust of wind whined through the trees. It was a good night for a séance.

Gilda looked at herself in the mirror. The red velvet evening gown hung from her small frame like a heavy curtain. Her black eyeliner and red lipstick looked suitably mysterious. *This time it will work,* she told herself.

Entering Gilda's room, Juliet looked like a haunted waif from a Victorian oil painting. She wore a white nightgown, her long, pale hair tumbling over her shoulders.

"Greetings," said Gilda.

"Wow!" Juliet gasped.

With her pale skin, red velvet dress, and purple-red lipstick, Gilda resembled a young vampire. The single candle she held in her hand cast a macabre light on her painted features.

"You look so different!" said Juliet.

Downstairs in the parlor, the grandfather clock chimed twelve times.

"Please be seated there on the floor," said Gilda, pointing to a spot next to the Ouija board. On either side of the board, Gilda had placed a pillow and a lit candle.

Juliet sat down on one of the pillows. Gilda plopped down on the other side of the Ouija board, crossed her legs Indian style, and faced Juliet.

"What is this thing?" Juliet asked, staring at the mysterious letters and numbers on the board.

"You mean you've never seen a Ouija board before?"

"I've heard of them, but I don't think I've ever seen one."

"It's a tool to help the dead communicate with the living. When it works the way it's supposed to, it's kind of like a psychic telephone."

"A telephone?"

"See, we both place our fingers very lightly on this thing—it's called a planchette—and when your aunt's spirit wants to speak to us, she'll send vibrations that make the planchette move across the board to highlight the answers to our questions. She can say yes or no, or she can spell out special messages."

Remembering the Principle of Amplification, Gilda placed the faded snapshot of Melanie next to the Ouija board. "Now," she said, "if anything strange happens—say, if I begin to levitate, or if the room we're in suddenly changes shape—it's important not to panic."

"You think you're going to *levitate?*"

"I've read that it sometimes happens during séances, so I just wanted to prepare you. Ready?"

"I guess."

Gilda and Juliet placed their fingertips lightly on the planchette and closed their eyes. In the flickering shadows and yellow glow of the candlelight, their faces looked slightly ghoulish.

"I'm actually kind of scared," Juliet whispered.

"Then let's get started before you lose your nerve." Gilda took a deep breath. "Spirits beyond the grave, please hear us. We would like to speak to Melanie."

The planchette remained still.

Juliet giggled.

"Stop it," Gilda whispered.

"I'm sorry; you're just being so *dramatic.*"

"Spirits beyond the grave," Gilda repeated, "please hear us. We would like to speak to Juliet's aunt—Melanie Splinter—who died near this very spot, in a fall from the tower in this house!"

Juliet stopped giggling. She suddenly felt very cold.

The Ouija board shook slightly.

Gilda's eyes flew open. "Are *you* doing that?!"

"No. I mean, I don't *think* I am."

Gilda felt a tingling sensation at the back of her neck. As if on cue, a familiar sound began from behind the wall of the room—the hollow echo of footsteps ascending a winding staircase.

This may be my first real communication with an actual ghost! Gilda braced herself for anything and reminded herself of one of Balthazar's rules: *A psychic investigator must remain calm at all times.*

The steps grew louder, then stopped suddenly, as if pausing just on the other side of the wall.

Gilda and Juliet stared at each other, then at the wall.

"Who is here with us?" Gilda asked. "Is that Melanie?"

With surprising force, the planchette slid quickly across the board to highlight the word *yes.*

"Wow!" said Gilda, forgetting, for a moment, to focus on maintaining a more formal demeanor as the leader of the séance.

"Oh my God," Juliet whispered. "It's really her!"

"What is it that you want to say to us, Melanie?"

The entire room seemed to vibrate with fearful anticipation, and Gilda prepared herself to feel her body float up from the floor or for the whole room to elongate like a stretched rubber band. More footsteps and rustling sounds came from the other side of the wall.

Gilda and Juliet held their breath for nearly a minute, watching and listening, but the sounds ceased. Gilda remained sitting firmly on the floor, and the planchette remained still.

"Maybe she doesn't have anything to say to me after all," Juliet whispered.

Minutes passed. Silence and the quiet sniffing sounds of Juliet's shallow, nervous breathing were the only answer. The girls sat patiently for what seemed a very long time, but the ghost would say nothing more.

20

The Message

Too exhausted to remove her makeup and séance gown, Gilda flopped down on her bedspread, feeling defeated. Although she and Juliet had come close to communicating with Melanie's ghost, the séance hadn't yielded the spectacular results Gilda had anticipated.

"Mind if I crash in your room?" Juliet asked Gilda tentatively. The séance had set her nerves on edge, and she hesitated to venture alone down the dark hallway that led to her bedroom.

"Sure—suit yourself." Gilda moved over on the queen-size bed to make room for Juliet.

Juliet sat down on the edge of the mattress. "You're sleeping in that dress?"

"Too tired to change," Gilda slurred.

"Well, *I* think the séance was pretty spooky," said Juliet, sensing Gilda's disappointment with the results and feeling that she should at least try to say something encouraging.

"But the point isn't just to 'be spooky' like the séances at slumber parties! I really thought we were about to make contact with Melanie and discover some specific information." Gilda yawned wearily. "Maybe I don't really know what I'm doing as a psychic investigator."

Juliet felt unsure how to respond since she had been skeptical of Gilda's psychic investigation skills from the very beginning. On the other hand, she sensed that Gilda's method of persevering through blind trial and error might eventually lead to some real discovery. Having always been an extremely cautious person herself, she couldn't help but feel some admiration for Gilda's willingness to experiment—her willingness to risk *failure*.

"You're probably learning as you go," Juliet said tactfully. "Besides, if it wasn't for your investigative skills, I would probably never know that my aunt was going to be sent to a place called Lilyvale. In fact, I'd probably still think I was crazy just for wondering if this house is haunted!"

"That's true," said Gilda, feeling more hopeful. "So you're actually admitting that you're *happy* I came to visit?"

Juliet paused. "Okay," she said. "I admit I'm happy you came to visit."

"Then I admit I am, too."

• • •

Gilda sat outside in the dark, staring up at the tower. A blond woman approached her—a childlike woman who looked exactly like Juliet. Somehow, Gilda knew that the woman was dead—that she was actually Melanie.

"Do you want to come in?" the woman asked, placing her slim fingers on the locked door leading into the tower.

"But there's no key," said Gilda.

"I'll let you in." The woman opened the tower door easily. Gilda hesitated for a moment, and then followed her.

Inside, the tower smelled of sweet, stale perfume—an aroma that reminded Gilda of the church lilies at her father's funeral.

I must pay attention to every detail I see in the tower, Gilda told herself. But somehow she could only focus on the white feet of the woman who led the way up a narrow stairway.

"Where are we going?" Gilda asked.

"I do this again and again," said the woman, ignoring Gilda's question.

They finally reached the top of the stairs.

"It's almost time."

Gilda found herself in a room that contained a small writing table and her typewriter. She heard the sounds of someone typing and immediately felt happy; it was her father sitting at the typewriter! *But what was her father doing inside the tower?*

Gilda walked toward him and sat on his lap, the way she

used to when she was just a child. How nice it was to feel her father's arms around her again. How reassuring it was to feel the soft fabric of his favorite flannel shirt.

"What are you writing?" Gilda asked, noticing that her father's face was unshaven, and that he had all the hair on his head again. In fact, he looked just like he used to look in the days before he was sick.

"Just typing some letters," her father replied.

"Do you get the letters I write you?"

"Sure."

"Then why don't you write back?"

"You know how slow the mail can be," her father replied calmly. "Don't worry; eventually you'll be able to read my letters."

"Did I tell you I'm a psychic investigator now?"

"I'm proud of you, honey," her father said.

Then the blond woman appeared again. She stood before an open window, the night wind blowing her nightgown around her thin body.

"Why are you doing this?" Gilda asked her.

The woman didn't answer; she simply perched on the window ledge and then pitched forward into darkness without another word, as if she were merely diving off the edge of a swimming pool into water. Gilda ran to the window in time to see her plummeting like an angel crashing to earth, her gold hair and white nightgown streaming behind her.

"Wake up!" Gilda heard her father say. "You should wake up and listen."

Gilda awoke to find Juliet sitting up in bed, wearing the same frozen, blank gaze she remembered seeing when she first discovered Juliet's eerie habit of talking in her sleep. Juliet seemed fixated on something in the darkness.

"What are you doing?" Gilda asked. She squinted into the darkness, trying to determine what Juliet was looking at, but she could perceive only the dark shadows of furniture.

Juliet didn't reply. "He hides things," she said.

"*Who* hides things?"

"I know, Aunt Melanie," Juliet continued, "I'll look."

Juliet was talking to her aunt Melanie!

Gilda had a gut feeling that she must write down everything Juliet said. *Wake up and listen,* her father had advised her in her dream.

Gilda scrambled out of bed, then searched frantically in the darkness for her notebook and a pen. She only succeeded in tripping over the Ouija board, falling to her knees, and knocking over two candlesticks, which rolled across the floor noisily. Gilda sighed, assuming that the commotion must have broken Juliet's trance.

But Juliet seemed to be hypnotized—completely deaf to everything except the dream conversation in her mind.

"I see your eyes," said Juliet, now whispering, "your eyes on the ceiling."

Your eyes on the ceiling? The strangeness of Juliet's words intrigued Gilda; it was as if she were reciting some cryptic poem.

Gilda found her way to her writing table and searched in the darkness until she could feel the typewriter keyboard under her fingertips. She hesitated a moment, wondering if the sound of the machine might break Juliet's trance, but decided to take the risk. She quickly typed as many of Juliet's words as she could remember.

Juliet now stood up and walked stiffly—as if her limbs were made of plastic—toward the corner of the room. She reached out, attempting to touch something in the blank space in front of her. "The angel," Juliet said. "The angel will speak and unlock you."

Something about this statement made Gilda's heart beat a bit faster. She quickly typed this phrase so that she wouldn't forget it, and then watched Juliet, waiting for her to continue.

But Juliet said nothing more.

"Juliet? Are you awake?"

Juliet did not respond. She turned, walked back to the bed, curled up into a fetal position, and fell into a silent sleep.

• • •

Juliet dreamed that a small piglet was chasing her through the house. When she stopped to confront the high-strung animal, it jumped into her arms and oinked joyfully. Juliet kept trying to put the piglet down, but somehow it wouldn't *let* her. "Please leave me alone," Juliet pleaded, but the piglet wouldn't listen.

Juliet suddenly awoke and felt disoriented until she remembered that she had been sleeping in Gilda's room. There, a few feet away from her, was Gilda, snoring loudly. *Her snoring must be why I dreamed about a piglet,* Juliet thought. On the floor, there was the scattered evidence of the séance: the candlesticks and the Ouija board, which now looked like an ordinary game board—more like Monopoly or Trivial Pursuit than a special instrument for speaking with ghosts.

Still asleep, Gilda snorted with great feeling.

Juliet shook Gilda's shoulder. "Gilda," she said, "wake up."

"Mmmmph." Gilda rolled over on her side, turning away from Juliet.

"Gilda! Quit snoring!"

"I do *not* snore," said Gilda, awakening immediately. Secretly, she remembered a slumber party during which her friends had made a tape recording of her snoring and then cheerfully played it back for her the next morning. "Anyway," Gilda added, "look who's talking."

"*I* don't snore," said Juliet.

"But you *do* talk in your sleep," said Gilda, "and this time, I kept a record of everything you said."

"What are you talking about?"

Gilda sat upright. "You said some things that I thought might be clues."

Juliet laughed with a burst of glee that Gilda found annoying.

"What's so funny?"

"Go look in the mirror!" said Juliet, pointing at Gilda's head. "Your *hair!*"

During the night, Gilda's hair had molded into a gravity-defying shape from an overenthusiastic use of bobby pins and hairspray in her "psychic-investigator hairdo." Mascara and eyeliner had also left a raccoon mask of dark smudges under her eyes.

Gilda suspected that she looked ridiculous after falling asleep in her séance costume, but she decided to ignore Juliet's laughter for the moment. Instead, she stood up, stretched, and yawned, then walked over to her typewriter, where she solemnly examined the clues she had typed the night before.

```
he hides things
   your eyes on the ceiling
the angel will speak
   and unlock you
```

Gilda felt a rush of excitement as she scrutinized the typed words. "Juliet," she whispered, "I have a distinct feeling that these words are a *message* of some kind!"

"A message?"

Gilda nodded. "I think Melanie communicated something to you last night. Do you remember *anything* specific about talking in your sleep? Maybe a dream you were having?"

Juliet shrugged. "I *did* have a dream about a piglet just before I woke up."

Gilda frowned. "You mean you don't remember saying, 'The angel will speak and unlock you'?"

Juliet looked incredulous. "I said that in my sleep? Let me see that."

Gilda handed Juliet the paper, and Juliet stared at the cryptic words, feeling bewildered. "How weird," she said. "I don't remember this."

"Try to remember," said Gilda. "You said these things in the middle of a dream; they must mean something to you!"

Gilda began to pace back and forth. "You know," she said, "sometimes if you think really hard you can remember all kinds of details from a dream even though it initially seems as though you've forgotten the whole thing." She stopped to inspect her disheveled-looking reflection in the mirror.

As Gilda wiped dark smudges of makeup from her face with a tissue, she felt that she herself was on the verge of remembering a dream—a dream that had something to do with the tower. However, she also knew that if she didn't write down her dreams right away, they had a frustrating way of evaporating from her mind completely.

Gilda glanced at Juliet, who was still scrutinizing the cryptic phrases she had recorded with her typewriter. This jogged Gilda's memory: she had a clear image of her father sitting at the typewriter. *Hadn't her father told her to "wake up and listen" to Juliet?*

"I don't know," said Juliet, squinting at the typed words and then tossing them aside in frustration. "Maybe these words mean something, and maybe it's all just nonsense, like scrambled eggs from my brain."

"Or maybe this is our best clue yet," said Gilda, removing a stray false eyelash from the corner of her eye. "I think Melanie responded to our séance."

Juliet watched Gilda's reflection in the mirror as Gilda picked the last of the bobby pins from her tangled hair. "I suppose these words *could* have something to do with a dream I've had before," Juliet suggested. "In one of my dreams, there's a woman in the tower who I think is Aunt Melanie, and she says, 'He hides things.' Then she tells me that my father 'has the key' to something."

"The key to the tower?"

"Maybe. In the dream she's in chains, and she wants me to help her unlock them."

"That makes sense," said Gilda excitedly. "Maybe Melanie's spirit feels like she's a prisoner in the tower, and she wants you to help free her!"

Juliet chewed on a fingernail. "But I don't know what *I* could do to free her," she said.

"Well, maybe we'll figure that out once we find a way into the tower."

21

The Key

Dinner is served!" Rosa announced.

"Looks wonderful, Rosa," said Mr. Splinter.

Gilda and Juliet and Mr. Splinter sat at an outdoor table facing the overgrown garden behind the Splinter mansion. Perhaps as a result of Gilda's previous attempts to interrogate him, Mr. Splinter seemed more reticent than usual; this time, he didn't appear to feel any need to make conversation. The silence was broken only by the clinking noises Mr. Splinter made with his silverware as he cut his meat. Juliet was equally taciturn: she was strangely absorbed in a meticulous process of cutting her potato into tiny, dice-size bits and chewing each one a little too carefully.

Gilda sensed the enormous secret sitting right in the middle of the table—an invisible presence that made everyone feel vaguely terrified of speaking. What would happen if she suddenly announced to Mr. Splinter that they had received a message from the ghost of his dead sister?

"It's chilly," said Juliet, hugging her thin arms.

"Ah, the chill of a San Francisco summer," said Mr. Splinter, finishing the last bite of his steak.

Gilda ignored this banal exchange and gazed across the tangled garden to a perfect view of the tower covered in vines. A layer of mist hovered over the angel fountain, rosebushes, and lilies.

"Still enjoying your stay here, Gilda?" Mr. Splinter inquired politely (but a bit suspiciously, Gilda thought).

"Oh, yes. Indeed I am," Gilda replied, using an English accent on sudden impulse. The clipped articulation somehow seemed appropriate to the formal tone of the conversation.

Juliet glared at Gilda. Mr. Splinter looked momentarily surprised, then shrugged, as if he had decided that impulsively switching to an English accent was yet another one of Gilda's bizarre quirks.

He eats one type of food at a time, Gilda noticed, observing Mr. Splinter. She remembered that her brother used to do the same thing when he was little. Stephen would scream if his carrots touched mashed potatoes and gravy, or if his chicken was tainted by the touch of broccoli. Of course, Mrs. Joyce had not tolerated this for long, and had served nothing but stew, sloppy joes, and pizza until the phase ended.

"You know what I find fascinating?" Gilda decided to drop the English accent since Juliet wouldn't stop glaring at her. "I find angels just fascinating."

Juliet's fork made a loud clattering sound as it collided with her plate.

"Excuse me?" said Mr. Splinter. "Did you say 'angels'?"

"Yes. Angels. How about you, Mr. Splinter?"

"I beg your pardon?"

"Does the word *angel* mean anything special to you?"

"Can't say that it does. I'm not particularly religious, for one thing. Why do you ask?"

"Gilda—" said Juliet.

"Yes?"

"Why are you talking about *angels?*"

"I'm just making conversation," said Gilda.

Gilda turned her attention back to Mr. Splinter, who appeared to be transfixed by something in the garden. Evening sunlight had broken through the mist, casting the garden in an orange-red glow.

Gilda abruptly stood up, as if she were about to make a toast at a momentous occasion.

"What are you doing?" Juliet demanded, worried that Gilda was going to create some kind of embarrassing scene.

Gilda sat down, but she could hardly contain her excitement. Why hadn't she thought of it before?

There, in the middle of the garden, was the angel statue.

Gilda wanted to run from the table immediately to investigate it more closely.

Rosa returned to clear away the plates. "Would you like some coffee with your dessert, Mr. Splinter?" she asked.

"No, thank you," said Mr. Splinter. "You know how caffeine keeps me awake at night."

Gilda fidgeted. She wanted everyone to leave so she could tell Juliet that she had just found a potential clue, although she had no idea what its significance might be.

Rosa suddenly leaned close to Gilda: "There is a ghost there," she said.

"Where?"

Rosa pointed in the direction of the purple and blue hydrangeas surrounding the angel statue. "See it? A lady, walking."

Gilda saw only flowers and mist. Why couldn't she see ghosts like Rosa?

"Don't let Rosa scare you," said Mr. Splinter. "She loves her ghost stories."

"I call them as I see them," said Rosa.

"Well, *I* certainly don't see them," said Mr. Splinter. "Now, if you'll excuse me, I have some work to finish in my office. Don't stay outside too late, girls."

"We won't," said Juliet.

Gilda squinted fiercely in the direction of the hydrangeas, determined to see *something*. "Why can't *I* see the ghost?" Gilda protested.

As Mr. Splinter walked away from the table, he whistled a tune in a minor key, then suddenly broke into song: *"Angel eyes . . ."*

Gilda grabbed Juliet's arm. "Did you hear that?!"

"He just likes old songs," said Juliet. "You know—jazz?"

"I see," said Gilda. "It's an interesting coincidence, though."

"Rosa," Gilda ventured as the housekeeper gathered the last of the plates from the table, "is the ghost still there?"

Rosa squinted in the direction of the hydrangeas. "No. She's gone."

Gilda leaned closer to Rosa. "Do you think the ghost you saw was Juliet's aunt—the one who jumped from the tower?" she whispered.

Rosa thought for a moment, and then nodded. "Her head was tilted to one side, like this." She let her head fall to one side so that her ear nearly touched her shoulder. "It looked like her neck—it was broken."

Both Gilda and Juliet stared at Rosa with gaping mouths. "Really?"

"That is why I stay away from that tower." Rosa hastily crossed herself and turned to go inside the house before Gilda could ask further questions.

"Come on," said Gilda, standing up and grabbing Juliet's arm. "We need to check out that statue."

Gilda ran down a narrow path until she reached the marble angel. It stood nearly six feet tall with palms open, its face gazing up at the sky. From a distance, the angel appeared to be singing, but up close Gilda saw that something about the angel's open mouth and pained expression suggested a shout of protest or warning rather than a song of praise. The girls stared at the angel's tumbling locks of curled marble hair, the strong facial features that might be either male or female. Its hands were open in a beseeching gesture and the stiff, long wings that arched from the statue's back looked as if they would be too thin and narrow to keep the creature in the air had it actually been real. Something about the mouth particularly intrigued Gilda: the teeth had a horselike squareness.

"What are we looking for?" Juliet asked.

"I'm not sure," said Gilda. She examined the angel's large stone feet anchored under the sand, dried twigs, leaves, and loose change that now filled the waterless fountain. "Let's just see if we find anything." Gilda and Juliet picked up twigs and poked through pennies, nickels, and debris in the empty pool, but found nothing that could be considered a clue.

" 'An angel will speak and unlock,' " Gilda said aloud, trying once again to find some significance in the words themselves. *Maybe the word* speak *is important,* Gilda thought.

She gazed at the angel's open mouth, and felt a very strong tickle in her left ear. "Juliet," she said, "come here and give me a boost."

"What do you mean, 'give me a boost'?"

"I want to take a closer look at the angel's face, but it's too high. Just put your hands together like this, and I'll put my foot there and use that as a step up. Haven't you ever given someone a boost before?"

"I think you'll break my hands if you step into them that way," said Juliet.

"I'm actually very light," said Gilda defensively, "but I suppose your arms might be unusually weak."

"But your feet look kind of dirty."

"Well, I hope that nobody ever has to count on getting a boost from you in a life-threatening situation where there's anything so mind-shattering as *dirt* involved."

"But this isn't a life-threatening situation, is it?"

Gilda sighed. "All right, then I'll give *you* a boost. Come on, just hop up there and check out the angel's mouth more closely."

"You don't expect this statue to start *talking* to us or something, do you?"

"To be honest, I don't know what I expect," said Gilda.

"Okay; just don't drop me." Juliet stepped gingerly into Gilda's clasped hands and grabbed onto the angel's head for support. She braced one knee in the angel's outstretched hand. "I feel weird stepping on it like this," she said. "I feel like I'm *offending* it somehow. . . ." Her voice trailed off and she almost lost her balance, because now that she was face-to-face with the angel, she saw something that surprised her. Caught in the fading rays of the sunset, something *gleamed* inside the angel's mouth—something that wasn't marble.

"What is it?" Gilda asked. "What do you see?"

Juliet reached gingerly inside the angel's open mouth, half fearing, for a moment, that its stone teeth might suddenly chomp down on her hand. She pulled something from the mouth.

"I found it," she breathed excitedly. "I found the key!"

"Show me!" said Gilda, releasing Juliet's foot a bit too quickly.

The key was slightly rusted and surprisingly heavy—almost as large as Juliet's hand. It seemed very old and magical—the kind of key that, in a fairy tale, might open a treasure chest or lead into a completely different world.

The girls stood before the doorway leading to the tower. Clouds passing before the sunset turned the sky a dark shade of raspberry mixed with lavender.

Gilda was surprised to discover that she suddenly felt nervous. "I think we should get some supplies first," she said, hesitating to open the door. "I mean, this tower hasn't been opened for ten years, and who knows what we'll find? We need flashlights, a crucifix—"

"A crucifix?"

"In case of vampires or an evil spirit."

"*Vampires?*"

"Well, *who knows* what lives in there? Better safe than sorry."

In the last minutes of fading sunlight, Gilda and Juliet stood at the foot of the tower, carrying flashlights and Gilda's Polaroid camera (her *Psychic's Handbook* recommended this type of camera for photographing ghosts or "manifestations of spirits"). Juliet wore a baseball cap and a shapeless plastic poncho, and Gilda wore a grandmotherly sunbonnet with a shiny vinyl raincoat.

"I still don't see why we need to wear this stuff," Juliet grumbled.

"What if there are bats in there?" Gilda replied. "Did you ever think of *that?* Do you want a bat getting caught in your hair? And if there are bats, you can be sure there will be bat poop. Bats poop a lot!"

Gilda's imagination ran wild: she envisioned shielding herself from explosions of protoplasm and cringing from an angry onslaught of bats. Rosa's vision of a ghost with a broken neck had also unnerved her, and she felt a wave of self-doubt. What if she didn't yet have the skills needed to handle a real psychic investigation?

Gilda took a deep breath and decided to face this situation the way she normally faced frightening situations: by pretending to be brave.

Tucking her flashlight under her arm, she pulled the heavy key from her raincoat pocket and thrust it into the keyhole. She almost hoped that the key wouldn't fit and that the two of them could retreat back to the house.

"Listen," said Gilda, before she attempted to turn the key, "I don't know what we're going to find in there, but if it gets too dangerous, I'll give you the signal, and we'll leave right away."

Juliet nodded. "What's the signal?"

"I'll scream."

"Good one." Juliet also felt trepidation at the thought of entering the tower, but she feared violating her father's ironclad rule (*You are* never *to go in that tower!*) as much as she feared whatever supernatural forces she might encounter within.

The key fit. With a loud creak, the door swung open with surprising ease, revealing only darkness and a musty, metallic scent, much like the smell of an attic or garden shed mixed with a chemical odor. "It smells like something

I remember," said Juliet, "something from when I was really young."

They entered a small, circular room and waved their flashlights around. When their eyes had adjusted to the dim light, both girls screamed.

22

Inside the Tower

An eerie collage of faces and emotions peered at Gilda and Juliet from the walls. Each face had hair and skin of unnatural colors—blue, green, red, purple—but they all stared with the same intense eyes.

Juliet gazed into a pair of almond-shaped gray eyes that were very much like her own. The eyes stared out from a face that had blue-white skin, a crooked mouth, and was crowned by blond hair. It was a painting of a woman who looked very much like Juliet herself—or a version of how Juliet might look as an adult.

Juliet instinctively recognized her aunt Melanie's face. In fact, her aunt's face was all around them.

"It's her," Juliet said.

Gilda focused the flashlight on the bottom corner of the painting where a signature had been painted. "Hey—it says 'Melanie Splinter'! She's the one who painted it!"

"I know," said Juliet. "It's a self-portrait."

"Why didn't you *tell* me that your aunt Melanie was a painter?"

"Because I had no idea until now!"

Gilda moved her flashlight slowly around the circular room and saw an easel and a small table littered with crushed tubes of paint, plastic trays stained with a range of colors, and paintbrushes with dried, stiff tips. It looked as if an artist had left in the middle of an ordinary day's work and never returned. Gilda was startled to see two girls wearing raincoats and absurd hats until she realized she was gazing into a mirror.

"She must have used the mirror when she painted the self-portraits," said Juliet. "They're *all* pictures of her."

"It's strange," said Gilda, looking at an image of Melanie that had purple hair. "Each one looks so different."

"But I still recognized her face right away, didn't I? I think this stuff is cool. It's really modern."

As she inspected the various versions of Melanie depicted in the paintings, Gilda wondered if Juliet's aunt had been the sort of person who liked to change her appearance and identity. *If someone wanted to paint my portrait, which version of myself would I want to capture?* Gilda wondered. *Definitely not the ordinary me—the way I look when I'm going to school. Maybe I'd put on my séance outfit or one of my disguises.*

Juliet moved her fingertips lightly over one of the canvases. "I can't believe all these paintings are hidden in here! Why didn't my parents ever *tell* me she was an artist?"

Juliet felt a small heat wave of anger along with her excitement at finally discovering something real about her aunt. Bits of her aunt Melanie's life were emerging; the paintings were large missing pieces of a puzzle. But why had Melanie's true identity been withheld for so long?

Juliet suddenly remembered her father's pained expression whenever she showed him her own artwork as a child. Her teachers had said she had talent, but both of her parents seemed unimpressed. She sensed that her father disliked the fantastic, fairy-tale creatures she created: he preferred antique oil paintings that had a high "market value" or realistic photographs of things like sailboats and houses. Her mother's response was no better: she had always placed Juliet's drawings in a drawer rather than hanging them on the wall. "I don't like any clutter," she would say. "Just hanging a few mirrors here and there is best; that way you don't risk anything tacky." Juliet knew that both of her parents valued practical, financially rewarding business pursuits, and that, in their minds, drawing pictures had nothing to do with building a "brilliant career" and a "promising future."

"Gilda," said Juliet, "why do you think my father decided to keep these paintings locked in the tower?"

Gilda thought for a moment. "Well, for one thing, there's something *scary* about them when you consider the fact that

Melanie killed herself. I don't know about you, but they kind of make me feel like she's right here—looking at us!"

"Maybe that's it," said Juliet. "Maybe my father couldn't stand to see her face around him, looking at him every day."

"Especially since she never made it to that Lilyvale Facility that was supposed to help her. I mean, what if your parents had gotten her there *sooner?* Maybe they could have helped her, and she wouldn't have killed herself. I bet your father feels guilty about that."

Juliet remembered the soothing, glossy brochure from Lilyvale Residential Facility. She strongly suspected that Melanie would have resented the idea of "supervised activities" and having her personal belongings "subject to search."

"I bet she didn't want to go," said Juliet. "I bet she hated the whole idea. Maybe that's part of the reason she jumped from the tower."

In the middle of the room, an iron staircase spiraled up toward the second floor. Gilda hesitated, unable to ignore the feeling that something might be lurking in the uppermost section of the tower, waiting for them. "I guess we should check out the next floor," she said, trying to sound brave.

The girls' feet made loud creaking sounds that echoed as they walked. Gilda and Juliet looked at each other knowingly: *the familiar sound of footsteps.*

They entered the room on the second floor and discovered that it had also been used as an artist's studio. Thin streams of moonlight poked through cracks in the boards that concealed the windows. This room's walls were also covered with paintings and sketches, but these images were dark shadows compared with the vibrantly colored compositions in the room below.

"Weird," said Gilda. "They're all black."

Juliet scrutinized an image of a woman's profile facing an empty landscape. "It looks like she used ink instead of paint for these."

"How can you tell?"

Juliet shrugged. "I can just tell. Besides, there are bottles of ink right here on the easel."

As she stared at the moody image painted by her aunt, Juliet felt as if she were peering through a window that allowed her to see more clearly into her own past. A picture entered Juliet's mind—an image of herself and her aunt Melanie standing in the garden, looking at roses that sparkled with dewdrops, like jewels in the morning light.

"See there?" Melanie said, pointing. "That's a fairy."

And Juliet saw it, too, just before the tiny creature quickly hid its translucent wings under a rose petal.

"They live in the roses," Melanie explained.

"I want to catch it!" Juliet said.

"Oh, no," said Melanie. "You'll kill it if you try to catch

it. Just be happy that you caught a glimpse of a real fairy in your own backyard."

Juliet's mother appeared in the garden. Dressed for work, she wore her high heels and strong perfume.

"Mommy!" Juliet shouted breathlessly, running toward her mother. "Aunt Melanie and I saw a real fairy in the garden!"

Her mother led Juliet away from the garden and peered earnestly into her eyes. "Listen, Juliet," she said. "You *didn't* see a fairy. Fairies aren't real."

"But I did. Aunt Melanie said—"

"Juliet, you may have seen a hummingbird or a butterfly, but you did *not* see a fairy."

"But—"

"You mustn't believe a word your aunt Melanie says," her mother had told her.

Juliet now felt that the shadow woman in her aunt's stark painting was the loneliest image she had ever seen.

"There's just one more room," said Gilda, staring at the stairway that curved up from the floor, leading the way to the room where Melanie had taken her last steps. Then she noticed that Juliet appeared to be paralyzed by one of the paintings.

"What's wrong?" Gilda asked.

"Oh, nothing," said Juliet, forcing herself to turn away

from the painting. "It's just—I'm starting to remember some things."

"What things?"

"I just had this memory of standing outside in the garden with Aunt Melanie."

"And?"

". . . and she saw a fairy."

"A *fairy?*"

Juliet nodded. "The funny thing is, I remember thinking that I saw it, too."

"Well," said Gilda, "my grandmother McDoogle used to say she believed in fairies, so who knows—maybe you did see one."

"All I know is that I *wanted* to see it," said Juliet. She reflected that even if her aunt Melanie had been mentally ill, the fact was that there had been something appealing about her. *For that moment, Aunt Melanie made the world seem genuinely magical.*

Gilda waved her flashlight at the opening leading to the stairs. "Should we check out the next level?"

"I'll go first this time," said Juliet.

When she had climbed high enough on the spiral staircase to peer up into the room on the top floor, Juliet stifled an impulse to scream again.

"What is it?" Gilda asked.

Juliet didn't respond.

"Juliet? Are you okay?"

"I think we've just found the meaning of the last clue," Juliet said, remembering the phrase *your eyes on the ceiling* as she cautiously entered the room.

It seemed as if she were gazing into a monster's eyes—an alien galaxy of blue-gray eyes that covered the walls and the ceiling, watching blankly, observing silently.

Each painting displayed nothing but a single eye. Juliet noticed that the eyes looked similar to those that had gazed at her from the self-portraits on the first floor, but these were disembodied: some were enormous, and some were tiny. Something about the eye paintings reminded Juliet of the medieval images of bizarre angelic creatures she had seen in museums—bodiless eyes and wings that gazed with a flat, all-knowing power.

Following Juliet, Gilda entered the room and caught her breath. She waved her flashlight wildly, as if she expected the walls themselves to come to life and attack her. The multiple eyes reminded Gilda of something disturbingly alien and insectlike—something that made her feel small and helpless. *Maybe this is how a spider's face looks to a small bug trapped in a web,* she thought. Feeling the need for some kind of protection, Gilda located the crucifix she carried in her pocket and held it in front of her like the priest she had once observed in the movie *The Exorcist.*

Both girls had the disconcerting sense that the painted eyes could somehow perceive them as they moved through the studio.

"What does it *mean?*" Gilda whispered.

Juliet shook her head. "I have no idea."

The paintings seemed to be the work of an obsessed, unhinged mind. In a museum, a similar display would have seemed a disturbing but interesting artwork, but in the tower, after dark, there was something genuinely horrifying about the eye paintings.

Gilda noticed a small table in a corner of the room. The table had a single shallow drawer, which Gilda opened. Inside, there was nothing but a piece of tightly crumpled paper.

"Hey," said Gilda, shining her flashlight on the paper after she had smoothed open its folds and creases. "I found a letter!"

It was from Melanie. Gilda noticed that her handwriting was neat and oddly geometric, as if she had purposefully shaped each letter as a tiny bit of art:

DEAR LESTER,

You're right; we can't go on like this.

I know I've become a terrible burden lately, and it isn't fair to you and your family. You need to move on and

LIVE YOUR LIFE WITHOUT ME, AND I NEED
TO MOVE ON AS WELL.

I HOPE YOU WILL BE ABLE TO FORGIVE ME
FOR LEAVING THIS WAY. I'M TRULY SORRY.

MY ONLY REGRET IS THAT I WAS NEVER
ABLE TO CAPTURE IN MY ART THE THINGS
I PERCEIVED IN MY LIFE. WHEN THEY
WEREN'T TERRIFYING, SOME OF THEM WERE
BEAUTIFUL.

NOW I'VE LOST THAT ABILITY, AND
EVERYTHING HAS BECOME VERY DARK. IN
FACT, I CAN HARDLY SEE ANYTHING AT ALL;
MY EYES WORK, BUT I HAVE GONE BLIND.
YOU MUST UNDERSTAND WHY I HAVE TO LEAVE.

LOVE ALWAYS
M

"It sounds like a suicide note," said Gilda, handing the
letter to Juliet. "But it's strange that it's still here, crumpled up inside this drawer."

As Juliet read the letter, she felt a combination of sadness
and revulsion. She imagined her father finding the letter,
crumpling it up, and slamming the desk drawer shut forever.

"I bet both of my parents were furious with her," Juliet
said. "There's nothing they hate more than changes of

plans and messy situations." And what could be a messier change of plans than a family member's suicide?

Juliet suddenly recalled her mother's attempt to explain Melanie's death: "Your aunt Melanie is gone," her mother said. Only a little girl at the time, Juliet remembered staring at her mother's frosty pink lipstick and feeling as if she did not understand at all.

"But when is she coming *back?*" Juliet asked. Just the day before, her aunt Melanie had promised to help her do some finger painting.

"I keep trying to tell you," the pink lips explained, "Melanie isn't coming back ever again. An angel has taken her away to heaven."

"Oh," said Juliet, still feeling confused. She decided to draw a picture of Aunt Melanie. She would send the picture to her aunt in heaven.

But which version of her aunt should she draw? After all, Juliet's aunt seemed to be many people; they all had long, blond hair, but one could never be certain which one might turn up. There was the playful Melanie who loved telling stories and drawing pictures, and then there was the weeping, angry Melanie who broke things and sometimes screamed for no reason. Recently, there had also been the Aunt Melanie who sat and stared at nothing.

Using some of Melanie's oil pastels, Juliet tried to remember the parts of her aunt's face. She knew the hair was yellow—almost white. The eyes were blue. *Or were they gray?* Juliet couldn't find a color that exactly matched her aunt Melanie's eyes. She compromised by using several colors together. Then she added an angel in the sky—an angel that had fierce eyes, enormous, colorful wings, and claw-hands like talons.

Juliet felt frightened by her own picture. The idea that an angel might simply decide to swoop down and take a person away at any moment was terrifying; it reminded her of a television program she had seen in which a rabbit ran in hysterical figure eights, trying to escape a large bird of prey that swooped down, grabbed it, and dragged its dangling body into the open sky.

Absorbed in her drawing, Juliet almost didn't notice her father looking over her shoulder. When she finally looked up at him, she saw that her father's face was wet with tears. How odd that her father was crying! Clearly, he didn't like her drawing.

"It's a picture of Aunt Melanie," Juliet explained.

"That's enough," her father said. "It's time to do something else."

Juliet reread the suicide note and wished for a moment that she had never discovered the glimpse of her aunt's state of mind. On the other hand, the paintings were evidence that Melanie's life had meant more than either the blurry photograph or the newspaper article describing her tragic death had suggested; even if her aunt had been mentally disturbed, she had also been an artist—a woman with a talent and a passion. *That, at the very least, is interesting,* Juliet thought.

The door leading back to the garden would not open.

"It's stuck!"

"Are you *sure?*"

"Of course I'm sure! It almost feels like someone's pulling on the other side!"

"Pull harder."

"I'm trying!"

Both girls tried to pull the door open, but it wouldn't budge. An unusually strong wind began to howl outside the tower.

"Where's the key?" Juliet asked.

"I think we left it in the lock when we first walked inside," said Gilda. "It's on the other side of the door." She attempted to pull the door open once more, but failed. She placed her hands on her hips and nodded wryly as if she were a police officer surveying a car accident. "Juliet, don't panic, but I think we're trapped."

"You mean we're *prisoners* in here!"

"We have to stay calm," said Gilda, speaking as much to herself as to Juliet. "Who knows how long we'll be in here. We don't want to use all the oxygen."

"Are you *kidding* me?" Juliet felt anything but calm. The wind that whined and shrieked outside the tower seemed to mirror her frazzled state of mind. "This is so dumb!" she lamented. "We should have brought something useful with us, like a cell phone, instead of raincoats and sunbonnets and that stupid camera!"

"Look, nobody stopped you from bringing a cell phone," said Gilda defensively. Secretly, she had to admit that this might have been a good idea.

Juliet sat down on the floor and rested her head on her knees, sulking. She felt an urge to throw a childish temper tantrum.

A psychic investigator must stay calm at all times, Gilda reminded herself, sensing that Juliet was ready to have some kind of meltdown. "Okay," she said, trying to sound positive, "let's take a good look at our options. Number one: We can try pounding on the walls and calling for help. I'm sure your father would eventually hear us and come open the door."

"You're forgetting that he takes sleeping pills at night, so he might not hear anything," said Juliet. "Besides, if he finds us in here, he'll kill us!"

"Good point," said Gilda. "In that case, we'll call that plan B."

Juliet sighed. "So what's plan A?"

Gilda stood up and began to pace back and forth in an

attempt to generate some inspiration. "This is an artist's studio, right? There must be some tools in here that we could use to break through one of the boarded windows."

Juliet shrugged. "Like what?"

"A knife or a hammer or something. We might as well look."

After stumbling over canvases and paints in each studio room for nearly an hour, the girls found themselves back on the third floor. By now, Gilda also felt exhausted—overwhelmed by a desire to sleep.

"Listen," said Gilda. "This is what we'll do. We'll wait until morning when there's more light, then we'll figure out a way to break out of here. Either that, or we'll just have to face the music and wait for your father to come help us."

Gilda squinted at her watch. It was midnight. Outside, the wind had died down, leaving a silence that felt ominous rather than reassuring.

Huddled close together, the girls sat on the floor and leaned against a wall.

"Do you think there's any chance we'll see her ghost?" Juliet whispered.

"Maybe," said Gilda. "In fact, she might be here with us right now and we just can't see her." This reminded her to pick up her Polaroid camera and hold it tightly, just in case she needed to snap a picture of any visible evidence of ecto-plasm.

"I don't *want* to see her," said Juliet. "I just want to get out of here."

Just then, they both heard the *thump, thump, thump* of footsteps slowly ascending the tower stairs.

23

Mr. Splinter's Discovery

Mr. Splinter suffered from chronic insomnia. Whenever he *did* finally fall asleep, he had a recurring dream that always left him feeling at once bereft and guilty. Sometimes the dream was so vivid and realistic that when Mr. Splinter awoke, he found actual pieces of the dream with him in his bed: a rose petal on his bedspread, a few blades of grass on his bare feet.

The truth was that Mr. Splinter often walked in his sleep.

As a child, he had sometimes sleepwalked right out the back door of the house and into the garden, where his mother would later discover him dozing forlornly on a patio chair or curled up in front of a rosebush. His mother subsequently locked all the windows in Lester's room and blocked his door shut, and the habit eventually ended.

In adulthood, Mr. Splinter occasionally awoke in the parlor or the kitchen feeling disoriented, but he never guessed that these occurrences signaled the return of his old habit of sleepwalking.

He was, however, aware of the unpleasant recurring dream:

In the dream, he was still a very young man. He sat in a stuffy room with his mother, who was slowly dying as the grandfather clock ticked away the seconds.

"Lester," his mother said, taking his clammy young hand in her withered fingers, "promise me you'll always take care of Melanie after I'm gone."

"I promise," Lester said, knowing that his sister was not like ordinary people; she couldn't be expected to take care of herself and live on her own. He thought of his sister as a magical, fragile creature. Throughout their childhood, he had been entertained by her frantic, intoxicating activities: she climbed the rose trellis outside the tower for no reason at all; she painted one of the walls in Lester's bedroom with an enormous, red *L;* she arranged a breathtakingly elaborate tea party for invisible guests. Melanie believed that people could visit one another in dreams, and she encouraged her brother to join her in a place she herself often traveled in her mind—a place with a violet lake and flowers that only bloom at night. "I wish I could draw you a picture of it, but I can't capture the way it *really* looks when I go there," she said. One day, Melanie suddenly had a pet—an enormous cat that resembled a cloud of blue smoke. When asked where she found the cat, she would only say, "He came in with the fog."

"You'll make sure Melanie always has a home, won't you?" Lester's mother insisted. "You won't let anything *bad* happen to her."

"I promise, Mother," he repeated. "Melanie and I will be fine."

Then something surprising happened in the dream: Lester's mother abruptly crawled from her sickbed into the grandfather clock and disappeared, leaving him alone.

Suddenly aged in his dream, Mr. Splinter found himself walking up the spiral staircase in the tower, which his sister had turned into a chaotic art studio. He looked at the stacks of her canvases and knew that the old Melanie was disappearing. She had recently destroyed hundreds of her early paintings in a fit of rage—the whimsical landscapes that used to fill the long hallways of her mother's house. Instead, she had taken to painting a series of self-portraits and images of disembodied eyes, believing that a long list of famous people had requested them. Mr. Splinter couldn't tell whether her artwork had become strikingly original or merely disturbing; he only knew that nobody had bought a single one of her paintings for some time.

Mr. Splinter was now a married man—a man with a

child, a job, and numerous responsibilities. His sister no longer seemed magical; she seemed ill.

"We simply can't take care of her anymore," Lester's wife had recently complained. "Besides, she's a bad influence on Juliet. Yesterday, she actually made Juliet believe that she saw a fairy in the garden! And what if she hurts herself one of these days? What if she hurts someone else?"

Mr. Splinter approached his sister, who looked thinner than ever in her faded, paint-splattered jeans. Her unwashed hair hung like frayed rope around her small frame as she crouched over a tiny picture of an eye, which she painted with painstaking detail.

"Melanie, did you take your medication today?" Mr. Splinter asked, knowing that the answer was no.

Melanie refused to look at her brother. She continued painting as if she couldn't afford to stop working for a single second.

"You know what the doctor said might happen if you don't take it," Mr. Splinter added.

"I already told you; I can't take that stuff! It makes me feel dead, and I need to *perceive* things if I'm going to get ready for this show. There are over fifty celebrities who are interested in my work!"

"Melanie, that show is all in your mind. You haven't had an exhibition in two years."

"I don't believe you."

Mr. Splinter felt tired. For several years, he had struggled to keep his promise to his mother, but he would fight no longer.

"Melanie," he said, "there's a place we'd like you to visit up north—just to see how you like it. We think you might be happier there. It's called Lilyvale."

Melanie looked at him with flat, gray eyes. "You promised Mother that you wouldn't send me away," she said. Then she evaporated.

Mr. Splinter found himself in his bed, awakened by the echoing of footsteps walking up and down a stairway. The steps seemed to come from the tower. He looked at his alarm clock: 2:00 A.M. What was Melanie doing in her studio so late at night?

Something worried him. A terrible idea entered his mind: Or was it a memory?

Wearing his pajamas, Mr. Splinter walked down the stairs to the parlor.

In the parlor, he found three familiar white-haired ladies dressed in flowing petticoats—the translucent inhabitants of the house who always sat on the velvet chairs drinking sherry at this time of night. Mr. Splinter never questioned their presence or thought of them as *ghosts:* they were simply part of the house during the small hours after midnight.

He was no more surprised to see them there than he was to see the grandfather clock.

"Good evening," they said to him, lifting their small crystal glasses.

"Good evening," said Mr. Splinter.

"So she's finally gone?" they asked, speaking as a group—a chorus of whispery voices.

"Who's finally gone?"

"Your sister, of course. You were supposed to look out for her. Your mother wouldn't like this one bit!"

"Melanie isn't gone," said Mr. Splinter.

"Oh no, she's gone," said one of the old ladies.

"You should check the tower. There's something going on there," said another.

"That's what I'm doing."

"You're already too late!"

Mr. Splinter hurried past the old ladies, whose clothing seemed to swirl about the furniture like dust in the moonlight; he rushed outside, into the cool wind.

Mr. Splinter heard a siren approaching from the marina at the bottom of the hill. Melanie had taken to locking the door to the tower while she was working on her art, but Mr. Splinter remembered her hiding place for the spare key—inside the mouth of the angel statue—the beloved statue she had helped a sculptor friend design.

But this time something was amiss: when he reached into the angel's mouth, he found that the key was gone.

Mr. Splinter walked toward the tower door, where he was surprised to find the key left right in the lock. He turned the key, but the door stuck. Mr. Splinter gave it a violent push and burst into the tower.

"Melanie?"

He ascended the stairs: *thump, thump, thump, thump, thump . . .*

"Melanie!"

As always, Mr. Splinter would be too late; Melanie would be gone, and he would be left in the tower alone, surrounded by his dead sister's paintings and feeling as if he were walking inside the fragile, abandoned shell of a creature that he had not tried hard enough to save.

But this time, something was different. He heard something—someone breathing. Maybe Melanie's death had been a bad dream. *This time she'll still be there, and I'll have a chance to fix everything.*

The sounds of sirens grew louder—maddeningly shrill whines that hurt his ears. Mr. Splinter hurried to the top floor of the tower, and there was Melanie, cowering on the floor. "Melanie—thank God you're okay."

The sirens became shrill voices.

People were screaming at him—two imps shining lights in his eyes so that he couldn't see.

Mr. Splinter awoke from his dream to find himself standing in his pajamas in the tower, faced with two shrieking girls—his daughter and that strange friend of hers, Gilda.

Gilda and Juliet had nearly passed out from fright at the sounds of a decidedly three-dimensional ghost ascending the stairs to greet them. Then—when they saw that it was Mr. Splinter—they screamed even louder, for he seemed to approach them with a Frankenstein-like blankness, as if he didn't quite see them or know what he was doing.

"He's *asleep!*" said Juliet, watching in horror as her pajama-clad father stumbled around the room.

"Melanie? Melanie—is that you?" he kept saying.

"Whatever you do, don't wake him up," Gilda warned. "If you wake up a sleepwalker, they either die or kill you or wet their pants or something." She wasn't sure whether this was actually true, but she had heard it at a slumber party and didn't want to take any chances.

But then Mr. Splinter woke himself up. He gazed around the room with a startled expression like that of a trapped animal. "How? What?"

Gilda felt sorry for Mr. Splinter. It was always embarrassing when adults suddenly looked as frightened as children.

"You were sleepwalking," said Juliet accusingly.

Mr. Splinter rubbed his eyes. Then he rubbed his whole face as if hoping to wake himself up from yet another bad dream until he realized that he was, in reality, standing in the tower with Gilda and Juliet. "I was sleepwalking," he said. "Well, that explains some things."

"What things?" Gilda asked.

Mr. Splinter thought of the leaves that had occasionally made their way into his bedsheets—the inexplicable dirt he had sometimes discovered on his hands or feet during his morning shower. "Just—things," he said.

"Mr. Splinter," said Gilda, shining her flashlight directly into Mr. Splinter's eyes, "how often do you walk in your sleep? Does this happen every night?"

"I honestly don't know, and please don't shine that flashlight in my eyes." Mr. Splinter groped along the wall, searching for a light switch. He found one, and light filled the room.

Gilda and Juliet felt silly; they had simply assumed that none of the lights worked.

Mr. Splinter cringed when he saw the eye paintings more clearly. In the light, they suddenly looked more cartoonlike than scary—almost silly. Gilda realized that the entire scene suddenly appeared quite ludicrous: she and Juliet in their raincoats and hats, Mr. Splinter in his red pajamas—each bleary-eyed from lack of sleep. If her own father had been there, he might have slapped his knee and had a big belly laugh.

The girls watched Mr. Splinter warily, wondering whether his confusion at finding himself in the tower had overwhelmed his anger at discovering that they had broken his strict rule about entering it.

After Mr. Splinter had regained some composure, he turned to face Gilda. "I can only conclude that you've been a very bad influence on my daughter, Gilda," he said. "I don't know how the two of you found your way in here, but you obviously knew that you were breaking one of the rules of the house. Tomorrow we'll make arrangements for you to return home."

"Wait a minute!" Juliet protested. "You can't send Gilda home! The summer's just started, and she's my friend. In fact, she's a relative! If she goes, I go."

"We'll talk about this in the morning, Juliet." Mr. Splinter turned to leave.

"Wait—why didn't you *tell* me that Aunt Melanie was a painter?"

Mr. Splinter ran his hands through his hair in a gesture of weary frustration. He turned to face Juliet. "Does it *really* matter to you that she was a painter?"

"Of course it does! She was my aunt and—and it isn't *fair* that you keep everything about her locked up in here!"

Mr. Splinter sighed and sank down onto a stool that faced an easel. "I suppose I was just trying to protect you from what I thought was a bad influence," he said, surveying the paintings that surrounded him. "Toward the end of her life, Melanie became a very disturbed individual. I thought her paintings might be too—too frightening."

"But I already *knew* that she must have been *disturbed*," said Juliet. "I knew that ever since I found out she jumped out the window! It would have been *nice* to know something good about her, too!"

Mr. Splinter clasped his hands together tightly and placed them over his mouth, as if he were trying to contain some powerful emotion.

"You and Mother have always been worried that I'm going to turn out just like her," Juliet added bitterly. "Haven't you?"

"That's not true at all," said Mr. Splinter, shaking his head. But he was thinking that his daughter's gray eyes were much like the painted eyes that peered at them from the walls and ceiling. He hadn't wanted to admit it to himself, but there had been many moments when his daughter looked so much like a young version of Melanie that he almost couldn't stand to look at her.

"Juliet," said Mr. Splinter, suddenly sitting up straighter and looking determined to assert his parental authority, "I understand that you're angry with me right now, but that doesn't excuse the fact that a rule is a rule. You know that this tower has always been off-limits, so there must be some consequence for your behavior." As he said the words, Mr. Splinter felt tired and false.

Juliet stared at her father. "That's all you have to say to me?"

"A rule is a rule," said Mr. Splinter weakly. Weren't good parents supposed to create structure? To maintain rules?

"Fine," said Juliet. "In that case, I'll be moving out tomorrow."

"Juliet!"

Ignoring her father, Juliet grabbed Gilda by the hand and hurried down the steps, leaving Mr. Splinter alone in the tower.

"So are you really going to run away?" Gilda asked, taking off her raincoat once they were back in the house.

"I'm coming home with you," said Juliet.

"Oh." Gilda knew that her mother hated sleepovers and unannounced houseguests. "I should probably at least ask my mom if that's okay first."

"Don't worry," said Juliet. "I have a credit card. I can buy my own groceries and stuff."

Gilda reflected that a credit card would probably make her mother more receptive to the idea, since she always complained about the price of meat and cereal. Gilda imagined bringing Juliet to school with her. All the kids in her class would be intrigued with the high-fashion waif from San Francisco. "She's my cousin," Gilda imagined herself telling people. "She lives with us now." Then she would tell everyone how she and Juliet solved the mystery of the ghost in a mansion in San Francisco—how they discovered her father's bizarre habit of sleepwalking—and they would be fascinated. At Christmastime, the two girls would return to San Francisco to visit Mr. Splinter, who would buy them elaborate gifts to appease his guilty conscience.

"I guess my mother won't mind if you come live with us," said Gilda.

"Great," said Juliet. "I'll start packing."

Mr. Splinter remained alone, sitting in the upper room of the tower for a long time. He had to face the truth: Despite all his efforts to bury the memory, he had been unable to erase the fact that he had failed to save his sister's life.

24

The Good-bye Letter

Juliet opened her suitcase, reflecting that she didn't own a single thing that seemed appropriate to wear in Michigan—the rough wilderness that was soon to be her new home. She packed a pair of jeans and a sweatshirt and then sat down on her bed to think.

"Juliet?" She heard her father rapping on her bedroom door. "May I come in?"

Juliet waited several seconds, then opened the door, but quickly turned her back to her father.

"I think we should talk," said Mr. Splinter.

Juliet shrugged.

"I suppose I owe you an apology," he said. "I wasn't very, um, sensitive to your feelings about your aunt Melanie—or your need to understand what really happened years ago."

"I'm going to Michigan to live with Gilda," said Juliet coolly.

"No, you're staying here because this is your home," said Mr. Splinter, staring at his daughter's angular shoulder blades.

"Some home." Juliet tossed her ballet shoes in her suitcase.

"This is your home, and I'm your father."

Juliet turned to glare at Mr. Splinter. "You probably wish you *weren't* my father."

"That isn't true," said Mr. Splinter.

Juliet pretended to fold a T-shirt very carefully, her back still turned.

"I admit, I'm not very *good* at being your father," Mr. Splinter added lamely.

Juliet shrugged. She took the ballet slippers out of her suitcase and frowned at them critically, as if imagining the outfit she might wear with them.

"I know I've never wanted to talk about your aunt Melanie," Mr. Splinter admitted, "and that wasn't fair to you. . . . It's just—I felt so *responsible* for what happened to her. I suppose I wanted to make the whole memory disappear."

Mr. Splinter watched Juliet, thinking that he no longer knew who his daughter really was. He felt as if he had just woken up from a long, bad dream, and sensed that he had missed an opportunity that had probably passed several years ago. Was he now in danger of losing his daughter as well as his sister? What could he possibly say that would make Juliet want to talk to him again?

"I think I'll arrange to have the boards taken off the tower," he ventured.

Juliet finally turned to look at him. "What for?"

"Well, I've obviously kept it locked up for too long. Maybe we can renovate it."

"What about Melanie's paintings?"

"I don't know," said Mr. Splinter, tentatively approaching Juliet and taking a seat on the edge of her bed to face her. "What do you think we should do with them?"

Juliet thought for a moment. "I guess we could put a few of them in the house. We hardly have any art on the walls."

"But—they're a little *unsettling,* don't you think?"

"That's what makes them good! Especially the portraits."

Mr. Splinter rubbed his temples. He obviously hated the idea of hanging Melanie's artwork in the house, but he was doing his best to stay open-minded in an attempt to reclaim his daughter's trust. "Well, maybe we can hang a few of them," he said, as patiently as he could manage. "I'm the first to admit, I didn't understand what she was trying to do with those paintings."

"I'm going to take art this year in school," said Juliet, speaking defiantly.

"You were always good at art."

"You and Mother never seemed to think so."

"Now, you know that isn't true, Juliet."

"It *is* true!"

"We always encouraged you to take courses that would help you get into a good college, but I'm sure we never told you that you aren't good at art."

"But what if I don't *want* to go to a good college? I mean, what if I want to go to an art school? Or no college at all?"

Mr. Splinter sighed, then tossed his hands in the air in a gesture of frustration. "We both just want you to be happy. I don't think either your mother or I ever *knew* that you wanted to pursue art!"

Juliet felt confused. She felt certain that her parents *had* discouraged her from drawing and painting, but perhaps they had done so without realizing it. "Well," she said, "I guess I never knew I was interested in art either—until now."

Mr. Splinter nodded, eyeing Juliet's half-packed suitcase. "At any rate, I do hope you won't be running away to Michigan."

Juliet pretended to concentrate on rearranging some of the clothes in her luggage.

"I would miss you," Mr. Splinter added awkwardly.

"I'll think about it," said Juliet.

Mr. Splinter turned to leave.

"Wait," said Juliet. "Can't Gilda stay longer? She practically just got here!"

"Yes—I suppose so. Gilda can stay for a while longer."

• • •

Shortly after her father left, a piece of paper appeared under the door of Juliet's room. For a moment, Juliet stared at it as if it were a large spider creeping across the floor. Finally, she picked it up and read it with a shaking hand. Her face wore an inscrutable, pinched expression that turned into a small smile by the time she reached the end of the letter.

Dear Juliet,

This is a letter from your aunt Melanie.

I'm writing because I never got a chance to say good-bye to you. Please try to forgive me for not being there in person to see you grow up.

I'm glad you found my paintings. You and Gilda did brilliant investigative work!

I thought you might also want to know a few more things about me since I'm not around to tell you:

1. My favorite color is purple. I urge you to draw some pictures using lots of purple every now and then.

2. I happen to know that your father's feet are extremely ticklish. (Do what

you will with this piece of information.)

3. The fairy we saw in the garden WAS
real.

4. I can't explain why I jumped out
the tower window years ago, but it was a
mistake.

5. Whenever you feel really down, do
what your cousin Gilda does and make a
peanut butter, chocolate syrup, and
banana sandwich.

Love always,

Aunt Melanie

25

Beach Bunnies

Today we're heading for the beach," Summer declared, "and I won't take no for an answer!"

The fog that had covered the city every day for several weeks had finally lifted, and with music blaring loudly from the radio of Summer's aging white convertible, the three drove across the Golden Gate Bridge and then through a forest of redwoods, where Summer deftly navigated the steep curves and hairpin turns of the road. Sitting in the backseat, Gilda struggled to control a growing sensation of car sickness.

"Woo-hoo!" Summer hooted. "Love these hills!" She peered into the rearview mirror. "Okay back there, Gilda?"

Gilda gave Summer a thumbs-up sign, not wanting to admit that she was focusing more on not throwing up than on the dramatic scenery that surrounded her.

"It's amazing out here, isn't it?" The car emerged from the forest, and Summer careened along a cliffside stretch of road where the ocean sparkled far below.

"I don't know about you two, but *I'm* starting to feel carsick," said Juliet. "Can you drive slower?"

For once, Gilda was grateful that Juliet hadn't hesitated to complain.

"Sorry!" said Summer. "My friends always say I drive too fast."

When they arrived at the beach, both Gilda and Juliet felt awed and intimidated by Summer, who lived up to her name in every way: she wore a yellow bikini and a thin, gold belly chain that showed off a perfect tan the color of light brown sugar; she had an enormous beach towel decorated with a giant pineapple; a fake diamond glinted from her pierced navel; she smelled of coconut suntan oil. Compared with Summer, Gilda suddenly felt ludicrous in her oversized, heart-shaped sunglasses and the zebra-print bathing suit that emphasized her snow-white skin—an outfit she had formerly considered stunning. Juliet concealed herself in an oversized T-shirt and an enormous, floppy hat that covered most of her face.

"My gosh, you two are as white as ghosts!" Summer gushed. "I'll have to show you how to use self-tanner next time."

"We're going for a vintage look," Gilda joked. "Kind of 1940s."

"Why would you want *that?*"

The three spread out their beach towels on the sand, and Summer whistled as a group of tanned, sinewy guys walked by. The boys smiled at Summer and waved. "Are those guys cute or what?"

"Nice butts," said Gilda, thinking that Summer would appreciate this sort of comment.

"You said it," said Summer. "I have a boyfriend, but I still love to *look*. You know what I mean?"

"Same here," said Gilda.

"You don't have a boyfriend," Juliet blurted.

"How do you know? I could have a hundred boyfriends for all you know."

Juliet shrugged. "I just *know* you don't have a boyfriend, that's all."

"Well, I'm sure *all* the boys are going to be crazy about you chicks next year in high school!" said Summer, who was now staring at the group of young men who had placed their beach towels strategically close to her on the nearly empty beach.

Juliet stared at the ocean as if in a trance, then suddenly flopped down and seemed to fall into a dead sleep.

"I'll be right back," said Summer.

Gilda watched as Summer stood up and boldly walked

over to say hello to the group of guys who watched her approach with frank appreciation for her svelte silhouette. Summer touched her hair and then convulsed with giggles at something one of the young men said. She was obviously in her element at the beach.

Gilda reflected that she herself had thus far shown very little talent for flirting with boys, and that she had never been much of a beach lover. For one thing, she always ended up sunburned, and if someone was going to get stung by a jellyfish or a stingray, the chances were good that it would be Gilda. Crowded beaches were sometimes interesting because it was possible to overhear gossipy conversations, but today—a Wednesday—Stinson Beach was silent and vast.

Gilda suddenly remembered a summer trip her family had taken to the Sleeping Bear Sand Dunes next to Lake Michigan. Her father had recently learned that he was sick, and for the first time, he didn't roll down the largest sand dunes or throw Gilda in the ice-cold water and then dive beneath the waves, pretending to be a shark that chomped her on the ankle. Instead, he sat on the beach and gazed out at the water.

"Sorry, kiddos," he said. "Your old pop is feeling poorly today."

"That's okay," said Gilda. "The water's freezing, anyway."

Her father perused a brochure about the sand dunes. "This is interesting," he said, and read aloud: "'Hikes around the area may reveal ghost forests—places where migrating sand dunes buried trees and then moved along, leaving only deadwood behind.'"

Gilda had been intrigued by the term *ghost forests* and the idea that the windblown dunes could move from place to place as if they were living creatures.

But something about ghost forests seemed to make her father sad. "It's really true," he said. "When you consider the big picture, we're really just here for a moment."

Feeling very small under the open sky, Gilda decided to distract herself with a productive activity, so she pulled her notebook out of her beach bag. She was planning to use her experiences at the Splinter mansion to write a novel with a few new plot twists added: for example, instead of discovering Mr. Splinter's habit of sleepwalking in the tower, there would be a very violent ghost who would actually *murder* either Juliet or Mr. Splinter just before a glamorous sleuth named Fiona Sparks (based on Gilda herself) stepped in to solve the mystery.

But Gilda's pen seemed strangely stuck. She couldn't come up with her usual flow of fictional ideas. Instead she wrote a letter:

Dear Dad:

I just wanted you to know that I solved my first psychic investigation. I think you'd be proud of me.

I've been wondering: do ghosts exist even when nobody's around to see or hear them? Or do people "create" ghosts with their own minds?

Balthazar Frobenius says that "ghosts are real to the person who sees them, and therefore they are real."

On an unrelated note, I can see why some people become "beach bunnies": you don't have to think about things or even talk when you're on the beach. You just sit here and feel good about being alive.

When Summer, Gilda, and Juliet returned to the Splinter household, they were greeted by a small commotion in the back of the house. Workers perched on tall ladders pried boards from the windows of the tower. On the ground, Rosa and several other short Latina women surrounded a priest who murmured a prayer in Spanish while making the sign of the cross in the air and sprinkling holy water on the ground. Rosa's lips moved silently as she crossed herself.

Mr. Splinter leaned against the angel fountain and observed the scene with a worried expression, as if he were watching a dangerous circus act.

Wearing her bikini top and a beach towel wrapped around her midriff, Summer approached the group in the backyard. "We're back from the beach!" she declared nonchalantly, causing both of the men on ladders and the priest to eye her bikini-clad figure with wary interest.

"Did you have fun?" Mr. Splinter asked politely. "Stinson Beach can be lovely at this time of year."

"It was nice," said Juliet.

"Did you go swimming?"

"Gilda tried," said Juliet, "but it was too cold for me."

"Well, our renovations have begun," said Mr. Splinter, gesturing toward the tower. "Juliet, tomorrow we can go inside and decide what to do with the paintings."

"I was thinking that we could try taking some of them to a gallery downtown," Juliet suggested. "I mean, Melanie probably would have wanted them to be seen by people. Besides, the portraits all go together."

"We could try that," said Mr. Splinter.

Juliet stared at the tower thoughtfully. "And then we could keep part of the tower as a real art studio, but we could make it much nicer than it is now. . . . Or maybe the room on the bottom floor could be turned into a breakfast nook."

"Cute!" Summer declared.

"I know; we should add a new door leading to the interior of the house so you don't have to go outside to get in.

Oh, and one of the rooms could be a reading room—a room with a window seat with velvet pillows."

"Oh, that sounds fab!" Summer gushed.

Mr. Splinter stared at his daughter, thinking that it was unusual to see Juliet become so visibly enthusiastic about anything. "I don't see why we couldn't do those things," he said. "Sounds like you have some great ideas."

"If you'll excuse me," said Gilda, "I'm going to go take a shower. I have sand in my nooks and crannies." She had once been appalled to hear her grandmother use this phrase following a trip to Lake Huron, but now she took a certain delight in saying it herself.

Gilda retreated to the house, feeling sticky and sunburned. She was glad that Juliet was excited about renovating the tower, but she also suspected that her cousin was the type of person who would now be fascinated by swatches of wallpaper and shades of paint—interests that Gilda did not share.

Nearly two weeks had passed since Gilda and Juliet had found their way into the tower. While the days of browsing in quirky boutiques and this latest beach outing had been fun, Gilda sensed that her visit at the Splinter household was growing a bit stale. The mystery of the haunted tower had been solved, and it seemed that a spell had been broken. There had been no further evidence of Melanie's ghost, and while the girls occasionally heard Mr. Splinter wandering through the house at night, they no longer heard the eerie sound of his footsteps ascending the tower staircase.

Gilda felt ready for a new location—a new mystery.

Or maybe I'm just homesick, she thought.

26

Going Home

•

The cabdriver threw Gilda's heavy suitcase in the trunk.

"Well, I guess this is good-bye," she said.

Summer gave Gilda a perfume-laden hug. Rosa kissed her cheeks and handed her a paper bag. "A hot tamale," she said. "There is no good food at the airport."

Juliet handed Gilda an envelope. "You can open it in the cab," she said.

"Okay."

Gilda gave Juliet a careful hug. She now looked much healthier than when Gilda had first met her, but her body still felt fragile and insubstantial, as if her skeleton were made of bird bones. "Thanks for that letter," she said.

"Don't thank me," said Gilda. "That letter was from your aunt."

"Then how do you know about it?"

"I'm a psychic investigator, that's how."

Juliet smiled. "Let's write each other this year."

"Sure."

"I have to go visit my mother in San Diego next week, so I'll *definitely* write you when my stepsisters start driving me crazy."

Through the rear window, Gilda watched the soaring tower and ornate façade of the Splinter mansion disappear as the cab descended a steep hill. When she could no longer see the house, she opened the envelope from Juliet.

Juliet had drawn Gilda wearing her séance outfit. In the red velvet evening gown and dramatic makeup, the character in the picture looked very eccentric and fierce. *I'm sure I'm better-looking than that,* Gilda thought. Still, she had to admit Juliet had captured a likeness.

Under the illustration, Juliet had written a note:

Gilda,

I'm so glad I met you! I haven't had this much excitement since forever.

I'll never forget you, and I hope we can stay in touch.

Your cousin and friend,

Juliet

When Mrs. Joyce picked her up at the Detroit airport, Gilda felt a surge of happiness as she smelled the familiar odor of stale cigarettes and rubbing alcohol in her mother's car. Her mom wore shorts and looked very freckled from the sun.

"Looks like you lost weight," said Gilda, thinking that *something* looked different about her mother, but she couldn't quite identify what. Was it just her imagination, or had her mother become prettier while she was away? And was she actually wearing mascara for a change?

"Oh, I may have lost a couple pounds," said Mrs. Joyce, maneuvering her way through the airport traffic. "My new resolution is to exercise more. Anyway, I missed you! It wasn't like you not to write lots of letters!"

"I got kind of busy."

"So—tell me about it!"

"Well," said Gilda, not knowing where to begin, "Mr. Splinter's house is *huge.*"

"I remember hearing that it's like a mansion," said Mrs. Joyce.

"It is," said Gilda. "And in the back of the house, there's this tower like something out of a fairy tale."

"How interesting," said Mrs. Joyce. "What does Lester use the tower for?"

Gilda hesitated. "Well, he had been using it to store his dead sister's belongings for the past ten years. She was a painter, and Juliet and I discovered that it was full of her artwork."

Mrs. Joyce gave Gilda a sidelong glance. It was a look she used when she suspected that Gilda might be embellishing the truth. "That sounds a little creepy," she said cautiously.

Gilda realized that it would be impossible to make her mother understand everything that had happened in San Francisco. Besides, the more information she gave, the more her mother would ask questions about things like parental supervision, respecting rules, and whether she had worn a seat belt while riding in Summer's convertible. Maybe it was better to keep the details of her first psychic investigation secret for the time being.

"And did you make friends with Mr. Splinter's daughter?" Mrs. Joyce asked.

"Of course I did," said Gilda. "I mean, she wasn't very *nice* to me at first, but we eventually became friends."

"It must be hard for her, living so far away from her mother."

"I don't know," said Gilda. "I don't think she gets along with her mother very well."

Gilda thought about Juliet, who was now on her own in the vast rooms of the Splinter mansion. She wondered if Juliet felt lonely without her.

Through the car window, Gilda observed the industrial

landmarks that lined the highway leading toward Detroit—sprawling factories, a giant rubber tire the size of a building, billboards advertising clubs with "live, dancing girls!" After San Francisco, Michigan seemed flat and mundane—a place where adventures rarely happened—but Gilda was nevertheless grateful to be home. The imposing surroundings of the Splinter mansion had been exciting, but she realized that she loved the pleasant security of riding in her mother's familiar old car. She loved her mother's freckled legs, thong-clad feet, and even the telltale whiff of cigarette smoke that lingered on her mother's clothes.

Then a disturbing thought suddenly made Gilda sit up straight in her seat. *"Hey!"* she shouted.

Mrs. Joyce slammed on the brakes, causing the car behind her to honk loudly. "What's *wrong?* You nearly gave me a heart attack!"

"I almost forgot to ask: HOW WAS YOUR DATE?!"

"Young lady, you are not to yell at me ever again while I am driving!"

Gilda scrutinized her mother's face and was annoyed to detect the quiver of a half smile. Clearly her mother had had fun on the date.

"It was okay," said Mrs. Joyce. "He's nice. I think you'd actually like him."

"I doubt it," said Gilda sulkily. She felt as if someone had just given her a hard shove. The highway beneath the car now seemed bumpy and coated with slippery grease. She obviously couldn't assume that everything would be the same at home. "Well," said Gilda, "does your new boyfriend have a *name?*"

"His name is Fred Pickens."

Gilda stared at her mother. "You're going to be Mrs. *Pickens!*"

"Of course not! Who said anything about marriage?"

"There's no way I'll ever change *my* last name," Gilda declared. "And if you have a wedding, you can find a bridesmaid from some other family, because you won't be seeing me in a big pink dress with a bow on the butt."

Gilda's mother sighed. "I knew you'd overreact. Am I not allowed to have any friends? Any companions?"

"You certainly don't need *boyfriends.* You have your rewarding career and two kids. That's plenty." She knew she sounded like a spoiled brat, but she couldn't help herself.

Her mother lit a cigarette. "See what you've done? I had actually cut way down on the smokes, and now you've got me started again."

"I guess old Fred doesn't smoke, huh? No ciggies for Mr. Pickens. No sirree!"

Mrs. Joyce ignored Gilda's comments and turned on the radio to a "lite rock" station that somehow made Gilda feel even more irritable. When she had left San Francisco, Gilda had felt like a real psychic investigator—a young, attractive woman with an intriguing, secret career. She was someone who had helped solve a mystery—someone with a glamorous future ahead of her. Now everything had become instantly banal.

As Gilda contemplated the unappealing idea of Fred Pickens, she suddenly missed her father terribly. *I've reached the point where I can go for days without thinking about Dad at all,* Gilda thought. *Then at certain moments, I miss him so much, you would think he had just died yesterday.*

Gilda's mother pulled into the driveway, turned off the ignition, and stubbed out her cigarette. "Gilda," she said, "I know you miss your father."

Sometimes her mother seemed almost psychic. Maybe it was genetic.

Gilda attempted a nonchalant shrug, but instead, her lip quivered uncontrollably.

Her mother reached over to give Gilda a hug, and Gilda's head collided clumsily with her mother's T-shirt. Her eyes felt like giant sea sponges. Where were all these tears coming from?

When Gilda pulled away a minute later, she left a large wet patch on her mom's blue shirt. She suddenly felt like an enormous toddler.

"Look," said Gilda's mother. "Nobody is ever going to

try to *replace* your father." She brushed a lock of damp hair from Gilda's face. "Nobody could possibly replace him. But that doesn't mean there will never be room to care about other people, does it?"

Gilda wiped tears from her cheek with the back of her hand. Even her hair was wet. A numb clarity was settling in her mind. *Things are going to keep changing,* she thought. *Getting over Dad's death was just the beginning.* Now her mother might have a boyfriend named Fred Pickens, and Wendy Choy probably wouldn't be the same after spending the summer at camp, and the truth was that her father was never, ever coming back, no matter how many letters she might write to him, no matter how many psychic investigations she might perform. . . .

"It's just"—Gilda sniffed—"sometimes I wish we could just *stop.*"

"What do you mean?"

Gilda wasn't exactly sure what she meant. On one hand, she herself wanted to grow up more quickly and have exciting adventures, but she also wished desperately that she could freeze time in some way so that everyone around her stopped *changing.* It seemed that as time moved forward, people only drifted further and further apart. "Lately it just seems like everyone's so busy with their jobs and boyfriends and everything," Gilda continued, "and I'm afraid we're just going to forget about Dad completely. That's what happened to Juliet's family, you know. After her aunt committed suicide, they got rid of all her belongings and decided that they would never talk about her again!"

"Gilda," said her mother, rummaging in her purse and then handing Gilda a crumpled tissue, "I can promise you that your father will *never* be forgotten."

Gilda blew her nose and wiped her eyes with the back of her hand.

"I know it's been hard for you and Stephen," said her mother wearily. "This killer work schedule of mine certainly hasn't helped things; I know I haven't been around enough to spend time with you." She sighed. "I could try to call in sick tonight—"

"No—I'll be fine," said Gilda, now feeling guilty for complaining. She knew that her family needed the money her mother earned from working overtime.

"Well, I have a day off next week," Gilda's mother said. "How about going to the movies or something?"

"Okay," said Gilda, still sniffling. She knew it was rare for her mother to spend money on frivolous things like going to the movies.

"It's been a while since we did anything fun as a family."

"That's okay," said Gilda. "Fun is overrated."

Gilda's mother frowned at her, thinking that her daughter often said the strangest things. "Well, you can be sure that if your father were here right now, he would be very proud of your trip to San Francisco. He'd be telling all his friends!"

Gilda smiled weakly.

"He never got to go there himself, so he would want to know every single detail."

I'll write him a letter with all the details, Gilda thought.

Juliet left her first art class feeling as if all her senses were heightened. As she walked along the bustling city street carrying a large sketchbook under her arm, she noticed colors, sounds, odors—but instead of cringing from her surroundings as she usually did, she merely observed without feeling afraid. She was aware of the hard soles of her sandals striking the sidewalk and her slightly labored breathing as she climbed a hill, hurrying to catch a bus. It was impossible to name the new feeling; it was simply the sense that for once, there *wasn't* something terribly wrong somewhere.

At first, Juliet had been terrified to go to the summer art class located at a downtown studio; after all, she would probably be the youngest person there, and what if nobody thought she was any good? But then she thought of Gilda. Gilda would shrug impatiently and say, "So what's the big deal? Just *go* to the stupid art class!"

As it turned out, Juliet *was* the youngest in the class, but it didn't matter. In fact, she sensed that she might have more in common with the nineteen-year-old boy with blue hair and a pierced nose and the silver-haired woman in her sixties than she did with most of the girls at her own school. *Maybe these are my people,* Juliet thought.

Juliet knew that her father didn't want her to wander through the city on her own, but she had a sudden impulse: she wanted to go to Chinatown. So instead of getting on the bus that would turn toward Pacific Heights, she followed a crowd of people aboard a crowded city bus that smelled of sweat and cabbages and managed to find a seat as the vehicle lurched into motion and creaked up the steep hill.

Juliet had been learning to sketch faces, and now she studied the people around her. Each face was a landscape of lines, contours, lumps, and shadows; each concealed a mystery or a sad story.

When the bus reached Chinatown, Juliet followed the herd of people that spilled through the narrow doors onto the sidewalk in front of a fruit-and-vegetable market. She paused for a moment, noticing that the lemongrass, snow peas, limes, and mushrooms of all shapes and sizes appeared very vivid in the late-afternoon sunlight—as if they radiated little rainbows of color. *That image would make a nice still life,* she thought. Then she wandered down the street until she found the Chinese temple that she and Gilda had visited before.

Juliet knew that what she was planning to do was irrational. Nevertheless, she had an idea that she felt compelled to carry out. She tried to imagine that she was in Chinatown with Gilda. *If Gilda were here,* Juliet thought, *she would walk directly into the temple without a second thought.*

In her pocket, Juliet carried a letter.

Dear Aunt Melanie,

I'll probably never understand why you decided to jump out of that window years ago. I guess things like that can't ever be fully explained. But I'm glad I know <u>something</u> about you now. I wanted you to know that seeing your paintings helped me; it made me remember things about myself that had been completely erased.

Your niece,

Juliet

P.S. The day I saw you standing in the hallway was so real. I still don't think I imagined it! I hope that you are at peace now.

Inside the temple, Juliet watched the corners of her letter turn brown in the flame of a candle. There was a small surge of orange-and-yellow light as the altar flame dissolved the words, leaving behind only an acrid aroma.

Good-bye, Aunt Melanie.

At home in her room, Gilda discovered an unopened letter from Wendy Choy that had been left on her bed:

Dear Gilda,

Thanks for your letter, and sorry it took me a while to write to you. I have to practice at least five hours a day here just to keep up with my lessons. My mother keeps calling to ask me, "Are you the best player at camp yet?" and I have to say, "No!" Then she says, "Practice more."

There are so many talented kids here. It kind of freaks me out. Maybe I should become a surgeon instead of a musician. Or maybe a secretary.

Omigod, don't freak out, but I have a boyfriend!!!!!

He's so cute. He's a little shorter than me and kind of chubby, but totally cute, with cute eyes and smile. He plays trumpet.

We kissed!!!!!! As you know, I've never done that before.

!!!!

To be honest, it felt kind of weird. Now he wants to do it every day. I don't see why.

The camp counselors saw us kissing, and now they

tease me about it. I pray to God they won't say anything to my mother, because she would be sure that kissing a boy is the reason I'm not the best performer here.

I've got a lesson now, so I'd better go.

Love,

Wendy

Gilda was surprised to feel a twinge of jealousy at the news that Wendy had a boyfriend, even if this boy *was* short and chubby. Wendy had never had a boyfriend before, so this development was alarming indeed. Did this mean Wendy might seek a completely new social life when she returned to school? Gilda also thought this was the most annoyingly girlish letter Wendy had ever written. Had Wendy tossed her brain into Lake Michigan? What kind of twit would allow herself to write the phrase *totally cute, with cute eyes and smile?*

<u>PROGRESS REPORT</u>

TO: GILDA JOYCE

FROM: GILDA JOYCE

RE: THE DISAPPOINTMENT OF FRIENDSHIP

Wendy has obviously changed completely while she's been at camp. I may have to

find a new best friend, because the next
thing you know, Wendy will be trying out
for cheerleading or dropping out of
school to become a teenage mom.

It's obvious that Wendy doesn't miss
me at all.
(NOTE TO SELF: Get some kissing experience
ASAP!)

Dear Wendy:

Congratulations on the boyfriend.

I must admit that I'm disappointed
to hear that you're not the best musician
at camp. I normally wouldn't say this,
but this time, your mother may be right.
The time you're spending kissing could
be spent practicing your instrument.
After all, your parents aren't rich,
you know. They're hardworking people
who simply want a little respect. They
could have just sent you to cheerleading
camp if they had known that all you want
to do is humiliate them by spending
all day smooching with every chubby
boy you meet, but they assumed you

```
wanted to improve yourself and get an
education.
    By the way, I just returned from San
Francisco, where I solved my first
psychic investigation.
    Remember that weird girl I wrote
you about (Juliet)? She's not so bad
after all. We kind of became friends.
Consequently, I didn't miss you as much
as I thought I would.
```

Gilda chewed her fingernail for a moment. She knew she wasn't being completely honest. The truth was that she did miss Wendy and wished she had some reassurance that they would still be best friends when Wendy returned from camp. Gilda found some white correction fluid and painted over the last sentence she had written. Then she typed over it:

```
The truth is, I wish you could have been
there.
```

Stephen peered into Gilda's room. "Want some pizza?" he asked. "I brought a whole pepperoni-and-sausage pizza home from work."

Gilda turned to look at her brother. Wearing a T-shirt that advertised JUMBO'S PIZZA, he smelled like a busy restaurant—a mixture of sweat, grease, and melted cheese.

"I thought you worked at Roscoe's Chicken and Fish," said Gilda.

"I do, but this is my second job. Actually, it's my third, because I've also been mowing lawns."

"Always the slacker," Gilda joked. "So you must be filthy rich by now with all those jobs."

"Well, *some* of us have to work for a living. *Others* of us get free trips to exotic cities."

"Hey, I *earned* my trip to San Francisco."

"Mom said you just invited yourself."

Gilda couldn't deny that this was true. However, she felt that the trip had ultimately been earned through her efforts to help Juliet solve a mystery. Of course, there was no point in trying to explain her psychic investigation work to her brother; he would be even less likely to believe the details of her adventure than her mother.

"I'm saving money to buy a car," Stephen explained as he and Gilda grabbed plates, napkins, and slices of pizza in the kitchen.

Sitting across from her brother at the kitchen table with the pizza box between them, Gilda remembered how

Stephen and his father used to look at the automotive section of the classified ads in the paper every Sunday, and how the two often spoke of the various used cars Stephen might purchase after he turned sixteen. She guessed that Stephen must miss those conversations now.

Gilda watched as her brother folded a large piece of pizza in half and then gulped it down like a sandwich. "You know," she said, "I never noticed it before, but you eat pizza the same way Dad used to."

"The best way to eat it," Stephen replied with his mouth full.

For once, Stephen didn't flinch or sulk when she mentioned their father. With this note of encouragement, Gilda decided to bring up another topic that had been nagging her ever since she returned home. "So," she ventured, "it sounds like there have been some new developments around here while I was away."

"Like what?" Stephen asked, grabbing another slice of pizza.

"Like this Fred Pickens character!"

"Oh, that guy." Stephen took another large bite of pizza.

"You've *met* him?"

"Just once," said Stephen, wiping some tomato sauce from his chin. "He came over to pick Mom up."

"And?"

Stephen shrugged. "He's a nice enough guy, I guess. Kind of a doofus, though."

"What does this Fred Pickens *look* like?"

Stephen shrugged. "Average. Bearded guy."

"He has a beard! Why didn't you tell me that right away?"

"So what if he has a beard?"

"Men with mustaches and beards are always hiding something."

"That's stupid."

"It's true! Facial hair is like a little disguise. Especially if the hair covers a man's mouth. Was it a really *long* mustache and beard?"

"It was a normal beard. Are you going to eat that piece of pizza or not?"

"And what *color* was his hair?"

"I don't know. Brown, I think. Brown with some gray in it. Look, I'm sure you'll have a chance to spy on him the next time he comes over."

"Oh, don't worry—I will," said Gilda, picking up her slice of pizza, and then putting it down on her plate again without taking a bite. "You know," she continued, "for all we know, this Fred could become our new father someday."

Stephen flinched, but he quickly shook his head, dismissing the idea. "First of all," he said, "he would be our *stepfather,* not our father. Second, that won't happen anyway because Mom wouldn't marry a doofus. And third, they practically just met, and this whole thing is none of our business. Besides, she's been in a really good mood lately, and it's been nice not hearing her asking me to do five million extra chores for a change—so in my opinion, maybe this Fred isn't so bad if she wants to hang out with him."

Gilda couldn't help reflecting that this was possibly the longest series of sentences Stephen had spoken to her in quite some time. In fact, she couldn't remember when they had actually sat down at the kitchen table together to talk instead of watching TV while they ate. It was nice. Really nice. Was it possible she had actually *missed* him?

"I suppose you make some fair points," Gilda admitted. Perhaps she was blowing things out of proportion. *Whatever happens, Stephen and I will have to deal with it together,* she thought. She surprised herself by hoping this was a sign that they were going to be closer friends again.

<u>PROGRESS REPORT</u>

<u>TO</u>: <u>GILDA JOYCE</u>
<u>FROM</u>: <u>GILDA JOYCE</u>
<u>PROJECT #1</u>: <u>PSYCHIC INVESTIGATION</u>--"<u>THE GHOST IN THE TOWER</u>"

STATUS: INVESTIGATION SUCCESSFULLY
COMPLETED

PROJECT #2: NOVEL-IN-PROGRESS--"THE GHOST
IN THE TOWER" BY GILDA JOYCE
STATUS: Although only one page has been
written thus far, the novel is off to
a splendid start. With her go-getting
attitude, designer clothes, extensive
dating experience, and outstanding psychic
abilities, the novel's main character,
Fiona Sparks, is sure to be a big hit.

NOTE TO SELF: Don't forget to add some
gory scenes and a love interest.

DEADLINE: With steady work, I'll be able
to finish the novel by the end of the
summer--just in time to leave the
manuscript on Mrs. Weintraub's desk
on the first day of school.

Gilda put on her cat's-eye sunglasses and ran out the front
door. For some reason, she felt unusually happy as she
walked down the familiar neighborhood sidewalk.

She decided to stop at the Gas Mart first, just to see whether Plaid Pants had gotten fired yet and whether he had continued to wear his hideous trousers well into the middle of the summer. *Maybe he also owns plaid shorts,* Gilda thought. Next, she would go check on Mrs. Frickle. With any luck, she would be wearing her pink wig today.